The Maverick

Carrie Alexander

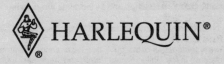

HARLEQUIN®

TORONTO • NEW YORK • LONDON
AMSTERDAM • PARIS • SYDNEY • HAMBURG
STOCKHOLM • ATHENS • TOKYO • MILAN • MADRID
PRAGUE • WARSAW • BUDAPEST • AUCKLAND

ISBN 0-373-71042-9

THE MAVERICK

Copyright © 2002 by Carrie Antilla.

Visit us at www.eHarlequin.com

Printed in U.S.A.

For the scholar and the woodsman, my mom and dad, who taught me the love of books and the benefits of hard work.

CHAPTER ONE

THE SILVER-AND-BLACK MOTORCYCLE zipped through downtown Treetop, Wyoming, at fifteen miles above the speed limit. Deputy Sophie Ryan was so startled she flinched, spilling her coffee and dropping her car keys. From Sophie's vantage point in the parking lot of the True Brew coffeehouse, she shouldn't have been able to recognize the driver.

Yet she was afraid that she had.

Maverick. The name flashed through her like lightning—as shocking and electric as the man himself.

The presence of Luke Salinger in Treetop—after fourteen years!—was too much to accept all at once. Sophie didn't want him here. She truly didn't. But there was no denying that she was transfixed by the possibility. Steaming latte soaked the front of her police uniform, and she was too stunned to feel it.

Squeezing the half-empty foam cup, she stared blankly after the speeding motorcycle. Even though Range Street had returned to its usual early-morning tranquility, the air seemed to reverberate with the bike's annoying buzz and hot blue exhaust fumes. Sophie shuddered. Every self-protective sense that she'd honed in the years since Luke's departure went on red alert.

Her mind raced. Try as she might, she couldn't convince herself that some other member of the defunct

Mustangs motorcycle gang had chosen to take a joyride through town for old time's sake.

For one thing, it was only quarter to eight. That let out the likeliest candidate, Damon "Demon" Bradshaw, who rarely rolled out of bed to open his run-down bike shop before noon.

The motorcycle in question had been black and chrome, sleek, stylish, fast. Snake Carson's bike was a big, ugly chopper that sounded like a dump truck. And ever since Skooch Haas had found religion he'd sooner wear a dress to bible school than break the speed limit.

While the driver had been little more than a blur, Sophie's observation of details was keen. She'd seen enough to identify dark wavy hair, whipped by the wind since it was a little too long to be reputable, a possible Mustangs tattoo on the left biceps, and a long, lean body clad in denim and brown leather. Which meant she could also eliminate Punch Fiorelli, who'd gained fifty pounds in the past decade, and Bronc Lemmons, who was in the hospital, sick and bald as a colicky baby from his second round of chemotherapy.

Sophie took a shaky breath. Other than the deceased and the incarcerated, that left one member of the Mustangs unaccounted for. And he happened to be the only man on earth for whom she'd never been able to rationalize—or completely stifle—her tangled, tumultuous feelings.

"Maverick," she said through her teeth, remembering with a spurt of pain a time when he'd left her scared, alone and, as she'd soon learned, pregnant. She clenched her fist. The last of the coffee gushed from the cup in a hot brown waterfall.

Luke Salinger was back in Treetop, and the town would likely be the worse for it.

There was no question that Sophie's stable life had just been turned upside down.

It was a minute before she came back to herself with a snap. Briskly she brushed at her stained uniform shirt, disgusted with her stricken reaction. One glimpse of Luke "Maverick" Salinger and her composure had cracked like the flimsy foam cup, releasing such a torrent of memory she'd been rendered mute and motionless. She would have to do better than that if she hoped to protect her family and hard-won reputation from the resurrection of the old scandal.

Nor could she continue to stand idly by while Luke flouted the speed limit. She was the only sheriff's deputy on patrol this morning, and, speeding ticket aside, there were those fourteen-year-old charges of arson, vandalism and B & E still lingering on the books....

It was up to Sophie to apprehend Luke Salinger. She reached for her fallen keys. How ironic.

Kelsey Carson stepped out of the side door of the True Brew, her cheeks pink and glossy from the steam of the espresso machine. "Whoa. That was so cool," she said. Her butter-blond ponytail swung as she scanned the empty street. "Who was he? I saw him zoom by from the kitchen window. Sweeet!"

Sophie straightened, keys in hand. Her law enforcement training demanded she give an impromptu lecture reminding the teenager that breaking the speed limit was dangerous, not cool. As she spoke, she couldn't help remembering the days when she'd been as pretend-tough, rebellious and impressionable as sixteen-year-old Kelsey. She'd thought that Luke was as sweet as apple pie à la mode, and ten times as cool.

Kelsey wasn't listening anyway. "Yeah, yeah, yeah. But who is that guy?"

Sophie grimaced. "I'm not sure, but I do know that he just broke the law."

"Hmm." Kelsey slid her hands into the pockets of her droopy camouflage pants and turned a measuring stare on Sophie. The gold ring that pierced her eyebrow winked in the sunshine. "He seemed familiar. Made me think of the photos of you and my dad and the rest of the Mustangs. From the old days."

Sophie stiffened. If even Kelsey—who'd been a toddler at the time—could recognize the marauding motorcyclist for what he was, it wouldn't be long before news of Maverick's return hit Treetop like an earthquake. Old rumors would rumble. Under the pressure, Sophie's good reputation would crack wide open. By the end of the day, the gossips would be in cataclysmic ecstasy.

"But he was too buff." Kelsey frowned. "No way was he my dad's age."

"Well, don't forget I'm nearly your dad's age," Sophie said, and Kelsey looked at her with blank incomprehension, making her feel every day of her thirty-one years. "Okay, I've got to go." She handed the teenager the mangled cup.

Kelsey's eyes sharpened. "Are you gonna arrest him?"

"We'll see." Sophie moved brusquely to her patrol car. She gunned the engine, the back tires spitting pebbles and dirt as the car sped out of the lot. From somewhere behind came Kelsey's excited whoop as she ran back into the coffeehouse to spill the beans.

"Nuts." Sophie buckled her seat belt one-handed, squinting into the sunshine splashed across the blacktop at the eastern end of Range Street. "Real smooth, Deputy Ryan." She snatched her sunglasses off the visor, keeping to the speed limit until she reached the outskirts of town, where she stepped up the pace. The motorcycle was long gone, but it wouldn't take much of an investigation to turn it up. She knew how Luke thought.

Or so she'd once believed.

Don't think about it. She sandbagged the rush of returning images. *You're on the job. No time for Memory Lane.*

She was fairly certain that if he'd just arrived in Treetop he wouldn't head directly out to the family ranch, where his older brother, sister-in-law and grandmother, Mary Lucas—the matriarch who presided over the conjoined Lucas and Salinger families—still lived. Luke's mother had died the year before he left; his father, Stephen Salinger, handled the family finances out of Laramie, the state's capital city. After all this time, Luke's welcome home might be as turbulent as Sophie's churning emotions.

She swallowed, aware of a swiftly rising apprehension that had set her nerves on razor edge. Normally she was completely calm and levelheaded on duty, even in the few crisis situations she'd handled. It would be prudent to consider her emotional involvement in this particular case before charging forward like Colonel Custer at the Little Bighorn. The comparison was apt. Her history with Luke was nearly as devastating.

She cast a doubtful glance at the police radio, presently broadcasting the usual soothing static that meant there was nothing happening in Treetop that needed her attention. If she called into the station and requested aid—

Hell, no. Sophie tightened her fingers on the steering wheel, the highway smoothly unreeling beneath the patrol car's tires. Sheriff Ed Warren would have a good belly laugh at her expense if it turned out that the renegade motorcyclist wasn't Luke Salinger at all and she'd asked for backup to write a measly speeding citation. She got enough grief from her boss as it was without handing him further ammunition to question her competency.

Sophie gritted her teeth. She'd bring in Maverick on her own. Call it payoff.

The low-slung cedar roof of the Thunderhead Saloon caught her eye. She slammed on the brakes and spun the wheel, making a sloppy turn into the parking lot as the patrol car bumped on and off the crumbling curb. The saloon didn't open till later, but the Thunderhead's grill did a brisk morning business serving massive breakfasts of fried eggs, steak and short stacks to truckers and area ranchers. She'd likely find Punch—one of the former Mustangs—behind the griddle, flipping flapjacks and pinching the waitress's bottoms. If he'd come this way, Luke might have stopped by to say hello.

Wagon wheels framed the walkway into the Thunderhead, the weathered spokes softened by the larkspur, oxeye daisies and purple asters that were among Theresa Fiorelli's recent improvements to the family business. The interior was dark and masculine, but freshly scented with a lemony polish that had the wooden floors, walls and furnishings gleaming like the burnished hide of a bay quarter horse. More of Theresa's handiwork. Before she'd swooped in with ideas about spiffy new decor, talent shows and karaoke nights, the business had been strictly utilitarian.

Sophie took off her sunglasses and went directly to the kitchen with a token wave at the bustling waitresses. Theresa was working the griddle, frowning in concentration as she poured precise dollops of batter in ruler-straight rows. She paused briefly to lift an eyebrow at Sophie. "Deputy."

"Morning," Sophie said, glancing around the immaculate kitchen. The stainless steel appliances shone like the chrome on Maverick's bike. "Punch isn't here?"

Theresa's frown deepened. "You just missed him. Some hooligan in leather busted in—"

Sophie's head snapped around.

"—and what with all the hollering and back-slapping you'd think this was a locker room." Theresa wiped her hands on her apron, most of her attention focused on the problem of a malformed blueberry flapjack. She was a perfectionist who was still adjusting to her recent elevation from waitress to wife of the proprietor. "We've got six orders up and Punch decides to take a motorcycle ride, of all things." The griddle sizzled as she scraped away the imperfect flapjack, pausing briefly to wave the gluey spatula at Sophie. "What is it with men, anyhow?"

"Darned if I know." Sophie found herself grinning. "I live with two of 'em and don't have a clue about how their brains work."

"You tell it, sister," said Ellen Molitor, a rangy, big-boned waitress with an incongruous snub nose. She dumped a tray full of dirty dishes near the sink with a clatter and ran a hand through her frazzled graying hair. The motion made the third button on her uniform blouse pop open. Ellen looked down into her meager cleavage and shrugged. "Tips," she explained to Sophie with a wink. "They're good for tips." She chuckled. "Men, I mean."

"Where's your hair net?" Theresa's voice was sharp.

"Lookee you." Ellen grabbed an order of scrambled

eggs and a slab of ham so big it hung off the edge of the plate and sashayed out of the kitchen, her flat behind swinging like a cow bell. ''Miss Fancypants,'' she shot over her shoulder.

Theresa sputtered.

''Which direction did they take?'' Sophie asked hastily, not wanting to be caught up in kitchen politics. ''Punch and Mav—er, this other guy?''

Biting her lip as she began carefully flipping the flapjacks, Theresa could do no more than bob her head in a vaguely easterly direction. When one of her perfect creations landed on another in a gloppy mess, Sophie slipped out of the kitchen before she took the blame.

Ellen waylaid her near the door. ''Maverick's back, you know, Soph.'' She squeezed the deputy's arm. ''I thought I should warn you.''

''I know.'' Sophie felt the need to blink. ''I already saw him.''

''He still looks good. Real good.''

Sophie blinked again. Must be something in her eye. ''He was going too fast for me to tell.''

Ellen peered beneath the brim of Sophie's taupe trooper hat. They'd once worked together, sharing bad tips, sore feet and tales of woe. ''You're not carrying a torch, are you, hon?''

''Of course not!''

''You can admit it if you are.'' Ellen rested the tray on her hip and patted the younger woman's arm. ''We've all been there. Even when a man's no good, it's awful hard to let go.''

No matter how many times Sophie blinked, moisture continued to well in her eyes. *Damn that Maverick,* she thought, trying to use the biker-gang nickname as a sobering slap in the face. She had to stay tough and mean, not surrender to misbegotten sentimentality. *Think of Joey. Think of what sort of trouble Luke's return could cause for your son.*

"It's been fourteen years, Ellie. My relationship with Luke was over long ago." Sophie closed her eyes and swallowed. "Frankly, I'd hoped never to see him again."

"If it were me, I might be sorta—" Ellen gave her shoulders a little wiggle "—excited that he was back. I reckon that man's brand lasts a long time. Even longer than fourteen years."

"I wouldn't know," Sophie said, although she knew very well that some brands were permanent. Defiantly she thrust up her naked ring finger. "I've never been branded, so to speak."

"I wasn't necessarily speaking of wedding rings." Ignoring a customer's call for more coffee, Ellen bent slightly to search Sophie's eyes. The waitress must have seen something Sophie hadn't wanted to reveal, because she nodded knowingly and said, "Yep, there are brands that last a whole lot longer than church vows." She snorted. "And since I've been divorced twice, who'd know better 'n me? All the same, if my first love came around to visit, I believe I might give it another try. First love goes the deepest, doesn't it?"

Sophie averted her gaze. *Branded.* By God, she was *not* branded. It wasn't as if she'd been pining after Luke like some wimpy dishrag of a woman. She'd dated plenty of other men. Or enough, anyway. Only once had she come close to marriage—and that had been ten years ago when she'd been feeling guilty for depriving her son of a father figure.

So, yeah, she'd admit to a certain reluctance to trust men. Which was normal, given her reality. They'd been hard, the lessons that Luke—and others—had taught her. She'd struggled. She'd fought. And she'd survived.

She certainly did not need a man to *complete* her. Luke Salinger least of all.

Almost entirely on her own, she'd worked her way up from a string of low-paying jobs to a two-year stint as one of the Thunderhead's waitresses, then on to her law enforcement training and the job with the Treetop Sheriff's Department. She'd also raised a fine son—no thanks to *anyone* named Salinger.

At that, speculation on how Luke's brother, Heath, would react to Luke's return made a shudder run through her body. Trouble was brewing, sure as shootin'.

At least she was dry-eyed now. Dry-eyed and loaded for bear, as her father would say. She gave Ellen a tight smile and swept out of the restaurant, jamming her sunglasses back in place. Within the day, Luke would be locked up where he belonged and the whole town could gossip to their heart's content about the welcome that Sophie Ryan had given him.

Reluctantly, self-consciously, she touched her backside before climbing into the car. *Branded?* Branded, her...her...her *foot!*

Demon Bradshaw's business, a grungy motorcycle shop, was Sophie's next stop, half a mile farther down the state highway that bypassed the small but bustling town of Treetop. She didn't even have to get out of the car. One turn around the swaybacked shack that housed the shop and the sorry excuse for a log cabin out back was enough to see that neither Demon nor his old lady had stirred. Demon's Harley was parked near the porch, the only thing at the Bradshaw place that was well cared for. Earlier that morning one of Sophie's fellow deputies had passed the word that there'd been a major kegger at the Jackpine Lake campground last night. It was safe to assume that Treetop's diehard partyers were still in bed, sleeping another one off.

Sophie knew where to go next. If Maverick and Punch were on an "auld lang syne" bike ride, they'd surely take the switchback, a blacktop county road that snaked upward in a series of sweet curves, rising in elevation until it reached a summit that offered one of the best views in the state. From an altitude of eight thousand feet, the town of Treetop would be a doll's village nestled in the valley below, most of it screened by the brushy evergreens that crowded the hillsides. Luke would get a grand overview of the valley, the river, and, in the far distance, the rangelands of the family ranch he'd chosen to abandon.

If he cared enough to revisit what he'd abandoned, that was.

Sophie blinked again behind her dark lenses. It was natural to get a little emotional about Luke's return. He'd been her first love. Her greatest love, to be completely honest. That didn't mean she had to forgive and forget.

She'd tried to forgive him for leaving her, especially once she'd matured enough to understand that he'd been nearly as young, reckless and shortsighted as she. But she'd never been able to forget—not what he'd meant to her, nor what he'd done to her.

"And I *won't* forget," she whispered, going on automatic as she steered the car around the curves of a road she still knew better than the back of Luke's hand.

Luke's hand. A vivid memory flared—the day that Luke, then only eighteen, had first let her drive his motorcycle, his hands covering hers on the grips as their bodies pressed close, the bike's speed and power vibrating through every inch of her as they climbed the scenic switchback.

She'd been sixteen and fresh out of a foster home, living with her neglectful father again, acting out her anger and rebellion, although deep inside what she'd really craved was to find a place for herself that felt safe. Luke had seemed like a god to her then—smart, handsome, filled with the kind of heat and energy and passion that lit up everything and everyone near him. He'd illuminated her drab life, chased away the shadows.

Hovering at the fringes of the ragtag band of rowdy young men who'd formed the Mustangs, she'd begun to crave Luke even more than safety. And eventually he'd regarded her with something other than a casual friendship. During her seventeenth summer, his nineteenth, they'd fallen head over heels in love. He'd shown her all his secret places in the countryside, warmed her with his fervent dreams of their future. On a star-filled night they'd made love at a hidden mountain lake, and she'd finally understood what it meant to be loved, cherished…and safe. In Luke's arms, she'd finally felt safe.

Ah, the folly and blind passion of youth.

Despite her attempt at sarcasm, Sophie saw the fawn-colored hills through a haze of tears. She flipped off her glasses and swiped at her eyes. It would be such a relief to put the past out of her mind forever, but she couldn't let herself do it. She needed to remember—to remember everything. That was what would give her the strength to keep Joey safe and close.

Another irony: Safety was once again what Sophie valued most.

But *this* time she wouldn't let Luke divert her purpose.

The resolution sounded reasonable enough. But when she rounded another of the switchbacks and sighted two motorcycles not far ahead, her unruly heart gave an instinctive lurch of recognition. Perhaps even of pleasure.

Maverick's back.

She took up the radio mike and called in her position. She switched on the siren. The lead motorcycle—Luke's—sped up for just a moment, then gradually slowed. Punch had already pulled over and was taking off his helmet as Sophie slowed to park on the shoulder, fifty feet back. Ordinarily, she'd play it cautious when confronting two bikers, but these were guys she knew. One she trusted. She stepped out and called to Punch, telling him to move away from his bike and wait by her car. It wasn't a by-the-book procedure, but she didn't have to worry about turning her back on Punch. It was the long slow walk over to Luke's bike that she dreaded, suffering his intense stare.

He didn't turn to look as she moved away from her vehicle. Did he know it was her? Had Punch already told him about her? Her stomach was alive with the flutter of a hundred wings—moths to the flame. Although she couldn't forget the searing pain of getting burned by Luke, she had no control over her fickle impulses either. The memory of what it had been like to have his arms around her was flooding back, drowning her resolve to be tough and mean and ultra-professional.

Damn you, Maverick, she thought, no longer certain that she meant it.

Her footsteps on the blacktop sounded like gunshots in the clear mountain air. Wind whistled through the twisted pines, catching at the curly wisps of her uncontrollable hair. Although Luke didn't turn, she recognized the rearing-mustang tattoo on his tanned left biceps. It matched her own tattoo—the one that only Luke knew about.

Sophie licked her lips, her police training kicking in as her hand went automatically to the holstered sidearm hanging from her gun belt. As if a gun could protect her from the lethal Salinger charm!

"Sir," she said. Her voice grated like pebbles under a boot heel; she swallowed and tried again. "Sir, I want you to step off the bike. I need to see your license, proof of insurance and regis—registra—tion…"

Her voice faded. Her vision blurred, her ears buzzed. Luke had swung his leg over the motorcycle and stood. He was taller than she remembered, more formidable. The shocking reality of his presence slammed into her with all the force of a runaway boulder tipped off the grandest of the Tetons. She could not believe that he was here. After all these years, he was standing right in front of her.

Then he turned to face her, and he was not at all the Luke Salinger she remembered.

CHAPTER TWO

IT'S THE EYES. Sophie's stomach dropped. Such flat steel-blue eyes couldn't belong to Luke Salinger. There was no fire, no spirit, no passion—only the cold-blooded stare, appraising her without a spark of recognition.

A silent cry ripped loose from the bonds of her tight control. What had happened to Maverick? Where was the man she'd once loved with all her heart?

Gone away, grown up, never coming back.

Her shock bottomed out. She realized that she'd been staring for too long and licked her dry lips. "Luke Salinger," she said with no inflection and just a faint tremor.

He nodded.

Sophie felt disconnected from reality, as though she were weightless, as insubstantial as smoke. Yet Luke was the mystery here. She remembered a time when purpose had burned in his eyes, lighting them like a neon sign, charging himself and her and all the rest of the Mustangs with such an excess of energy that trouble was bound to follow.

The spark was gone. He was deadened.

Miserable but trying not to show it, she swiped her hand across her pants before extending her palm. "I need to see your license, registration and proof of insurance."

He removed a flattened billfold from his back pocket

and slipped the driver's license from its plastic sleeve. Taking the card, she examined it carefully, her eyes flickering between Luke's watchful gaze and the name and photo on the ID. The license had been issued in California. She read the address. Los Angeles? It wasn't easy to imagine the Luke she used to know putting up with the plastic superficiality she imagined ran rampant on the coast. But then, *this* man was a stranger to her. For all she knew, the Luke who'd despised the greed of conspicuous consumption had become a status-conscious spendthrift who shopped Rodeo Drive and ate goat-cheese pizzas at a hundred bucks a pop.

Except that he didn't look soft and pampered. He was tough, rugged, stringent.

Physically, he'd changed, but not by much. Although he hadn't thickened the way most men did by their mid-thirties, he'd…hardened. The muscles in his arms and legs and the broad chest beneath an expensive but battered brown leather vest and white sleeveless T-shirt appeared to be as hard as iron. Forged in fire, she thought, glancing briefly into his face. Aside from the shock of his unrecognizable expression, he was as handsome as ever. Only now his skin was tanned and weathered, drawn tight over strong cheekbones and jaw. Not a single strand of gray had sprouted among the dark hair barely restrained by a blue bandanna.

The Luke Salinger she remembered had been more boy than man. That was no longer the case. But the old attraction trickling through her veins was terribly familiar.

Sophie cleared her throat, desperate to distract herself. "Please move away from the bike. Stop. Wait there for just a moment, please." She stared at her feet as they turned and walked her back toward the patrol car without any conscience decision from her addled brain. Luke's indifference flummoxed her. Even after fourteen years, was it possible for him to have completely forgotten her? The one thing Luke had never been was *lukewarm*.

Punch Fiorelli had been watching them, frowning. "Uh, say, Sophie?" Sheepishly he scrubbed a hand across his big, firm belly. "We weren't going much past the speed limit. You wouldn't give tickets to two old Mustangs, now, wouldja, honey?"

She said, "You're in the clear, Punch," and slumped behind the wheel of the black-and-tan patrol car, boneless as a jellyfish. It was a minute before she gathered herself together and examined the license with a more objective eye. Hesitating to call it in to the dispatcher, she tapped the laminated card against the steering wheel, watching through the windshield as Punch approached Luke and began talking, gesturing at her car. Luke shrugged, nodded. Punch slapped him hard between the shoulder blades, a slap that would have made most men flinch.

Luke didn't waver. He was looking in Sophie's direction. Between the distance and the glare of sunshine on the glass, he shouldn't have been able to see her face very well. But she knew with a panicky certainty that he *did* see her. He saw inside her, to her dreams and fears and secrets. And he...

He didn't care.

Her last shreds of hope, already as brown and brittle as fallen leaves, disintegrated into crumbled bits of nothing. Whatever had happened to change Luke into a stranger, it was clear now that his return had come too late for both of them.

Sophie closed her hand around his license and other

papers and reached for the radio mike, intending to have him run through the computer for additional outstanding warrants. He'd changed immeasurably. It was possible that he was a fugitive wanted in six states other than Wyoming.

"YOU DO REALIZE that you were speeding when you drove through town," Sophie said in her curiously toneless voice, tipping up her chin to glare at him from beneath the flat brim of her trooper hat. "I'm going to issue you a citation."

"A fine welcome," Luke said, flippant, uncaring.

Her eyes narrowed. "By your own choice."

She was different...yet the same. Little Sophie Ryan, with the tough-girl attitude that would forever be betrayed by her Cupid's-bow mouth, the girlish sweep of her lashes and rampant curls the color of butter-brickle ice cream. At the same time she was strangely alien to him in her police uniform with its stained shirtfront and the badge on the pocket and the holstered gun she kept touching as though it were a lucky rabbit's foot.

Did he scare her?

The thought disturbed him. Her betrayal being what it was—a knife in the gut no matter how many years had passed—he still didn't care to come across as the kind of man she had to fear. He knew Sophie's heart. So tender and damaged. Intimidation wasn't his game.

What was hers?

She licked her lips, a nervous reaction he remembered well. She'd licked her lips, her eyes like saucers, the day he'd asked if she wanted to take a ride on his bike. She'd been barely sixteen, too young and uncertain to be as jaded as she'd put on. Straight off, he'd seen beyond her cocky attitude to the wounded psyche of a girl who was as untethered and searching as he.

"Can you step over to the patrol car, sir?"

Punch seemed anxious. "Hey, now, Soph—"

"No problem," Luke said, holding up his hands and walking away with Sophie cautiously trailing him. He couldn't see her expression very well because of the hat, but he could feel the worry and confusion—and maybe attraction—emanating from her. He responded with equally mixed emotions in spite of their past, to such a degree he began to wonder if he'd sped through town in order to attract Deputy Ryan's attention. Of course he hadn't known she'd be on patrol, but just the same...

Apparently, a man could hope even when he knew there was no logic to it.

"Place your hands on the hood," she directed. Her boot nudged his. "Spread 'em."

Luke knew the stance. The command amused him, coming from Sophie's baby-doll lips. Without even trying, he remembered the taste of her mouth, the velvet stroke of her tongue. The clarity of the memory was agonizing. Shouldn't he have forgotten by now?

"What is this?" Punch blustered. "C'mon, you can't—"

Luke chuckled mirthlessly. "Deputy Sophie's arresting me, Punch. Don't interrupt a woman at work."

Sophie gave him an abrupt shove between the shoulder blades. "Funny guy," she said, and started patting him down. She was efficient about it, but the effect her hands had on him as they ran over his body was anything but professional. Through his swift arousal, he felt her fingers slip into his back pocket. A small sound followed—the snick of his knife opening.

He looked over his shoulder. Sophie's left hand tightened on the back of his belt as she held out the knife, the silver blade flashing in the sunshine. She hesitated for a moment, saying nothing, her eyes accusing him.

The corners of his mouth twitched at the thought of her considering him a dangerous character. "A trinket," he said with a shrug.

She pocketed the knife. Gave him another shove. "I called in your license, Mr. Salinger. There are no outstanding out-of-state warrants on you." The back of her hands ran lightly over his legs, down, then up the insides, skimming across his thighs. After an infinitesimal hesitation, she cupped his crotch, her fingers skimming for a weapon. The intimate touch lasted for only a split second, but in that one tick of a moment his response leapt at the speed of light. Fire shot to his groin, producing a slight twitch, a thickening rush of desire. She gave a small gasp and pulled her hand away, her cheeks flaring as pink as the cotton candy he'd once fed her at the county fair.

"Yeah, aside from the one nasty breaking and entering charge, I've been a very good boy." His voice was rough, mocking, certain that Sophie's reaction to his old arrest would be as cold as a bucket of ice water. He needed to douse the fire between them right now. Or, heaven help him, jail would seem like a reasonable alternative.

"You're not getting off so easy this time," she snapped with frigid precision. He silently complied when she jerked his arms behind his back and clamped a hard metal bracelet around his wrist. "You forget. There's more than one charge. Add vandalism, arson and evading arrest and you're looking at a nice stay in the state pen, Mr. Salinger."

"Neither the Salingers nor the Lucases do hard time," he pointed out with fake good humor, which seemed to make her even colder and angrier. "When push comes to shove, they bribe the judge."

She yanked at his wrist and clicked the other handcuff into place. "Judge Cobb retired. We'll see if Judge Entwhistle is as lenient."

"Aw, Soph—handcuffs? Do you really need handcuffs?" Punch spread his upturned palms. "This is Maverick—you remember Maverick. Hell, you and him used to be—"

"Old news," Sophie said. "If Mr. Salinger didn't want to be arrested he shouldn't have come back to a town where there are charges against him on the books. I'm just doing my job."

"Man, when did you get to be such a hard-ass?" Punch complained. "Shucks, girl, you used to ride with the Mustangs! We don't turn on one of our own."

"All that was a long time ago," Sophie said. She stole a quick look at Luke. "Things have changed."

Not as much as either of them might have wanted. He thought of the fleeting touch of her hand between his legs. And his instantaneous reaction.

"*Everything's* changed," she added under her breath.

In the shadow of the hat brim, her eyes were large and liquid, betraying a modicum of shyness despite her position of authority. There was still a beguiling air of innocent femininity about her.

Only the appearance of it, Luke reminded himself, trying again to be ruthless.

He scowled, unable to reconcile his memories of the teenage Sophie with both the woman she was now and all that he'd been told of her since he'd skipped town.

Fourteen years was too immense a span to leap when doubts were nipping at his heels.

One question was clanging inside his head. *What if he'd been wrong about her?*

Sophie read him his rights in a flattened, disaffected voice, then hustled him into the patrol car. Punch gave her a hard time, sputtering and complaining, looking ready to carry out his nickname. The burly Italian calmed down some when Luke asked him to look after the motorcycle, but he continued to glower at Sophie, muttering under his breath. She unconcernedly went about her job, slamming shut the back door and climbing behind the wheel. She swept off her hat, started the car and reached for the radio all at the same time, and was soon reporting her progress to the dispatcher as she spun the steering wheel one-handed. The tires squealed. She trod on the gas, aiming the car straight down the mountain.

Luke watched the scenery for a while, silent as a stone while he tried to work out the ramifications of his arrest on his unsuspecting family. Tough to concentrate on what would be a replay of the same old recriminations and accusations when Sophie was sitting a few feet away. His gaze kept straying to the curve of her fragile neck, framed by a crisp collar and the wild corkscrew curls that had come loose from her hair clip. She held her shoulders and head with a stiff military precision—no more broody teenage slouch. And she'd filled out some, was stronger and more substantial than the reed of a girl she'd been the last time he'd seen her. She'd become physically confident, he decided. Brisk and competent, certain enough of herself to handle a job that called for a typically male brand of aggression.

Little Sophie Ryan had truly become a cop, just as

Heath had claimed. Luke shook his head in amazement, even though it might not be such a strange career choice when he considered her final gesture toward him.

He wasn't especially worried about the old charges she'd arrested him for. In fact, he'd assumed that his grandmother had smoothed that over years ago. Not out of a particular concern for him, but to protect the precious family name. For all the affection between them, he'd never been as valuable to Mary Lucas as the family's history, longevity and status, which she'd preserve at all costs.

Roughly fourteen years ago, he and a few of the Mustangs had broken into a lawyer's office in Treetop. For Luke, the mission had justified the means. He'd been too narrowly focused to foresee how quickly the break-in would escalate into a free-for-all, particularly when his liquored-up friends were involved. Demon and Snake had started trashing the place—supposedly to cover their tracks. Luke had grabbed what he'd come for and hustled them out as quickly as he could. Too quickly, it had turned out, because he'd overlooked the lighted lamp that had fallen off the desk onto a sheaf of upended files. They'd been long gone before the fire had started.

Being young and stupid was no defense. He was guilty. No one would believe it now, but back then, as rebellious as he'd been, he'd intended to turn himself in after learning about the fire. All he'd wanted was to see Sophie first. To tell her that it would be okay, that she should stay strong and wait for him even if he was sent to jail.

He remembered driving to her dad's dumpy trailer on what had turned out to be his last night in town. The crisp autumn air had been tinged with the scent of snow, and there had been a wildly romantic notion of inviting Sophie to run away with him floating around inside his head. The patrol car parked in the Ryan's weed-choked driveway had stopped him like a brick wall.

First he thought that Sophie was merely being questioned. But the snatches of conversation he'd caught through the thin aluminum sides of the trailer seemed to tell a different tale. By all appearances, Luke's girlfriend—loyal little Sophie—was ratting him out.

He'd let impulse take over, leaving Treetop in a fury so hot it had shriveled his breaking heart into a coal. That had always been his way—covering pain with burning anger. Learning the art of icy detachment had taken years.

In his early days on the road, when he had no idea where to go or what to do, a small part of him had clung to the hope that the situation wasn't what it seemed. Sophie had been put into a no-win position— his fault all the way. But when he'd called the ranch, his older brother Heath had reported the ugly truth of Sophie's actions. The word had spread throughout Treetop. To save her hide, Sophie Ryan had told Deputy Ed Warren everything she knew. As a result, charges were being brought against the Mustangs.

Given Luke's culpability, he might have forgiven her that…if she hadn't done worse. Again, Heath had been the reluctant messenger. It seemed that Sophie had not only betrayed Luke in spirit, she'd betrayed him in body.

The end.

To this day, Luke didn't know which hurt more— leaving Sophie or loving Sophie.

But what if he'd been wrong about her? What if he'd

been wrong to believe in secondhand gossip instead of the heart-and-guts proof of their actual relationship?

No. There was evidence, the kind she couldn't hide.

Luke coughed. "I hear you've got a kid."

Sophie's alarmed eyes met his in the rearview mirror; the car shot dangerously fast around one of the switchback curves. She slammed her foot on the brake, sending the back end fishtailing into a soft sandy spot on the shoulder of the road.

"Take it easy," Luke said, just before he was flung across the seat as she bumped back onto the road. By the time he'd awkwardly righted himself, pushing himself up with his hands cuffed behind his back, she'd gotten the car under control and was proceeding as if he hadn't spoken, her lips tightly pursed. He sought her eyes in the mirror, but she wouldn't look at him.

"A boy," he said.

Her fingers clenched on the wheel. "Let's keep this strictly business."

"Not possible."

Her head jerked sideways and he caught a glimpse of her pale face and stormy eyes, brimmed by thick brown lashes. "What did you say?"

"You and I will never be strictly business."

"Fourteen years without contact certainly indicates otherwise."

"Nope. Fourteen years without contact only means that we both went cold turkey. Now that I'm back..." He let the smoldering heat inside him flow into his intense stare. It was amazing how physical desire could blot out one's doubts. "Things are bound to be different. There's a wicked temptation in proximity." If she hadn't cuffed him, he could have run his finger along her exposed nape to remind her of the sparks that flew between them. It was obvious that maturity had only deepened the attraction.

His fingers flexed. Was her skin still as smooth as satin? He'd always been astonished by how soft she was beneath her rough cotton blouses and cheap denim jeans. His sweet little Sophie had been a pink rose bristling with thorns.

She caught her breath. "Don't—" She exhaled noisily. "Don't you even think of starting up with me again, Luke Salinger. I'm not interested."

"Well, well. Little Sophie's learned to stand up for herself."

"I finally figured out that no one else would do it for me."

"Yeah." He remembered the patrol car parked in her driveway on that fateful night. With all her defiance, why hadn't she stood up for him? Although he'd never have dreamed of asking her to lie, it had turned out that he'd *wanted* her unflinching support. Had counted on it. Discovering that not even Sophie was prepared to back him up had seemed like the final cruel blow.

Years later, he understood that the situation hadn't been so black-and-white. He'd made mistakes himself. Bad ones. Perhaps even irreparable.

"Life sure is a bitch, huh, Little Soph?" he said coaxingly.

"Don't call me that," she snapped, uncoaxed. "May I remind you that I'm your arresting officer?"

"Something you've been waiting to do for a long time, I'd wager." He kept his tone nonchalant. Even so, he could tell by the way she cocked her head that she'd caught the underlying accusation.

"What's that supposed to mean?" she asked, softly menacing.

"Only that a jail cell's where you think I belong. Maybe you always did."

She didn't answer. Didn't speak for a long while. When finally she did, he couldn't tell if the quaver in her voice indicated guilt or regret or maybe even longing. "Oh, Luke," she said. "Why'd you come back?"

"Hey, babe, you don't sound happy to see me."

She slammed the flat of her hand on the steering wheel. "Try to be serious, please. I need to know why you've come back after so long. What made you—" A shudder coursed through her. "Why?"

He hesitated, wondering about the worry in her voice. It was as if she feared him. And that didn't make sense.

"Haven't you heard?" he said mildly, settling on the easiest of his reasons for returning to Wyoming. "The Lucases are having a family reunion at the ranch. A black sheep is just what they need to complete the happy get-together."

Watching her face in the mirror, he caught the relief that flashed over her features. It was gone before he could fully weigh it. "And that's all?" she prodded, her brows beetled.

He shifted, trying to find a comfortable position. The links of the cuffs jingled. "Looks like I'm going to have a date in the courts as well. Thanks to you, Deputy Ryan."

"I'm sure the family lawyer will take care of the problem in a snap." She'd probably meant to sound gruff, unaware that a hint of concern had crept into her voice. "Judge Entwhistle is tough but fair. She'll take into account your clean record." Sophie cleared her throat. "As long as it's completely clean, that is."

"You mean, have I been carrying out a lawless rampage for the past fourteen years?" He shrugged. "Nope.

I'm squeaky clean. Other than for a recent speeding ticket.''

She smiled. Then quickly sobered. "So what have you been doing all this time?"

"A little bit of everything."

"In the old days, that meant carousing, disturbing the peace, malicious mischief..."

"A guy learns to be more discreet when he's on the lam."

"On the lam for fourteen years?" Sophie braked at the highway intersection. "Some life."

"Yeah, it's been real fulfilling," he growled, taunting her. What did she care? She'd cast him aside, hadn't she?

"You always did suit your name," she said softly. "Apparently you're still an untamed maverick." Her chin tilted, showing him her narrowed eyes. "When are you going to grow up, huh?"

"Like you? Little Sophie Ryan with her uniform and her handcuffs and her big, bad gun?"

She twisted around in the seat. "At least I've stayed in one place and built something good and lasting for myself! I've lived up to my responsibilities!"

Luke was taken aback. "Sophie?" he said quietly, puzzled by her vehemence.

A truck stacked with hay bales rattled past. She stepped on the gas and pulled out behind it with a spin of the tires—obviously her driving hadn't improved just because she was now piloting a patrol car. "Forget I said that. I was only blowing off steam."

He insisted. "What responsibility have I shirked?"

She hunched her shoulders. "I expect your family could answer that better than me."

"Maybe." But he didn't think that was what she'd

meant. He went silent for a few minutes, trying to evaluate the situation from Sophie's viewpoint, with the aid of years of hindsight. If she'd been as angry and mixed-up as he, shouldn't he be able to find enough compassion to forgive her own lapse—or lapses, according to Heath—of good judgment?

I don't know if I can. He'd been Sophie's first lover; his possessiveness had run strong. The shock of her betrayal had been the only way he'd made the break, and still his unreasoning desire for her had remained—a torturous emotion to live with, driving him to dangerously escalating extremes in his work as a stuntman, all part of the effort to get her out of his mind until he'd finally smartened up and realized that seeing her again was the only way to know for sure.

"I left you," he said. "You're still holding a grudge about that?"

She gave a short, hard, dismissive laugh. No answer.

They were passing Punch's place, nearing the town. In a short while Sophie would turn back into Deputy Ryan and Luke would have missed his chance. He had to speak now—or forever hold his peace.

"I wanted to take you with me, you know."

She went as quiet and watchful as an owl, her rounded eyes reflected in the mirror.

"My brown-eyed girl," he whispered, lost in a sudden swirl of bittersweet memory. Slow dancing with Sophie in the gravel parking lot of the Thunderhead since she was too young to go inside, her head flung back, her dark eyes on his. Speeding on his motorcycle, taking the switchback at a reckless speed, her arms wrapped tight around his waist. Hours spent lying together in the long grass of the Boyer's Rock pasture, the sun-warmed earth their refuge, their cradle. Trading kisses, whispering confessions, studying the stars.

Sophie blinked. Several times. "Sure you wanted to take me. So much so that you left town without even saying goodbye." Her voice was clotted with wary resentment.

Yet hopeful? he wondered, then deliberately reminded himself of why he'd left her behind in the first place. According to Heath—and other walking, talking evidence in the form of her son—she'd not only spilled her guts to the sheriff, she'd quickly found "consolation" with a string of other men.

Luke refused to let her see how badly that tore at his insides. *Ice water in my veins.* "Well, jeez, Sophie, I guess I figured that if you were willing to turn me in to the sheriff, keeping me as your boyfriend was not a top priority."

She stopped the car in the middle of Granite Street, two blocks from the police station. Luckily there was very little traffic, as was usually the case in Treetop.

"Luke…" she said, turning to stare at him over the top of the car seat. Slowly she shook her head. "I didn't."

Anguish clawed at his gut. "You didn't?"

She was adamant, proud, passionate—his Sophie, his brown-eyed girl. "No, Luke. I most certainly did not turn you in to the sheriff!"

SOPHIE TURNED THE KEY and sat dully in her thirteen-year-old hatchback—same age as her son—waiting for the engine to stop rattling. A wisp of smoke rose from the tailpipe.

She sighed. There was no way she could afford a new car this year, not if she intended to heat the house during the long, cold winter, keep Joey in jeans, sneakers and pizza, plus pay tuition for the last two courses she needed to complete her degree in social work. If going to college part-time had given her any smarts at all, she'd have chosen a field that paid better. Having a career that meant something to her and the world at large was more important to her happiness in the long run, but in the short run, her old car was ready to plunk its last ker-plunkety plunk.

Sophie's head throbbed. Maybe her dad could work on the engine again, keep it going a little longer with another bubblegum-and-rubber-band miracle.

She pushed the door open with a creak and stepped out, tired to her bones. Aside from the wicked headache, it wasn't a physical exhaustion as much as a mental one. The psychological trauma of Maverick's return had done her in.

Facing her father and son was what she dreaded next. If Archie "Buzzsaw" Ryan had made his rounds to the Thunderhead and the liquor store instead of moldering in his trailer out back, he'd have heard the news. Word wouldn't have reached Joey as fast. Even if it had, he wouldn't really care about an adult he'd never met. Unless some busybody had started up with the old rumor about Luke Salinger being Joe Ryan's father...

Rolling her head to ease the tight muscles in her neck and shoulders, Sophie clumped up the porch steps of her two-bedroom wood frame cottage. Coming home usually gave her a boost. The small house wasn't much, but it was hers—at least the mortgage was—and she'd worked hard to make it into the kind of safe, cozy home she'd never known, growing up. Today it just looked like a money pit—a conglomeration of loose shingles, dripping faucets, crumbling plaster and buckling linoleum. If she hadn't splashed bright jewel-toned coats of paint on every surface to distract the eye, there'd be no disguising that the place was coming down around their ears.

"Hey, Joe?" she called from the pumpkin-colored front hall, even though the silence told her that her son wasn't home. She checked the clock. Time for a bath before she had to start dinner. If ever there was a day when she needed to be cleansed of her cares and woes, it was today.

Luke already knows about Joey.

The thought had pulsed at the back of her mind all day, a red-for-danger strobe that had given her the vicious headache. As the tub filled, she popped a couple of aspirin, staring at her face in the mirror over the sink.

"He doesn't know everything," she told her bleak reflection.

But he soon will—someone's bound to repeat the rumor, argued the voice that had taken control of her pounding skull. *What will you do when he shows up, asking if it's true?*

How badly did she want Joey to have a father?

"I can't think about it now." Sophie stripped off her uniform and dropped it in the hamper. She'd have to remember to bring the ruined shirt to the dry cleaner's tomorrow morning—another expense she could do without.

As if it mattered in the larger scheme of things. After this morning, she had worse problems than coffee stains to think about. Confronting them made her headache intensify. She could have sworn it was gnawing away her brain.

Luke suspects.

She winced in pain.

Heath Salinger knows.
The townspeople think *they know.*
Gad, her head was going to explode.
But everyone's wrong—including me.

CHAPTER THREE

TYPICALLY, JOE RYAN came home with a clatter and crash—backpack flung to the floor, high-top sneakers kicked off against the wall, a brief stop to power up the TV at top volume, a noisy forage through the kitchen, gabbing loudly all the while whether or not there was a response from Sophie. Only his garrulousness had abated recently as he took more and more to locking himself in his attic bedroom, rap music pounding the slanted walls, immune to his mother's entreaties for either a little bit of peace and quiet or a return of their old rapport. While Sophie figured Joe's moods were the usual teenage funk, she missed the boy he used to be: sweet, funny, affectionate—a chatterbox.

"Hey, Mom, what's for supper?" Joe hollered from the kitchen, sounding as though his head was buried in the refrigerator.

Sophie had left the bathroom door open a wide crack. "Casserole," she yelled, which was what she always said when she hadn't planned a menu or shopped for ingredients. There was usually something on hand that could be made into a casserole.

Joe groaned. "Not again."

"Unless you want to fire up the barbecue?"

He groaned louder to be sure that she'd heard.

She muttered. "Then don't complain about the casserole."

A creaking sound followed by the shushing slide of stocking-clad feet in the short hallway told her that Joey was trying to creep upstairs without her hearing. "Joe," she called. "Stop and say hello before you go up to your room."

"'Lo," he mumbled from outside the bathroom door.

A few years back—more like four, Sophie realized with a pang—Joe used to sit with her while she soaked in the bathtub. He'd chatter about his day at school and why the pond changed color and how come Grandpa only had one arm and what he'd dreamed about last night, which at the time was usually spaceships or vampires. Now she was lucky if she could get a "'lo" out of him.

Today she needed more. "Can you talk to me, please, Joey? Tell me that you got an A on your first biology quiz and that you and Grandpa cleaned out the garden shed like you were supposed to all summer."

"I got a B+, and Grandpa wasn't here when I got home from school so I went over to Fletcher's and played basketball. Okay?"

"You'll do the shed this weekend."

"Yeah." Agitated, Joe rattled a bag of tortilla chips in time with his jiggling leg. He was all twitches and fidgets these days, a perpetual motion machine. "Can I go now?"

The silhouette he made hovering in the dim hallway was disturbing to Sophie's tenuous peace of mind. Anyone looking for it would see her son's familiarity to the Salinger brothers—the lanky frame, the handsomely carved profile, the height. Luckily Joe's eyes were brown like hers and not Luke's steel blue. That would have been a dead giveaway.

Joe raked one hand through the scruff of dark hair

that flopped over his forehead. "Huh, Mom? Can I pleeeze go to my room now?"

Sophie squirmed in the bathtub, rubbing at the goose flesh that had sprung up on her arms despite the steamy water. "Then nothing interesting happened today?"

"Mo-o-om…"

"Okay, you can leave," she said, relieved. "Way to go on that B+." But Joe was already gone, galloping up the twisting steps like a gangly runaway colt. His door slammed. Two seconds later, music blared. Sophie listened for a few minutes to be sure he hadn't sneaked in a banned CD—she knew more about gangsta rap than she wanted—before tuning out.

Reprieve. She closed her eyes and slid lower in the tub. She had time to think of what—if anything—she should tell her son about his father.

Gradually the hot bath eased her tight muscles. Total relaxation beckoned, but one thought kept intruding. Joey had said that his grandfather was gone. Which meant that Archie would return knowing of Luke's reappearance. The Lucases—even though the younger generation carried the name Salinger, they were still considered Lucases through and through—were the kind of family that the citizens of Treetop loved to gossip about. Every lurid detail of Sophie's chase and arrest of the black sheep would be dissected over dinner tables all over town. Archie would glare at her across the table and wave his stump around, dredging up his ancient complaints about the Lucases and how they'd done the Ryans wrong. It would be the Montagues versus the Capulets all over again, and Sophie was exhausted just imagining it.

"Nuts." She hoisted herself out of the tub. One way or another, Maverick's return was going to force her into a showdown with everyone in her life. And out of it, she supposed, thinking of Luke with an unwelcome but nonetheless compelling fascination. She shivered.

"Branded," she whispered, blotting herself with a towel. Her fingers went involuntarily to the Mustangs tattoo on her rear end. *Get a grip*, she scolded herself. *It's just a tattoo. Not a brand.* She wrapped the towel around herself, hoping that out of sight would equal out of mind, and went to get dressed.

Sure enough, by the time Sophie had concocted a kitchen-cupboard casserole and was slicing sweet potatoes to look like french fries—as if that would fool Joey—Archie Ryan had arrived in a temper. A short, stubby, muscular man in canvas work pants and an untucked plaid flannel shirt, he stomped past the kitchen window, ignoring his daughter's wave. He went straight to the trailer she'd persuaded him to park in the backyard because that was the only way she could keep an eye on him.

After putting the sweet potatoes in the oven to roast, she called for Joe to set the table, knowing very well he couldn't—or wouldn't—hear her over his loud music. She sighed in exasperation before climbing the attic steps to bang on his door until it rattled.

Archie was next. However, as soon as Sophie stepped outside the back door, the mud-speckled red motorbike leaning against the garden shed caught her eye. And held it.

Getaway.

She plopped down onto the back step and rested her chin on the heel of her palm, letting herself imagine climbing aboard Joe's peppy little bike and taking off for the hills, leaving behind her cantankerous father, her complicated son and all her other responsibilities. She'd go straight to the Rockies and climb toward the sky, the Continental Divide being the closest thing to heaven on earth that she knew of. Already she could feel the wind in her hair, the thrum of the engine, the adrenaline coursing through her bloodstream....

Sophie shook her head. She hadn't dreamed about such things in years. Luke was to blame, Luke and his seductive pledge that he'd wanted to take her with him.

Fourteen years too late.

"Goddamn you, Maverick," she said, rising to stalk across the straggly grass to pound on her father's dented door. "Supper," she barked. "Now or never, Dad." Without waiting, she returned to the cottage where Joe was miraculously setting the table. She wrapped her arms around his skinny shoulders and gave him a tight hug that was mostly a comfort to herself. He slipped away, smiling sheepishly.

The screen door wheezed. "What's to eat?" Buzzsaw demanded in his distinctive gravelly voice, already scowling at her from beneath the creased brim of his grimy straw cowboy hat. He had a grizzled week-old beard and stormy brown eyes that turned mean when he'd crossed from pleasantly buzzed to downright drunk.

Sophie was no longer intimidated. Time and circumstance had tipped the scales of power in her favor. She swept off her father's hat and set a green salad on the table. "It's been a long, hard day. We are going to sit together and have a nice dinner without complaint or ill comment. We will be polite and courteous and talk only of pleasant subjects. Isn't that right, Dad?"

Archie grunted as he went to his place.

Sophie took that as agreement. "Joey, will you say grace?"

"Oh, Mom."

She smiled—pointedly. "Pardon me. I meant, Joe, my dear, handsome, obedient son, will you please say grace?"

Joe took one look at her steely smile and ducked his chin to comply. He knew his mother's limits.

Even Archie seemed to understand; occasionally a glimmer of a clue pierced his thick skull. They ate dinner in a near silence that Sophie found very restful. The only discussions were those she initiated, consisting of topics such as the cushions she was needlepointing for the window seat in her bedroom and the gorgeous acorn squash Bess Ripley was selling from her produce stand at the railroad junction.

When they finished, Joe helped wash the dishes one-handed—a towering ice cream cone occupying the other—and then begged to be excused to play computer games. Because he asked so nicely Sophie agreed, even though she couldn't understand why he didn't want to be outside on such a beautiful evening. She thought of Luke then, locked up in one of Treetop's little-used, cement-block jail cells. Luke, who belonged to the outdoors more than anyone she'd ever known.

It wasn't like this was the first fine September evening he'd spent in the lockup. The Mustangs' penchant for petty crime had kept them all checking in and out of the jail on a rotating basis. Luke had always been the first to make bail or pay his fine, thanks to Mary Lucas and her attorneys-on-retainer.

There was no reason for Sophie to feel sorry for him.

She put the last plate away and slammed the yellow cupboard door. She raked her hair back from her face, hoping the taut pull of skin over her forehead would yank her out of the momentary funk.

Instead her thoughts returned to the shock of seeing Luke again. How he'd alternated between lazy taunts and the bitter accusations that had shaken her already-wobbly resolution to distance herself.

What had become of Luke? Her Luke—handsome, vital, burning with the joy of life?

Sure, he'd always been wild. But he'd never been... bad. Not at the core. Not like Demon Bradshaw, who the sheriff's department currently suspected of selling illegal firearms, among other nefarious dealings. So far they hadn't been able to put together enough evidence for an arrest.

"That's not Luke." Sophie let out a deep breath and released her hair. She pulled the drain and wiped down the counter, her eyebrows drawn together in a scowl that was an unconscious copy of her father's.

"Hey, girl," Archie called from the front porch. "Come on out here."

Figuring she'd put it off long enough, Sophie went to the door, wiping her wet hands on the back pockets of her denim pedal pushers. "Ice cream, Dad?"

"Uh, no." Guiltily Archie slipped a can of beer to his left side, holding it there with the stump of the arm he'd lost in a logging accident on Lucas land approximately thirty years ago. Sophie made no comment. Aside from the occasional sniping argument when her temper wore thin, she'd given up expecting her father to change his ways. Only middle age and bouts of ill health had mellowed his bad habits.

She sat beside him on the purple porch swing and gazed out over Granite Street, waiting for the well-named Buzzsaw to start in on the grief the Lucases had caused him. Birds twittered and hopped in the old plum tree that made a canopy over the small front lawn, pecking at the last of the rotting fruit. The saw-toothed leaves shimmered against the deepening sky.

For once Archie was subdued. "I hear that good-for-nothing Lucas boy's back in town."

"He's a Salinger, Dad. His mother was a Lucas."

Archie snorted. "Same thing. They're all rotten, don't matter what name they go by. It's in the blood."

Sophie tensed. The front windows were open. Joe might overhear their conversation from the living room. The bleeps, small explosions and mechanical screams of his computer video game reassured her that his attention was focused elsewhere—on virtual mayhem instead of the real kind. "I wouldn't condemn them all," she said. "But, yes, I did arrest Luke Salinger."

Archie drank deeply and emitted a satisfied *ahhh*. "For speeding?"

"I gave him a citation for that. I arrested him on old charges—breaking and entering and arson. Remember the fire that damaged the law office? Fourteen years ago, next month."

"Humph. That boy always was trouble, with his fancy motorcycle and his law-breakin' ways. I hope you got the sense not to have any more to do with him." Sophie's past relationship with Luke—an alliance Archie had done his best to prevent—hung between them with all the levity of a lead balloon.

She fingered the frayed edge of her pedal pushers. "Well, Dad, I expect I'll be seeing him in court."

"Court." Archie guffawed. "You think them muckety-mucks are gonna let that case get to court? Old lady Lucas will be in the judge's chambers calling in favors—"

"Hush, Dad. I don't want Joey to hear."

That shut Archie up. He and Sophie had never talked

about the identity of Joe's father, partly because Archie had thrown her out of the trailer in a drunken rage when he'd found out she was pregnant. He'd been deep into a bad streak then, drinking non-stop. Only seventeen and not yet graduated, Sophie had been almost relieved to go through the pregnancy on her own, in a rented room at Lettice Bellew's boardinghouse. Archie hadn't seen his grandson until Joe was three years old. And it wasn't until he and Sophie had made their uneasy peace many years later that he'd become a regular fixture in their lives.

Archie's brows met in a deep frown. "Girl, what are you gonna tell the boy about, uh…"

Sophie held her breath, but her father didn't finish the question. In which case she wasn't about to volunteer an answer.

"Them Lucases," he growled, lapsing into familiar territory. He thrust out his stump, the sleeve of his shirt knotted where the elbow should have been. "You know what they done to me, girl. By rights I should be settin' pretty with a big pension, but nosiree, old lady Lucas is as mean as a junkyard dog, holding tight to every penny unless she's gonna see some return…"

Sophie tuned out her father's voice until it was no more than an annoying whine at the back of her brain. The truth of the matter was that Archie had snuck a few beers the day he'd had the accident with a chain saw that had resulted in the loss of his arm. Mary Lucas, a new widow at the time, had taken over running the Lucas cattle ranch and logging operations. She'd paid the hospital bills and given Archie a generous settlement—considering the circumstances—a goodly portion of which he'd promptly drunk up on a months-long spree. Even so, he persisted in blaming his troubles and sketchy work history on Mary Lucas and her extended family.

Sophie had heard it a thousand times before. Gently she pressed a hand on her father's good arm. "Shut up, Dad, and take a look at the sunset. Isn't that pretty?"

Archie barely glanced at the apricot glow that lit up the mountainous horizon before continuing churlishly, "Listen to me, girl. Call 'em Lucases or call 'em Salingers, that family will stomp you under their boot heels for so much as smiling at them the wrong way. You steer clear—"

"I've got a badge, Dad. Even Mary Lucas has to respect the law."

"Sure, sure, go ask Sheriff Warren about that. He's been doing their bidding ever since they helped him get elected top dog, just like every sheriff before him. How'dja think my accident report got cleaned up so no one named Lucas was to blame?"

Sophie simply shrugged. Argument was useless when her father got this worked up.

"That's right," Archie said, nodding so vigorously the swing started to sway. "I tell you—"

"Joey!" Sophie said in relief when her son made the mistake of poking his head out the door. "Join us. Please."

Joe rolled his eyes, but he came outside and sat on the porch railing. The golden-pink light of the setting sun washed across his narrow face and baggy white T-shirt. To Sophie he was beautiful—not that she dared say so out loud when he'd become so touchy about expressions of affection. Silently she ached with her immense love for her son. Too much, she sometimes thought, for one heart to hold.

When Joe had been born she'd known with a protectiveness so fierce it scared her that she would do anything to keep her baby from suffering the kind of upbringing that she'd had—one that had become essentially homeless, parentless and loveless after her mother had died when she was only five. Right from the start, though, she'd denied Joe a father, even if it hadn't been entirely by plan. Could she continue to deny him the truth as well, especially now that Luke was back home and the can of worms had been opened again?

Listening to his grandfather's diatribe, Joe cocked his head in such a way that Sophie was reminded of Luke so explicitly that she wondered why no one else noticed. Or commented.

Probably some of them did, but only behind her back.

The Lucas brand, she thought, growing doleful as she twisted a thick curl of hair around her index finger. She'd always worried about what Mary Lucas, the dominating family matriarch, might do if she knew for sure that Joe carried her blood. As of yet, her eldest grandson Heath hadn't produced an heir. For a long time now Sophie had watched and waited, knowing more about Heath's personal life than she cared to because she was friendly with his wife, Kiki. It was Sophie's greatest fear that one day Mary Lucas might began to look elsewhere for her heir.

And there would be Joe Ryan, hidden in plain sight.

The Lucas brand was more trouble than it was worth, in Sophie's estimation. Joe wasn't one of their heads of cattle, mineral mines, or uncut trees. He wasn't their property.

She would never let that family stamp their brand on him!

If that meant she had to deny his parentage, so be it.

"TELL ME ABOUT SOPHIE RYAN," Luke said when the deputy came to collect the hard plastic supper tray. For fifteen minutes he'd been standing at the high, narrow window of his jail cell, looking out at the sky, thinking of Sophie and her amazing statement of innocence regarding the criminal investigation. She hadn't uttered one world of explanation to defend, or prove, herself, only brought him in silence to the station, booked him, fingerprinted him and locked him up.

And Luke believed her.

It remained true that someone with inside knowledge had dropped a bug in Ed Warren's ear. But that someone had not been Sophie, despite the incriminating words that Luke had overheard and somehow misinterpreted.

Of course it hadn't been Sophie. He was a jackass for doubting her on that count. He'd been so blinded by jealousy over reports of Sophie's swift recovery from their love affair that he'd believed without proof the gossip that claimed she'd served up the Mustangs to the authorities.

He cursed. Even if she *had* cracked under interrogation, could he blame her? She'd been seventeen, alone and abandoned—by him. The fault had been his, no other's.

Face it, man. He stared at the lacy upper branches of a tall cottonwood tree, the only thing he could see from the window besides the sky. The leaves shook like coins in the gilding rays of the setting sun. *You acted like a first-class heel. A selfish hothead. A coward.*

It was no big surprise, then, that Sophie wanted nothing to do with him aside from his arrest.

Deputy Boone Barzinski was absently studying the uneaten dessert on Luke's tray. "Sophie Ryan..." he mulled in response to Luke's request. The redheaded deputy scooped up a dollop of bread pudding with his forefinger.

Luke made fists around the iron bars of his cage. "How long has she been a deputy?" He was beginning to wonder how much of Heath's secondhand information was accurate.

"Oh, well, now..." Boone licked his finger. He seemed good-natured, but not the sharpest tack in the hardware store. "Maybe four years. No, five. Or six?"

"She's unmarried?"

"Yep. I mean, nope. She's not married."

Luke's eyes narrowed. "Boyfriend?"

Boone colored; Luke discerned that the deputy had a crush on Sophie. "Uhh, I think she's...unattached," he mumbled.

"She's got a son."

"Well, you know." Boone's glance skipped across the congealed contents of the supper tray. He lowered his voice. "An unwed mother. Nowadays these things happen even to good girls, am I right?"

"Good girls?" Heath—Luke's main contact in Treetop for more than a decade—had said that Sophie's inclinations had leaned rather drastically in the opposite direction.

"Saint Sophie—that's what some of the guys in the department call her. Because she doesn't...you know. Uh, share her favors. She hardly even dates." Boone's brows arched up a high forehead bisected by a horizontal tan line. "They say she's practically a nun, even though there's, well, her son and all as evidence of, uh, whatever. I dunno. I was hired only last year, so I couldn't actually say..."

Luke stared—hard. His knuckles were stark white. "How old is Sophie's son?"

Boone blinked nervously under the scrutiny. He waggled his head back and forth, as if silently counting with each nod. "Junior high age, I guess. Joe's a good boy. Plays guard on the basketball team. Sophie's awful proud of him."

"Twelve?" Luke asked sharply. "Thirteen? That old?"

"Maybe."

"And what about the father?"

Remembering his professional capacity, Boone drew back, squaring his sloping shoulders in the taupe deputy's uniform. "Uh, say, what do you care anyhow?" His color deepened, turning even the pale half of his forehead pink. "Sophie doesn't put up with loose talk. She'd have my hide if she knew I'd gone and blabbed—"

"No harm done." Luke stepped back from the bars. "Sophie and I used to be friends. I was wondering how she's been doing, that's all."

"Oh. Right." Recognition—and something more—flared in the deputy's eyes. "You're the one who—" Boone slammed shut his mouth. "Er, uh, okay. You set for the night? Sure you don't want to make a phone call? We got lights out at ten."

You're the one who— The unfinished statement was jangling in Luke's head like a fire alarm, but he nodded and drew further back into his cell. When Deputy Barzinski returned an hour later to put out the lights Luke was still standing in the same place, silent but alert, his eyes on the narrow rectangle of indigo sky.

Sophie, he repeated to himself. Sophie…

He was the one who—what?

JUDGE HARRIET ENTWHISTLE prided herself on being eccentric and independent, as well as tough. She ran her court her way and hang what the judicial review board had to say. There were cases where a woman's good sense had to overrule the guidelines thought up by city folk who, when it came right down to it, knew beans about country-style justice.

The particulars of the bail hearing of Mr. Lucas Salinger—fugitive, notorious hometown boy, grandson of the judge's favorite canasta partner—had convinced Harriet that this was such a case. Her quandary was how to adequately satisfy what was one of the participants' most unusual need for personal justice with what the law demanded.

"Let me see if my poor ole brain's got this straight," the judge said, glaring from the bench at the assorted players, not out of any actual ire, but just on general principles. "The injured party in this case, Sampson and Devore, Attorneys-at-Law, have been out of business for eight years, and they never wanted to press charges in the first place. Oddly enough." Lucas money had passed hands there, she'd wager. "Mr. Salinger—" the judge regarded the leather-clad defendant sourly "—skipped town before he could be fully questioned. Our good sheriff seems disinclined to reopen the investigation." Sheriff Ed Warren bobbed up, smiling like a politician. "For reasons that fail me," Judge Entwhistle intoned, and the sheriff dropped down again, his smile gone stale as day-old doughnuts. "However, the charges against Mr. Salinger were never officially dropped, leading Deputy Sophie Ryan to make an arrest when Mr. Salinger reappeared in town."

Judge Entwhistle paused to scan the arrest report, neatly filled in by Deputy Ryan, whom the judge was prepared to favor above the rest of the yahoos standing before her. Sophie Ryan had testified in the circuit court many times. She was always respectful, well-prepared and honest, unlike some of the law enforcement personnel, who were so puffed-up with machismo they thought a starched uniform and a sidearm were enough to persuade even a judge to their point of view. Nevertheless...

Mary Lucas had asked for leniency, and Mary did know how to play a mean game of canasta.

The judge looked up. Every eye in the courtroom was trained on her face, which put her in a better mood. "And finally, we have the prosecutor—" the fresh-out-of-law-school pipsqueak brightened expectantly "—who also is disinclined to prosecute the case, considering the time span and Mr. Salinger's clean record and gainful employment thereafter. Is that right?"

The prosecutor agreed.

Judge Entwhistle addressed Luke Salinger. "I'm of a mind to see that you get what you have coming to you, young man, fourteen years too late or not." She scrutinized the defendant, trying to decide if he was as lawless as the case signified or merely temporarily misguided, as according to Mary Lucas.

After a nice, lengthy silence, the judge cleared her throat. "Which leads to my ruling. I've decided to continue this case indefinitely. In the meantime, Mr. Salinger, you're free to go." The judge tapped her gavel at the sudden rise of chatter. "However," she said heavily, silencing the courtroom, "I also intend to keep you under close supervision, Mr. Salinger." She twitched a scolding finger, deciding to take a left turn off the rule book. "As a matter of fact, I do believe it would be wise to appoint a watchdog to see that you behave yourself. By order of this court, I place Mr. Lucas Salinger under the charge of—''

Mary Lucas set her cane and rose from her seat in the first row, a proud, tall, gaunt figure in a Western-cut business suit.

''—Deputy Sophie Ryan,'' the judge finished with a flourish.

A collective gasp rose from the crowd. Several mouths dropped open in shock, including Sophie's. Judge Entwhistle favored the young deputy with a woman-to-avenging-woman smile. ''Deputy Ryan will see that you pay for your crimes, Mr. Salinger. I wish you both the best of luck.'' A satisfying smash of the gavel. ''And that's all she wrote, people. Court is adjourned.''

CHAPTER FOUR

MARY LUCAS STABBED HER CANE against the marble floor. "Of all the foolish notions!"

A small smile flickered across Luke's face. He'd completed the paperwork of his official release to find his grandmother waiting for him outside the courtroom doors and Deputy Sophie Ryan set like a guard dog near the exit at the other end of the hall. In between were a surprising number of townspeople, some of them friends, many of them busybodies, all of them loitering to see firsthand what would happen next.

Which was why Luke smiled. One glance at Sophie and he knew what was going to happen next—something he'd been waiting to do for fourteen years.

"I'm certain our lawyer can handle the situation," Mary continued. She cast her grandson a sharp look. "If you had called, I might have heard about your unfortunate incarceration in time to deal with it properly."

"I'm sorry, Grandmother. I would have called, but I didn't want to involve you." Luke—he'd been named after his mother's side of the family—bent slightly to kiss the old woman's cheek. She held herself stiffly and gave an abrupt "Harrumph," but her stern bluish-gray eyes had suddenly developed a softening sheen.

Luke stroked a hand between her shoulder blades, reassuring himself that she was okay. He'd expected that in her late seventies his grandmother would have become noticeably older, but other than the cockeyed gait that precipitated the cane, she was the same tall, spare, tough old bird that she'd always been. Of course, she was not the type to give in without a fight, not even to old age.

Mary looked him up and down. "I certainly hope that this is the last of it, young man. Now that you're back where you belong, I'll stand for no more of your malingering. Unless you've changed your mind about our business dealings—" Luke's shrug conceded that he hadn't "—you'll take your place at the ranch." She tapped her cane for emphasis. "Yes, yes. That'll do. Running the ranch was never Heath's strong suit. But you'll be fine at the job, Luke. Just fine."

"If I choose to stay, we can discuss it."

The imperious angle of her head drew his attention to her feathery cap of white-as-snow hair. One sign that she'd grown older; when he'd left, it had been dark gray. "You'll stay," she insisted.

"I'll consider it."

Mary looked deliberately to the other end of the hallway, where Sophie stood by the double doors that led outside. "Oh, I think you'll definitely be staying."

Suspicion rankled. Luke's gaze skipped across the curious faces of those loitering in the long hallway. Every muscle in his stomach clenched. Did they all know something that he didn't?

"You heard Harriet's ruling. You're to stay under court supervision." Mary nodded with a good amount of satisfaction, apparently realizing that the judgment hadn't been so foolish after all.

"Oh, right. That." He doubted that the ruling was legally enforceable, but for now he saw no reason to protest. It might be enjoyable, having Sophie as his watchdog.

"You *will* stay. I'm an old woman now, Luke. I've had all of your rebellion I can take. I need to see that my family is safe and settled, capable of carrying on to the next generation..." Again, Mary glanced toward Sophie.

A second shot of suspicion darkened Luke's thoughts. "Don't get any ideas in that regard, Grandmother."

Mary's thin lips curled in what passed for a smile. Her gaze shifted. "It's not *ideas* that should concern you," she insinuated.

Luke cocked his head. "Meaning?"

"Meaning that it's time we had a serious talk, young man."

After fourteen years apart, he could see the sense in that. Unfortunately, Mary Lucas's "serious talks" usually entailed him buckling to her will. There was no listening or back and forth; only orders. She'd wanted him to study mining, mineralogy and business at Wyoming State. When that failed, he'd been instructed to focus on ranch work, then to surrender his motorcycle for the reward of a brand-new Chevy Blazer just like his brother's. Although Luke had tried to explain to Mary and his frequently absent father that he wasn't suited to the life they expected him to lead, not even his skirmishes with the law had seemed to convince them. His father put Luke's troubles down to a bad reaction to his mother's death, sure he'd get over it in time.

It had been more complicated than that. But explaining would hurt his father, and Luke couldn't do that. Mary Lucas knew the truth, but she admitted only what suited her. She put his maverick ways down to grief and the sowing of wild oats, too bullheaded to believe that she couldn't domesticate him to her purposes.

During those days, Sophie had been Luke's only comfort. His eyes sought her out as surely as a compass points north. He moved toward her without conscious intent, brushing past the curious onlookers. Snake Carson stepped into Luke's path, tattooed and muscled, grinning and calling him Maverick, saying something about Mustangs sticking up for each other. With a friendly slap on the shoulder, Luke made his way past the diehard member of his old motorcycle gang. Plenty of time for that later.

Someone pushed a door open to enter the courthouse. A slanting ray of bright September sunshine washed over Sophie. She turned away, squinting, tugging on her hat brim, the girlish curve of her cheek as firm and downy as a golden-pink apricot.

Luke put his arms around her. Struck with resurgent emotions, he wanted to sweep her up and carry her down the broad concrete steps. Only the years of misunderstanding that stood between them restrained the impulse.

She let out a squeak at his unexpected touch. He said, "Come outside with me," giving no time for objection as he led her out the double doors. They clanged shut, cutting off the rising babble of voices. With only seconds to spare, he pulled Sophie off to the side. In the cool shadow of the portico, his lips covered hers. Sweet bounty. Her mouth was open, soft, caught by surprise. And warm, so warm…like liquid sunshine. His arms curved around her narrow back, drawing her closer.

The kiss was full, but too brief. By the time Sophie's instinctive response had deepened into womanly knowledge, she'd regained herself. Luke felt her struggle against his embrace. Her head snapped back. She gave him a push that he allowed to propel him back a few steps.

Flushed, fuming, she said, "How dare you!" and swung at him wildly. Luke stood his ground. Her open palm cracked against his cheek.

Sophie's eyes widened. For an instant she looked appalled, but then her face closed down. Without a word she turned on her heel and charged down the steps, stopping only when the doors opened and the others began pouring out.

Luke leaned against a pillar, his arms folded across his chest as he watched her inner struggle. He supposed he'd been wrong to kiss her without warning. But there were some temptations a man could resist for only so long. Sophie had always been his weak point.

The crowd was milling around, reluctant to leave when it was obvious there was much unfinished business between Sophie and Luke.

Ignoring them, Sophie stomped back up the steps. "Don't you ever do that again," she said to Luke in a low, sharp voice. Her brown eyes snapped with indignation.

"You don't mean that."

"Oh, yes I do." Her rigid control was new to him. They'd both learned their lessons, perhaps.

"I'm a sheriff's deputy now, Luke, whether you like it or not. Sworn to uphold the law. Which means I have authority over you—"

"Not when it comes to kissing."

Her narrowed eyes warned him to hush. *"Kissing,"* she hissed, leaning closer, "doesn't come into it. What we have is a professional relationship. That's it." Her expression was not as confident as her words. *"That is it,"* she repeated for emphasis.

Yeah, sure. He was convinced.

"I don't appreciate you trying to undermine my reputation—my authority, I mean—with adolescent stunts like…like…"

"Kissing?"

"I can't believe you did that. Someone might have seen!"

Luke spread his hands, as if he were blameless. "Sorry. It dawned on me that I'd forgotten to give you a proper hello."

She tamped her trooper hat back in place, eyeing him belligerently from beneath the brim. "After so many years, a handshake would have sufficed."

"Not for Deputy Sophie." He gave her a lazy, two-finger salute. "Apparently only handcuffs do it for you, ma'am."

"Well, gosh, Luke, what did you expect?" She was baffled. "A big Welcome Home party? Was I supposed to be stuck here in Treetop, unchanged, waiting breathlessly for the day you'd return for—" She swallowed the next word, but he thought it might have been *me.*

His pulse raced. Maybe it wasn't too late to right an old wrong.

Sophie wasn't as hopeful. With an effort, she reassumed her distant, objective detachment. "Too bad Judge Entwhistle chose today to go soft. You'd be sentenced to ten years of hard labor if it had been up to me."

"Exactly what crime would you be punishing me for?" he asked softly.

She sucked in another breath, her unschooled response apparent in the glitter of her eyes and the high color flaming in her cheeks. After a moment, she looked away. Too late.

She despises me, Luke thought. Suddenly he knew that his abandonment had been harder on her than he'd imagined, never mind Heath's party-girl reports. And that in spite of it she'd stood her ground, living out her pain and humiliation under the scrutiny of the local denizens, some of whom had labeled her "trailer trash" before she'd learned how to talk.

She had guts, his Sophie. Whereas he'd taken the easy way out, even though it was becoming apparent that the path he'd traveled had cost him more than he'd known. Sophie had paid a high price too, but gained a new confidence and self-respect in exchange. She had found her place in the community, while he was still a freewheeling vagabond.

The question was: After fourteen years and inestimable miles, had they wound up in the same place? With—considering the thin line between love and hate—equally strong feelings for each other?

Did he still love Sophie Ryan, the feisty little brown-eyed girlfriend of his misspent youth?

She'd never left his heart, hard and shriveled though it was. But he was smart enough to recognize that the woman she'd grown into might turn his memories and fantasies of her as topsy-turvy as a carnival ride.

A ride for which the lady judge had just handed him a ticket. Which was not at all the harsh, swift justice Deputy Ryan had wished for, that was certain.

Luke smiled.

"Don't smile at me," Sophie warned, knowing she sounded foolish. It took all of her willpower not to wipe his kiss off her mouth, where it lingered like the warmth of a summer day.

The courthouse doors opened. More of the spectators filed out. They gave Sophie and Luke a wide berth, not out of caution, but out of amusement. She seethed, struggling with her anger and frustration.

Luke had made a laughingstock of her—again.

"Keep an eye on him, Deputy," someone called, eliciting laughter. "Don't let him get away this time!"

Snake Carson guffawed. "Handcuff him to your bedpost."

Sophie gritted her teeth. Ever since their time with the Mustangs, Snake had treated her like a pesky mosquito worthy of a good swat. The several hundred dollars' worth of traffic citations she'd written him went unpaid, as if she were playing pretend, her badge made of tinfoil, her uniform only a costume. Someday, she vowed, she'd prove herself to Snake, to the Mustangs, and to every single person in Treetop who looked down on her.

For now, she had to settle for jingling the handcuff case clipped to her equipment belt. "Better watch out, Carson. If you don't pay your fines you'll be next."

"G'wan, Soph." Snake was a large, muscular man in a tight black T-shirt, baggy camo pants and Army boots that had never seen Army duty. He was also the kind of arrogant bully who'd never been properly challenged. She suspected he wasn't as tough as he liked to imagine.

The biker held up his tattooed arms, fists clenched, biceps bulging. "You can cuff me to your bed any day of the week, sweetheart." A smattering of uncomfortable laughter accompanied his leer.

Luke turned his steely, unblinking stare on Snake. It curdled the ex-Mustang's bravado as swiftly as it had Sophie's, even though Luke didn't say a word.

Snake did, but only one. A surprisingly high-pitched "Hey" popped out of his mouth as he lowered his arms. His lips clamped shut in embarrassment.

When Luke looked back at her, there was a strong light in his eyes. *Possession,* Sophie thought. A chorus of breathy exhalations rose from the onlookers as though they'd all reached the same conclusion. It didn't matter one iota that Luke hadn't uttered a word, or even raised the mask of his icy non-expression.

Branded. They all know I'm branded.

Her throat was raw, her nerve endings screaming. The injustice of it inflamed her. She was the one with the gun, the handcuffs, the badge, the authority—and she was still the one who was branded. It wasn't fair.

Life was never fair, she brutally reminded herself. Especially not for women who were all too often at the mercy of their biology.

Sophie thought of Joe—her sacrifice and her reward. Her burden. Her heart. And she thought of the judge's unconventional ruling, a ruling that pretty much gave Sophie the leeway to handle Luke how she saw fit.

Well, fine. The iniquity of life being what it was, there was still the law. Although men like Luke and Snake and Demon sometimes made the law seem as strong as the paper it was written on, let Luke try anything under *her* watch and he'd soon find out just how ruthless a woman scorned could be.

"All right, everyone," Sophie said in her brusque deputy voice. "The show's over." For now. "Let's clear the steps." She made shooing motions as if the townspeople were a bunch of sheep who needed to be herded in the right direction.

She turned when Luke gingerly took his grandmother's arm. "Just a moment, Mr. Salinger. I'd like to speak with you."

Mary Lucas nodded. "Good day, Deputy Ryan."

Sophie touched her brim. "Ma'am." The frankness of the older woman's cool-eyed regard was as discomfiting as ever. "I—um, I'm sorry I had to arrest Luke on his first day back, but…"

"It was your job." Mary waved a hand that had retained its elegance despite being roughened by work and gnarled by age. "Yes, yes, of course. I understand."

Sophie drew herself up. "I intend to follow Judge Entwhistle's instructions. Luke won't be getting into any trouble while he's under my watch."

Although Mary was not normally one to bow to outside authority, she did not seem perturbed by Sophie's pronouncement. "Indeed. My grandson needs to be kept on a short leash."

One corner of Luke's mouth quirked, but he didn't protest, either. It seemed that he'd learned the value of holding his tongue. Even so, Sophie rather missed the way he'd once jumped into every conversation with all guns firing, so fervent about his beliefs that he couldn't understand how anyone's view could possibly differ from his own.

Despite the guardedness, she doubted he'd changed all that much. If he was like the other Mustangs, he was taking her as seriously as a tiny Chihuahua nipping at his heels, unworthy of too great a defense.

Sophie huffed. "Indeed he does need a keeper. Don't worry. I'll see to him."

Mary Lucas brushed away her grandson's helping hand. "Between us, I expect we'll manage, Deputy

Ryan.'' Setting her cane with a careful precision, she started down the steps, her head held high.

Sophie had the funny feeling a deal had just been struck. Only she didn't know the terms.

She followed Luke, who was following his grandmother, ready to help in case she should falter. In the way of small towns, Sophie knew that Mary Lucas had badly bruised her hip in a recent fall from a green horse someone of her advanced age shouldn't have been riding in the first place, but that the prognosis was good for a full recovery.

Typically, Mary refused to use her temporary infirmity to her advantage, even in Luke's case. She gestured for him to rejoin Sophie and proceeded along the sidewalk without them.

Luke turned, disconcertingly good-looking even though he wore the same clothes as yesterday. His dark hair brushed the collar of the leather vest, curling slightly at the ends in a way that made Sophie's fingertips tingle with a desire to comb it. She was going to have to watch herself as closely as she watched him.

''Okay, Deputy, what do I have to do?'' he asked. ''Check in with you like a parole officer?''

She tucked her traitorous fingertips into fists, not exactly sure of how to handle the unorthodox situation. ''You might start by telling me what your intentions are.'' One of the possible interpretations of the phrase scrambled her thought processes. ''That is, I meant...'' She swallowed, her throat still as raw as a slab of fresh-cut beef. It was a funny thing how emotions of the heart manifested themselves in physical symptoms. If she spent an extended time around Maverick she'd likely find herself in the hospital, languishing with an incurable case of lovesickness.

Lovesickness? Good God.

"Why have you come back?" she blurted.

There was a pause before he answered. "Not for any funny business."

Hmm. Was his hesitation born of caution, or deception? She shrugged. "Given your record…"

He grinned. "You have good reason to doubt me."

He didn't have to look so pleased with himself.

"You'd better keep a very close eye on me," he said with a sly intonation.

Sophie tilted her head back to regard the sky. "Am I the only one who's taking this seriously?" she asked the bountiful cumulus clouds. It was much better not to look at Maverick. The smallest things about him—the flicker of his lashes, the tiny curved line that too many wry, lopsided grins had cut into the side of his cheek— knocked her off center.

"Seriously?" he said. "I don't need a baby-sitter, if that's what you and the judge had in mind."

Sophie steadied herself. "That's fine, because I'm a deputy, remember?"

"So you've said. Repeatedly."

"You don't think I can do my job?"

He looked her up and down. She felt far too aware of the feminine curves that filled out her uniform. More than her fingertips were tingling by the time he finished. The smile line in his cheek deepened, though he didn't come right out with a full-fledged, wolf-licking-his-chops grin. "Anything I say now will get me into trouble."

Sophie wanted to feel stolid and obdurate, not like a weightless butterfly shimmering in the sky, vulnerable to every turn of breeze. "Try me." She touched her tongue to her upper lip. "I can take it."

"I think...you've grown up very nicely."

"*Grown up* being the operative phrase."

He slid his hands into the front pockets of his jeans, rocking slightly on his heels. His face was still, but his eyes danced. "I was emphasizing *nicely*."

She frowned to disguise the pleasure flickering inside her.

"Don't be like that," Luke said. "I was giving you a compliment."

"The point is my competence, not my appearance."

He shrugged. "You asked, darlin'."

"Luke," called Mary from the open window of her big old Ram pickup truck.

"Two seconds, Grandmother," he said without taking his eyes off Sophie. He was only looking at her, but it was the sort of "looking" usually aimed at bikini-clad babes. With the added impact of the old-style Maverick magnetism. Sophie hadn't experienced anything like it since he'd skipped town, and while she knew she should be demanding to be taken seriously, at heart she exaulted that he hadn't completely changed.

Luke was still Maverick—intense, vital, electric Maverick.

And she could feel herself opening like a sunflower under his brilliant illumination.

SEEING THE LUCAS RANCH again was like getting slammed in the chest with a sledgehammer. Luke's heart ached. For the moment, he let himself forget that his place in the family had been purchased at a high price. He believed that he was coming home.

The ranch looked good—too good. Almost enough to make him wonder why he'd left. The road turned in a wide arc between the gate and the house, sweeping past the stand of quaking aspen, alder and birch where he and Heath used to play Davy Crockett and Jim Bridger. The trees were already decked out in yellow and orange for autumn, whispering of winter with each shake of their leaves. A blue jay squawked and flashed its brilliant wings, scaring a flock of goldfinches up into the branches. The sight spread warm fingers of bone-deep satisfaction inside Luke. He'd missed this place.

A grassy slope rose toward the grand house. The original Lucas homestead had been built in a natural hollow of the land, where it was sheltered from the scouring wind. A practical, commonsense approach. After the family had prospered, the fancy new house, a three-story Georgian with rows of tall windows across the front, had been constructed on the rise. It overlooked the ranch in majestic splendor. To the east, the ranch land spread flat like a bolt of cloth flung across a table. To the west, ridges and red granite mesas were dotted with pines twisted by the cruel winds.

Mary Lucas surveyed the land with a satisfied air. "Good to be home," she said, not quite a question.

Luke drove onto the apron of paving bricks that stretched across the front of the house. Low brick planters bristled with multi-colored asters and chrysanthemums. "It's the same."

"I expect you'll notice a few changes." His grandmother directed him to park near the steps. "We had to take down the old hay barn and rebuild. Roof was caving in. Lightning split the tree by the pond. That firewood lasted us two winters."

"The one with the rope swing? That's a shame."

Mary shrugged. "We have no younger generation to enjoy it."

The irony was apparent only to Luke. "Heath's slipping up on the job, huh?"

"Kiki." Snort. "That's his wife. Too delicate and flighty by half. It takes a strong woman to bear a Lucas child."

"Especially with the weight of all previous generations on your back." Luke stepped out of the truck and slammed the door, not waiting for a response. Mary Lucas was not the doting grandmother type, looking to cootchie-coo a baby out of maternalistic yearnings. Her maternal instinct was for the land. All she cared about was continuing the family line for posterity. By any means necessary, up to and including paying a brood mare—or an expensive stud—to do the job.

Luke welcomed the harsh reminder. It kept him from getting sentimental.

His grandmother had opened her door, but was willing to wait for him to help her step down. He put his hand on her elbow, alarmed by the thin layers of skin and fat that barely padded her fragile bones. "Careful, Grandmother."

She shook him off once she was on level ground. "I might have one foot in the grave, but I'm not dead yet. If you've come back to inherit, it'll be a long wait, young man."

You wish, old lady.

Luke refused to rise to her bait. "No problem. I assumed you went to the lawyers and changed the will years ago," he said, then couldn't help adding, "Leaving it all to Heath. As it should be. He deserves it."

She stiffened her neck. "I reward loyalty."

"But you revere blood."

She refused his bait as well. "Rightly so. The Lucases have an honorable history in this state. Jefferson

Lucas homesteaded this land at the turn of the century. His nephew was a state senator during the days when politicians were honorable. Even your father has managed to double our net worth.''

"Pretty good, considering he's only a Salinger."

"The Salingers are an important family as well. I approved the match." Mary nodded, her cane tap-tapping up the stone steps. They'd never had the confrontation he'd intended, so Luke couldn't figure out whether she didn't know or simply didn't care that he'd discovered the dirty little secrets that hadn't made it into the public version of the Lucas family history.

She must know why he'd broken into the law office, he decided. He'd hinted at it, fourteen years ago, the day before he left for good. She was being stubbornly blind again, counting on him to keep the truth buried.

"Heath's name might be Salinger, but he's also got a mighty strong strain of the Lucas blood. I'm sure in time he'll have a fine son, if that silly young wife can manage to carry it."

Luke couldn't be sure, but he sensed that his grandmother was trying to convince herself more than him. Were there problems in paradise?

The door opened. "Luke?" said the man who stood at the threshold with his arm around a pretty little gal who must be the sniped-about Kiki. "Good lord, Luke. Why didn't you tell us you were coming back? We had to hear it from the sheriff! It was fortunate that Ed had the sense to inform us of your arrest before you were railroaded straight into a prison sentence."

"It's all over and done with." Mary waved a dismissive hand. "We won't talk about it again. Luke's home, that's all that matters."

Luke nodded. "Hello, Heath."

For one instant, Heath hesitated, his handsome face creased with speculation. Possibly worry. Then he stepped forward and hugged his brother, saying, "Good to see you, good to see you," with his voice choked by a strong show of emotion. He held Luke at arms' length, studying his face. "You've changed."

Luke offered a wry grin. "School of hard knocks." He tapped his knuckles against Heath's trim midriff, taking in the minutely receding hairline and expensive cut of clothing. Heath gleamed with health and vigor, from the shortly cut dark-blond hair to the tips of his polished cordovan loafers. "You look like a contented married man."

"I am that." The older brother held out an arm to his wife, gesturing her over with a twitch of his fingers. "This is Katherine Van Everen Salinger. Kiki for short. My wife."

"Kiki for short." Luke took her hand. "Pleased to meet you, Kiki."

"And you." Kiki was petite, with a slender frame and a small-featured face. Though she seemed deferential to Heath, there was also a witty spark in the exotically shaped green eyes that boldly stared out at Luke from beneath a thick bang of dark hair before her lids dropped in belated modesty. She went up on tiptoe and kissed him on the cheek, a tiny bird peck. "It's astounding. After all these years, I finally meet the long-lost brother." She patted Luke's hand with cool, dry fingers, then withdrew. "Welcome home."

"Yes, of course. Welcome home, Luke!" Heath happily slung an arm around both his wife and brother and guided them into the house on Mary's heels. "You'll want a look at the house first."

Luke was most interested in the ranch itself, but he

went inside willingly enough. His grandmother asked Kiki to see that Luke was properly settled. "All this folderol is too distracting for me. I have work in the study."

Fine lines of exhaustion radiated from the elderly woman's compressed lips. The events of the day had been rough on her. Impulsively, Luke touched her hollow cheek. Mary's eyes softened to a misty blue. "Go ahead, Grandmother. We'll visit later." He suspected that she needed to sit and rest more than she needed to work, but he could allow her the small vanity.

She hesitated, looking as though she might say something welcoming or loving before departing. Instead she came out with a stern, "Get a haircut, young man."

Luke had to laugh. "How is she?" he asked Heath as soon as Mary had made her way through the graciously appointed living room to the study that overlooked the working side of the ranch. Command Central, the brothers had jokingly called it when they were growing up. Mary Lucas had been widowed at forty and was firmly entrenched in her position of authority by the time the youngest generation was coming of age. Heath had always been fascinated by the workings of the business side of operations, while Luke preferred the ranch.

Heath didn't seem concerned. "You know Grandmother. She's a tough old buzzard. She rarely takes a day off."

"A seventy-five-year-old woman has no business near a horse." Kiki frowned in the direction of the study. "The doctors tell her again and again, but she won't listen."

"The leg will heal?"

"Maybe not completely," Heath said. "Arthritis is

settling in. Until this injury, she was damn spry, considering.''

Kiki's chin was lowered, but she was gazing at Luke from beneath her bangs again. "It will do her good to have you home, Luke. She's often said how much she misses you.''

He gave a huff of a laugh, uncertain of Heath's young wife's intentions. Everything that Kiki said seemed like a line from a play, words she'd memorized to make the right impression. "Doesn't sound like the grandmother I remember.''

"It's been a long time," Heath pointed out, unnecessarily. "You might have come home for the occasional visit. If only to lift Grandmother's spirits.''

"Show up, smile, and spread the platitudes?" Heath was good at that; Luke had never been, even before he knew how shallow such family courtesies truly were.

"Would that be so bad?''

"I never could keep a civil tongue," Luke reminded his brother. It was what Mary had said to him that last day when he'd tried to bring up the reasons behind his arrest. "If I'd visited, Grandmother wouldn't have liked what I might reveal. Better to stay away.''

"Then why come back now?" Heath blurted, dropping the hail-fellow-well-met act.

"Isn't the family reunion reason enough?''

"Look, Luke." Heath drew a deep breath. "We don't need trouble. Especially at the reunion.''

"Shh, now." Kiki ushered them through the large foyer and into a corridor that led to the kitchen. "We will have no tiffs on Luke's first day back. You must be hungry, yes?" She smiled at Luke. "The cook's off shopping for tonight's special menu, but I can make my new brother-in-law a sandwich, I think. Do you like mustard on your ham?''

"That would be fine, thanks."

Kiki's heels clicked across the ceramic tile floor. In the old homestead, the floor had all been wood, blackened with age and crisscrossed with scars and gouges made by the ranch hands' boots and spurs. No one wore spurs into this showplace. Since it had been built, only the family ate at the big house. The homestead, still standing, had been given over to the ranch foreman; his crew stayed in bunkhouses near the barns.

"Gilley's hanging in there?" Luke asked, watching Kiki fuss with a frill of lettuce. Bob Gilley had been the foreman of the Lucas Ranch for as long as Luke could remember. The man must be slowing down by now, like Grandmother. Luke wondered if Gilley, as tough as old saddle leather but even more proud, knew that Mary Lucas was making plans to install her blacksheep grandson as the new foreman.

Or was Luke's position to be nominal, a family figurehead running the ranch from an office the way Heath did? The idea was no more appealing now than it had been fourteen years ago.

"Gilley turned sixty-seven last winter. But he's still invaluable." Heath didn't put on pretensions about who was really running the day-to-day operations. Like his father, he preferred money managing to hands-on labor. He made frequent trips to Laramie, ground zero of the family business holdings that included cattle, logging and mining operations as well as a stock portfolio that demanded daily attention.

"Here you are," Kiki chirruped. She set a plate on the square oak kitchen table and went to open a built-in refrigerator. Stainless steel flashed in the afternoon sunshine pouring into the room through wide windows that overlooked a pasture dotted with Herefords. In the distance, craggy Chickenhawk Ridge was unchanged except by season, its lush grassy slopes fading to a soft fawn brown. The sight gave Luke a pang of longing for old times. Innocent days, when he'd believe he was the luckiest boy on earth to live on this ranch.

"Luke? Luke? Earth to Luke." Kiki's laugh tinkled like silver bells. "Now that I've got your attention, did you want a beer?"

"Sure." Luke picked one half of the sandwich off the plate and ate it standing by the windows.

Heath and his wife sat at the table, sharing a bottle of designer water that she poured over ice cubes with curls of lemon suspended in them. Luke was amused by the niceties, which included arrangements of fresh flowers in every room, pretty furleboughs hung on walls that had previously held only manly works of Western art, and a subtle fragrance that perfumed the air. Pot-pourri, probably. The house had been buffed, glossed and feminized. The style-conscious poseurs of L.A. had nothing on Kiki and Heath Salinger.

"So..." Heath submitted patiently while Kiki smoothed his collar. "What happened in court?"

Luke shrugged. "It was a farce."

"I knew Grandmother would get the charges dropped."

The memory of the judge's pronouncement and So-phie's flabbergasted expression made Luke smile. "That's not exactly how it went."

Kiki's eyes widened. "Will there be a trial? Oh my. Grandmother Lucas won't care for that." She shook her head, her dark silky hair swinging just above her shoulders. "Not at all."

"No trial. Judge Entwhistle freed me. But I'm on a sort of unofficial probation." He chewed the last bite of sandwich. "For the time being."

"Oh." Kiki seemed disappointed that there would be no fireworks. She dipped a pinkie into her water glass and bobbed the cubes until Heath reprimanded her with a look. "Sorry, honey," she whispered, touching the wet fingertip to her lip. Her gaze slid sidelong toward Luke again.

Heath scoffed. "The law didn't stop you last time."

"It's different now," said Luke.

"How?"

"My priorities have changed." He'd been thinking of only himself when he'd left Treetop. During his restless vagabond years, when he'd gone from job to job and town to town, he'd distracted himself with fast times and hard living. It was years before he stopped long enough to examine his inner demons. He'd wound up by chance in Los Angeles and jumped feet-first into a well-paid job in the movie business. Unfortunately, it had only fed his more reckless instincts. After six long years of risking life and limb, the escalating dangers had forced him to realize he'd never be at peace until he'd faced the past. Heath's call inviting him to the family reunion at their grandmothers behest had come at the right time. But it was seeing Sophie, experiencing their natural attraction again, that had doubly emphasized the rightness of his decision to return.

"Your priorities have changed," Heath repeated. "Does that mean you're ready to settle down?"

For one moment, Luke had thought his brother would say "do right by Sophie," but that must have been his guilt talking. After all, it had been Heath who'd urged him to forget about her. And her fatherless son.

"Depends what that entails," Luke said.

Heath took on the officious, I'm-trying-to-be-good-natured-about-this air that had always stuck in Luke's craw. "We'll be satisfied if you merely stay out of jail."

"Is that the royal we? You're speaking for the entire family?"

"It's not a difficult request." Heath laughed. "Except for you, I suppose." He glanced at Kiki. "Every family has a troublemaker. Luke, here, fills the bill for us."

Though Kiki had remained quiet throughout this exchange, she continued to watch the brothers intently. Weighing the family dynamics, Luke decided. He should save her the bother: the load was both immeasurable and unyielding. And yet…worthwhile. Regardless of his disillusionment, he was forced to admit that he wanted to be welcomed back into the family.

"You don't need to worry, Heath. I've been assigned a keeper."

"A probation officer?"

"No-o-o." Luke would normally have chafed at the idea of being checked up on, but since it was Sophie….

"One of the deputies will be looking after me," he explained. "Keeping me on my best behavior."

Heath blinked. "Not Sophie Ryan."

"The very same."

Kiki paled. "Sophie?"

"You know her?"

Kiki nodded, biting her lip. "We're, um, friends."

"I'm sure Grandmother can fix this," Heath said between clenched teeth. A muscle in his jaw twitched.

"She likes the idea," Luke said.

Kiki's chair scraped the floor as she jumped to her

feet. "Sophie would never agree to such an absurd assignment. Why, she—she hates you!"

"Now, Keeks, calm down, honey." Heath patted her behind. "This is between Luke and Sophie. No need for us to interfere."

She turned snapping eyes on Heath. Luke watched her consciously scale back the reaction while she and her husband exchanged a long look he couldn't interpret. Eventually Kiki swallowed, nodding. "I'm sorry, Luke. I shouldn't have said that. I was shocked, that's all."

"Sophie hates me?" He rubbed a hand across his forehead. He'd thought as much. Hearing it confirmed by a third party was disturbing, even though she had every right.

Kiki glanced at Heath for confirmation of her next line. "I spoke out of turn," she murmured.

"I don't imagine Luke thinks too highly of Sophie, either." Heath gave an awkward chuckle. "First she turns him in, then, years later, she arrests him. Neat trick."

"I'm not holding a grudge." Luke remembered Deputy Barzinski's remarks about Saint Sophie. He wondered whether Heath had exaggerated Sophie's bad reputation for his own purposes. Purposes that included keeping Luke away so Heath's position as crown prince was assured?

It was possible. Luke swore silently. He should have considered it before this.

Heath's eyes had narrowed, but it was Kiki who said, "You should stay away from her, Luke."

"Why? Because she hates me?" *Or because of her son?* he wondered.

The thought that Sophie's son might be his, however

remote the chances seemed since they'd always used birth control, was a new one for Luke. He'd mulled it all night in his jail cell, calculating how much that would upset his perceptions. Topsy-turvy didn't do it. The possibility was an earthquake of devastating scale.

He closed his eyes for a moment, thinking *Sophie, Sophie.*

Sophie and…Joe. Joe Ryan.

His son?

His blood?

What would Grandmother Lucas have to say about that?

"If you're not holding a grudge, then there's no need to bring up the bad old days," Heath said. He smiled. Kiki smiled.

Luke remained unconvinced, but decided to keep his own counsel for the time being. He'd trusted Heath for many years, but no longer.

Kiki carried the empty plate to the sink. "What have you been doing all this time?" she asked brightly. An obvious change of subject. "Heath said you were living in L.A. and working in the movies? How glamorous is that!"

"Not so glamorous when you're a stunt double."

Kiki shivered with excitement. "I'll bet I've seen you in the movies and didn't even know it."

"That's kind of the point. When there's a blur on the screen—that's me."

"I want to hear all about it. What movies were you in?"

"Not many you'd have heard of. I mainly did motorcycle stunts, and there aren't many pictures that call for—"

"*Mission Impossible 2,*" Kiki guessed.

"Afraid not. I never made the upper level of the A list. My work usually showed up in cable movies or straight-to-video action flicks."

"Still, how cool. Have you met many stars?"

"A few."

"Now, honey. Let's save the celebrity chitchat for another time. Luke would probably like to get to his room and wash off the jail stink." Heath chuckled to show he was joking.

Luke stood. "What I'd really like is to take a ride around the ranch."

"Sure, I'll go up and cha—

"I'll go alone," Luke said. "After dinner. If you don't mind."

"Not at all." Heath spread his arms, all benevolence. "This is your home."

It may be, Luke thought, turning to face the windows as the prospect of a new life—or a return to the one he'd always dreamed of—made his throat grow thick. In the past fourteen years, he'd been down many a wrong road, but he might have finally found his way home.

CHAPTER FIVE

BESIDES SOPHIE, Polly Childress was the only female employed by the Treetop sheriff's department. Bubbly, bright, curvaceous and barely twenty-one, Polly's official title was dispatcher, though she also served as receptionist, secretary, records and properties clerk, and even waitress. Every time Sophie heard Sheriff Warren bellowing for Polly to run over to the diner for a piece of pie, she wanted to stomp inside his office and smack him on the snout. Whereas Polly only giggled and said, "Oh, I don't mind," which was probably why she'd been hired in the first place. That and her ornamental value.

Sophie didn't know why she'd been given a job. Treetop politics and hiring policies tended to be a snarl of family ties and mutually beneficial favors. She had no pull in either area. Seeing as her boss was not the type to hire a female deputy on his own, someone must have pulled strings on Sophie's behalf. She suspected Mary Lucas. Reason enough not to dig deeper into the matter.

Polly waylaid Sophie the instant she stepped into the station, a utilitarian cement-block building on Canyon Street.

"Sheriff Ed wants to see you." The young dispatcher made saucer eyes. "Watch out. There's a bug up his butt."

"A nasty, stinging one, I hope." Sophie glanced at her wristwatch. "My shift starts in sixteen minutes. Fake me a phone call if I'm not out in ten."

"It's probably about this morning." Polly led the way to the door, sashaying her hips. She was dressed in skin-tight Lycra, as if she'd just come from a workout. "Gosh. The whole town's talking about you and Luke Salinger."

"Don't pay any attention, Polly. It's a dried-up old story the gossips don't want to leave alone." It wasn't often that Sophie told a bold-faced lie, but she was willing to do anything to squelch the rumors.

"I heard Luke's a total hottie," Polly whispered as she knocked once and opened the door. The sheriff snorted a greeting and sent her away to fetch him another cup of coffee.

Sophie declined Polly's offer of the same. She doffed her hat. "Afternoon, Sheriff."

Ed Warren was the sort of middle-aged man who'd always looked middle-aged. His hair was thin, his waist was thick and his attitude was stuck in the Stone Age. He wasn't an altogether bad sheriff, but he'd kowtowed to the powers-that-be long ago in return for election support. In Sophie's view, Sheriff Warren adhered to the letter of the law only when it suited his agenda. He cut various culprits slack according to a private system of friends and enemies. No Ryan had ever enjoyed favored-nation status.

"Well, well, well." The sheriff leaned back in his swivel chair and regarded Sophie sourly. "So the outlaw Maverick has returned and our lady deputy nabbed him."

Sophie had practiced her game face in the mirror that morning. She was able to give a nonchalant shrug.

"You know what they say. Old bikers never die and tattoos never fade away." And *lady* deputies worked twice as hard in order to be thought half as good.

Behind steel-framed glasses, Warren's pig eyes grew even beadier. He wasn't to be detoured from his ire. "Did it ever occur to you to check with me before you arrested him, Deputy?"

"Why would it? I've never asked permission before." She blinked blamelessly. "Is there some reason that Luke Salinger deserves special treatment?"

Clearly, it peeved the sheriff that he couldn't reply except to huff and shuffle papers on his desk. He certainly wouldn't admit that he was at Mary Lucas's beck and call, bound to protect her grandson from unfortunate prosecutions.

That hadn't always been the case. At the time of the law office break-in and fire, Ed Warren had been a gung-ho deputy looking to make a name for himself. He'd come down hard on Sophie during an interrogation concerning her possible role in the Mustangs' crime. First, he'd threatened to haul her in as an accessory. When that didn't work well enough, he'd insinuated that he would make both the Ryans' lives hell. Sophie would be sent back into foster care till she was eighteen, leaving Archie on his own, bound to break the law sooner or later during one of his drunken sprees. Deputy Warren swore on his mother's grave that he would be there to slap Buzzsaw in jail.

Sophie had pleaded. She'd sworn she knew nothing. She'd even come close to spilling her suspicions, but the thought of Luke in a jail cell had made her stop. In those days, her top priority did not lie with the law.

She shook off the old memories and refocused on the sheriff. He was railing about how Judge Harriet Entwhistle was a crazy old broad who sure as hellfire wasn't about to distribute orders to his deputies. That Sophie should go on about her regular duties and forget all about Luke Salinger. If there was any more trouble on the ancient case, the sheriff would see to it.

Sure, Sophie thought. Sheriff Warren would see only what Mary Lucas told him to see.

Having no choice, Sophie swallowed hard. "Whatever you say, sir." Lie Number Two.

The sheriff leaned forward and peered at her. "I'll be watching you, Ryan."

And she'd be watching Luke. She'd been shocked by his guilt involving the break-in and arson. Unless there'd been a damn good reason for it, he was remaining on her Local Suspects list.

"One misstep and you're out of here. I've let you slide up till now." Warren screwed up his mouth and singsonged in a high-pitched tone, "Gotta give the lady deputy special treatment." It was the same old song and dance she'd been hearing since her first day on the job when he'd made a big production of hanging a curtain in the locker room. It didn't matter that Sophie had not once asked for special treatment. Or, for that matter, needed it.

She set her hat back on her head. "Is that all, Sheriff?"

"Don't suppose you've made any headway on the dead horse deal?"

"I'm planning to go out that way this evening. Stop in at the closest ranches, see if anyone heard shots or noticed suspicious activity." A few days ago, two mustangs had been found dead up in the hills, off Bureau of Land Management land by a couple of miles. On Lucas land, in fact. Which wasn't necessarily significant. The Lucases owned parcels all over the state, but this particular piece happened to be listed under the Wildlife Preservation Act—safeguarding it from development.

"Teenagers," the sheriff said. "Taking potshots." He didn't consider the case a priority, especially since the carcasses had been a couple of weeks old. But Mary Lucas had sent down word that she wanted the incident investigated.

Sophie doubted that teenagers were to blame, particularly in light of her best pieces of evidence—the expensive rifle scope and .308 calibre shell casing she'd found among a rock outcropping that had obviously served as the shooters lookout point. The killer might have been one of the ranchers who believed the wild horses were a blight, but she doubted that, too. However, she'd learned not to volunteer an opinion until she had all of the facts, especially since her opinions were always shot down by the sheriff. "The report on the scope should be back soon."

"Came in this morning. I gave it to Deputy Hardin."

Sophie said nothing. Although they all shared the work since the department was so small, the sheriff knew quite well that the mustang case was hers. Making her defer to Deputy Rick Hardin, who was Ed Warren's macho ideal of a proper cop—but privately nicknamed Deputy Hard-on by Sophie—was yet another of his nagging attempts to give her grief.

"Waste of time and money," he groused, then waved at her. "All right. You can go."

Sophie planned to. As soon as she had her degree. In five years on the job, she'd overlooked more of Ed Warren's posturing rubbish than any self-respecting woman ought to.

EVENING SETTLED upon the town while Sophie watched from a lofty vantage point in the foothills west of town. The sun went down with an artistic flare, threading filaments of golden light through the pink clouds that had gathered along the mountain ridges. Gradually, the great dome of the sky deepened to purple-tinged indigo.

Sophie scanned the hills through binoculars. Her mind wasn't on the spectacular sunset. She was looking for suspicious activity. The wild horses had been killed nearby. She'd recovered a couple of slugs that were safely bagged and stored in the evidence room, awaiting tests if she ever found the rifle that matched the scope. The report said it was a specialty job, designed for a make of rifle that was not your run-of-the-mill Remington.

All was quiet. Peaceful. Yet unease continued to nibble at Sophie's composure. She couldn't shake it.

At first she put the feeling down to the case. Treetop was a law-abiding town, by and large. She didn't like the idea of a criminal—especially the kind of venal subhuman who'd kill a wild horse—walking around free.

But something else was going on. Her stomach was as nervous as it'd been her first day on the job.

Had to be Luke. Who else? He'd scarcely left her mind for the past thirty-six hours.

Setting the spyglasses on the hood of the patrol car, she leaned against the fender to survey the area. High land. Luke and she used to ride up into these hills to sight the herd of mustangs that roamed in and out of the area. A few times they'd been lucky enough to see them at full gallop, the foals bounding at the mares' sides, the small band a blur of streaming manes and tails and shining chestnut, sorrel and buckskin hides against the backdrop of the nourishing Wyoming green grass. Luke had put Sophie's palms to the earth to feel the vibration of the hoofbeats, and her heart had filled up with wonder. Their future was all about possibilities then.

She'd always be grateful to Luke for that. He'd shown her there was a better life to be had than the one found in a dumpy trailer with her hardscrabble father, each day as dirty and mean as the last.

What had happened to Luke's possibilities? Back then, his plan had been to persuade his family to permanently preserve this land for the horses—it was wild country, too remote and rocky for cattle ranching, too high in elevation for commercial timber. Word in town was that Heath Salinger had recently arranged for either geographical or mineralogical surveys to be taken.

A lot of the talk about the Lucases was speculation. This time, Sophie figured she'd be wise to check into the veracity of the rumor.

Movement in the distance. Hard to distinguish what, among the long blue shadows.

She used the binoculars, swinging them in small circles to find the object of curiosity. A horse and rider. She adjusted the lenses until the horseman sprang into sharp detail.

Luke.

Cantering this way.

She had time to leave, if she wanted to. As she hesitated, still watching Luke through the glasses, he lifted a hand in a wave. Damn. He'd seen her.

She lowered the binoculars, her heart beating like a tom-tom. *Better get used to it, Deputy. You're not his girlfriend, you're his keeper.*

And that was all.

Despite her reaction to his kiss, that *had* to be all. She couldn't risk more.

Luke and the horse had disappeared behind a small crop of greasewood, but the hoofbeats still sounded on the hillside. They were close. Impulsively Sophie knelt and laid her palm on the ground. Nothing, this time. Had she really felt vibrations from the running herd, or had it been her love for Luke, pulsing like essential lifeblood in her veins?

The horse came back into view. Luke was in chaps and a hat, with a rifle slung across the back of the saddle. Quickly, she clicked on her radio, speaking into the mike attached to her shoulder epaulet. Static cut the dispatcher's voice in and out, but she reported her whereabouts anyway, saying she'd return radio contact in no more than twenty minutes, as soon as she left the hills. Just a precaution.

Luke's horse slowed to a trot, cresting the last rise. Deliberately Sophie leaned back against the side of the car, one leg crossed over the other, hands on hips.

He halted the horse some yards away. Tipped his hat. "Evening, Deputy." His gaze went to the binoculars. "Keeping an eye on me, I see."

The sight of him made her stomach do another flip-flop. He'd always looked good on a horse.

"As ordered by the court," she said.

"Hmm. You're practically omniscient. How'd you know I'd be riding this way?"

"I could have been tracking you the entire time." They both knew that wasn't so. She narrowed her eyes. "What's the rifle for?"

"Just in case. There's been a bobcat stalking the high pastures. We lost a heifer."

"Got an up-to-date permit?"

"No, ma'am. You going to arrest me again?"

She stretched her pause like an elastic band, then finally conceded with a snap. "Not this time. But you must promise to get that permit ASAP. In the meantime, leave the rifle at home."

Luke swung out of the saddle. "I heard about the dead mustangs. It happened nearby?"

When he approached, she squared her shoulders and lifted her chin, halfway wishing she'd worn her body armor. As if that would be any protection. The closer he got, the more her insides prickled with awareness. Damn if she wasn't as electric as a transformer in a lightning storm. If Luke touched her, they'd both be sizzled to a crisp.

She pointed. "Maybe a hundred yards that way." Near Hidden Lake, but she didn't want to bring that up—too many memories. Keep him talking about impersonal subjects and she'd be okay. "Harve Buchanon lives the closest, half a mile away in his cabin on Bailey Road. If he heard the shots, he didn't pay them any mind." She shrugged. "Figured it was hunters."

"The weapon?"

She looked him in the eye. "Are there any custom-designed Steen Scout collector's rifles hanging around the Lucas ranch? It's a .308 and is missing a scope."

"I haven't had time to check the gun racks since I've been back." His smile was grim. "But I will."

Her gaze flicked to the rifle holstered behind his saddle.

"Be my guest." He studied her face. "You're also welcome to come by the ranch and interview the family and employees. You could even inspect for gunpowder residue."

"That's okay," she said hastily. "Sheriff Warren already talked to your grandmother."

"Invitation's still open. Any time. On duty or off."

"How does it feel to be back home?" she asked to keep herself from dwelling on what an "off duty" invitation might mean.

"Familiar, but strange. My grandmother's doing a time-warp thing, pretending the past fourteen years were only an extended vacation. She won't talk much, but that's her way."

"And your brother?" Sophie asked warily, unable to help herself. She had to know where she stood. Though she was leery of Mary Lucas, she feared Heath the most. He shared her secret shame.

"He's being very welcoming. But I still get the feeling he'd rather I didn't stay on. One man of the house is enough, you know?"

She nodded. "Makes sense. He got used to carrying on without you."

Luke's eyes were blue-gray even in the fading light. They riveted upon her face. "So did you." His voice as soft and caressing as the eventide wind, lightly tinged with bittersweet regrets.

Every hair on Sophie's body tingled in warning. She cleared her throat and asked with stubborn avoidance, "You've met Kiki, then?"

Luke blinked at her abrupt shift. "Sure did. I hear you two are friends."

"Of a sort." The friendly overtures had all been made on Kiki's side. Sophie's initial responses had been cool, prickly, barely civil. She'd never imagined becoming friends with Heath's wife. Too dangerous to the status quo. But Kiki had persisted, and eventually Sophie had relaxed around her, particularly when there were no insinuations about the past forthcoming from the innocent newlywed. Apparently Heath was playing his cards close to the vest. Sophie was relieved, but had remained cautious about what she said to Kiki. And she never accepted the woman's rare invitations to the ranch.

"Of a sort? What does that mean?" Luke asked.

"We're friendly, but we don't—" Sophie's teeth clicked shut. She'd almost said *share secrets.* "We're not best friends or anything. I'm too busy with work and fam—" Another dead end.

"Family?" Luke said, at the same moment she blurted, "You didn't like Kiki?"

"That's not what I meant," Luke said when it was clear she wouldn't continue. "Kiki seems sweet and kind. On the surface. Beneath it, I sensed she was being very careful. Sort of uptight? Is that the feeling you get from her?"

Yes. There were even times Sophie suspected Heath's wife of harboring ulterior motives. Not that it was any of Luke's business…

It had been. But he'd forfeited his rights.

"I suspect that it's not easy living with a grand-mother-in-law like Mary Lucas. Kiki's probably always walking on eggshells."

"She's brought a woman's touch to the house, that's for sure. It's a nice change."

Sophie's brows went up. She couldn't imagine Luke noticing. When she'd known him, he'd considered houses a convenience, somewhere to lay your head at night, a way station for refueling. Part of that had come from his love of the outdoors. Another reason, she believed, was his family's distant relationships. Heath and Luke were fairly close, but their parents had been rarely around, particularly when the boys were teenagers. Their grandmother was too stiff and stern to be considered loveable.

Sophie might struggle to make ends meet, but the two things that were always in supply at her home were love and affection. She was proud of that.

It hurt to remember that she'd imagined making the same kind of home with Luke. A good part of her wanted to welcome him back into her life, and Joe's. Let him be the boy's father. He was all that she'd wanted in a husband. Fourteen years apart hadn't changed her mind. It hadn't changed her body's natural desire for him, either.

Oh, nuts! Just looking at him, she ached with longing.

Sophie turned away abruptly, mumbling that she had to get back. She was too drawn by Luke's magnetic eyes to stand so close and not touch him. She wanted to feel her fingers twined with his. Her lips and breasts, his mouth and chest, meeting. Her hand to his heart. Counting the steady beat of their love.

Too late, too late.

She ducked around the car door, keeping her head down. Her throat was raw with wanting him.

"Don't run too far away," Luke said, catching his horse's reins. "We need to talk, Sophie Ryan. I'm only just beginning to realize how much."

Joe, she thought. Sooner or later, he was going to ask if Joe was his son.

"Talking won't change a thing," she insisted, which was a bunch of baloney. She turned the key, hoping that the engine would drown out his response. But it didn't.

"We can't change what's happened," Luke called. "But we sure as hell can change what will."

Sophie stomped on the gas. The tires spit gravel and

dust, but she could still see him in her rearview mirror, standing quietly beside his horse, tall and tough and tan, the one man in the world that she wanted.

And the very one that she could never have.

THERE WAS ANOTHER PAIR of binoculars on the mountain that evening. A four-wheel drive Blazer from the Lucas Ranch fleet was parked on an old access road that was no more than a pitted dirt trail, seldom used. The wielder of the spyglasses had sworn softly when Luke had cantered his horse over to Sophie. A rendezvous? So soon?

The watcher kicked the dirt. *I won't let this happen.*

The welcome-home family dinner had been an awkward affair, though they'd done their best to make the prodigal son comfortable. Better than the deserter deserved, certainly. Afterward Luke had gone to the barn to saddle up a horse for an evening ride.

It had seemed wise to keep an eye on him.

At first his course had been random, merely a reacquaintance with the ranch he'd left behind. His secretive escort had nearly packed it in, but then Luke had ridden off the main ranch and taken the trails that led to the westerly hills, where the family had acquired a few seemingly worthless sections over the years. The terrain had grown too rough for the Blazer to continue, but by then the police car had been spotted, parked on the county road that came in from the northeast. Screened by sagebrush and a thin stand of shadowy cottonwood trees, the watcher studied Sophie and Luke's body language through the binoculars, sifting for clues to their relationship.

Luke's actions looked conciliatory. Sophie was harder to read—it was too dark to see her expressions.

Any way you cut it, this wasn't good. Just having them together, talking, was dangerous.

How soon before they compared notes? How soon before the careful construction of lies and betrayals collapsed around everyone involved?

CHAPTER SIX

"YEEEE-HAW," yelled one of the cowboys from his perch atop the split-rail fence. Other male voices chimed in, urging Luke to stick as his mount crow-hopped around the corral, kicking up a dust storm with flicks of its dancing hooves.

The bay gelding shuddered under Luke's weight, its back hunched like a bristling alley cat. Luke held the soft rope reins in both hands, keeping a firm grip on the hackamore so the horse couldn't put its head up to rear, a maneuver that had so far tossed three of the ranch hands and earned the horse the nickname of Moon Doggie. To hear the men tell it, Moon Doggie reared so high his rider would either touch the heavens or take a moon flight under his own propulsion.

The green broke three-year-old wanted Luke off. He kept applying pressure with his legs and heels, making the horse go forward instead of back, sideways, up or down—directions the bay preferred.

Moon Doggie snorted and shook his black mane, his ribs working like a bellows. "Ya got him, Luke," Gilley shouted from the sidelines. "He's fixin' to settle down."

Luke slowed the horse to a trot, turning him in circles every time he tried to twist away from the rider sticking to the saddle like a burr. The fight was going out of Moon Doggie. Luke spoke soothingly. Another couple circles of the corral and the gelding would have had enough for this session.

Out of the corner of Luke's eyes, he saw a Blazer drive up. Heath and Mary emerged, drawn by the activity. Exiting, Heath leaned on the horn. The short hard honk distracted Luke for an instant—and startled Moon Doggie.

The bay gave one monster buck. Luke stayed on, but he'd been thrown forward in the saddle. The reins were momentarily lax. Seizing the chance, Moon Doggie's head went up, followed by his body as his front hooves clawed at the dusty air. Luke clamped his legs tight, but still felt himself slipping as the horse rose to a nearly vertical position.

He heard shouts of encouragement. Gilley jumped off the fence, into the corral.

The bay gelding dropped back down with springs in his hooves. The jolt reverberated all the way up Luke's spine. Moon Doggie would have gone right back up again, but Gilley gave him a whack on the hindquarters and he shot forward instead, rocketing to the opposite side of the corral. Luke regained control of the reins and pulled the heaving horse to a halt in a cloud of dust. A couple of the cowboys ran out to take hold of the bridle so Luke could dismount without Moon Doggie crow-hopping away from him.

He staggered a bit when he landed on solid ground. "Shew! Moon Doggie must not've reached the moon that time, 'cause I sure as hell was feeling the pull of gravity."

"Good job," Gilley said, slapping Luke's shoulder. "He reared up, but he didn't unseat ya. Tomorrow we'll give it another go. Dadgum, you'll have him doin' figure eights by the end of the week."

Luke slapped dust out of his jeans. "Who said I was getting back on?"

Laughing and joking at the prospect, the cowboys walked Moon Doggie back to the barn for a rubdown and a cool out. Gilley stopped to say how-do to Mrs. Lucas and brag about her grandson's ride. "Here we got us a fella who's been professionally trained to take a fall and dang all if he doesn't stay on."

Luke grinned. "Sorry to disappoint you.

"The hands were hoping to see a triple somersault." Gilley rubbed his whiskery chin. "What about you, Heath? Figgerin' on your brother taking a spill?"

"It was a good ride." Heath appeared blameless. "Sorry about the horn, man. My hand slipped. Such a little tap didn't upset the horse, did it?"

Luke agreeably said, "Nope, not at all."

"A rough ride's just the thing for you," Mary observed. "Get the feeling back in your bones. Bet you've missed it."

Luke put a hand to the base of his spine and gave a twist so it crackled. "Oh, I've got the feeling in my bones, all right. Thanks anyway, Grandmother."

She made a shooing gesture at him, her eyes twinkling beneath the brim of a fedora-style hat tied beneath her chin with lengths of soft fabric. The wind was keen for September, an early harbinger of winter. They were all dressed for the colder weather, but styled to suit the individual—fine leather driving gloves versus worn work gloves, designer label gear instead of Gilley's rawhide vest and Luke's faded denim jacket.

He buttoned it up. "Where are you two heading?"

"I'm taking Grandmother into Treetop. Business at the bank."

"You may come along, Luke," Mary said. "Afterward we'll stop for lunch at the place on the highway."

Luke nodded. "Maybe I'll do that."

Heath frowned at his brother's disarray. "Surely not in that state."

Mary snorted. "Why not? It's Wyoming."

"I meant—"

"I know what you meant, young man." Mary nodded goodbye to Gilley and marched off to the vehicle, her cane hanging unused over her wrist. "A little bit of dust won't worry the waitresses at the Thunderhead. Nor the bank, considering how much business we give them."

"If you say so." Heath hurried to open her door.

"What about Kiki?" Luke asked from the back, after they'd all been seated and Heath drove past the house without stopping.

"She went into town this morning for a doctor's appointment."

"Nothing serious?"

"Oh, you know," Heath said. "Girl stuff." He glanced sidelong at his grandmother. "Just a regular checkup."

She turned her head to look out the window. They were passing the Lazy Eight, a dude ranch that had been refurbished by new owners. A long string of riders was leaving the corral, heading up to a trail that wound through the golden aspen. "I didn't say a word. I've given up on the two of you."

"We haven't been trying that long, Grandmother. Don't be so impatient."

"It's my time that's wasting away," she said. "Not yours."

The great-grandchild quest. Luke leaned back against the plush seat, glad to be left out of the conversation.

Except that his mind went straight to Sophie. And her son. He still didn't know the particulars of that story, other than that which Heath had supplied long-distance. Suspect, now. It had been easier for Luke to believe the stories when he was far away. Seeing Sophie again, looking her in the eyes—those beguiling big brown eyes—had a way of challenging his previous conclusions.

They did their business at the bank with amazing alacrity, being shown directly into the president's office for the signing of a few papers. Luke paid special attention to the details just to rile Heath, but it appeared that there was nothing untoward going on. Their father Stephen was arranging a stock transaction that needed Mary's approval. If Heath hadn't been so officious about shepherding Grandmother through the process, Luke wouldn't have given the deal a second thought.

KIKI SALINGER SAT in Dr. Cotter's office, waiting for the verdict on her latest battery of tests. Why did they call it that, she wondered. Was it because her battery had run out of juice?

She sighed. It was four years since she and Heath had begun trying for a baby, almost from the day of their wedding. And all she had to show for it was more time spent in stirrups than the Lucas's busiest ranch hand.

Kiki shifted fretfully. She was certain, absolutely one hundred percent certain, that there was something wrong with her. It didn't matter that on previous visits her personal doctor and all the specialists had insisted that she checked out fine. The suggestion that Heath come in had been raised several times, but Kiki wasn't about to ask it of him. *Nosiree*. He'd take it as a blow to the ego, something her mother had told her that a smart wife avoided delivering under any circumstances if she wanted to stay married. Besides, as Heath had pointed out several times during their hurried arguments out of earshot of his grandmother, they had *plenty* of proof of his virility.

Kiki had tried to explain that virility and sterility weren't mutually exclusive, but she was no doctor. She didn't have the right words to make an impression. Heath just patted her on the behind and told her to go see Dr. Cotter again if that would placate her worries.

A silent prayer rose from Kiki's throat. *Please, please tell me already!* It was better to know than to exist on pins and needles, always wondering and worrying where she'd gone wrong.

She swallowed hard, staring blindly out the window behind the doctor's desk. The sky was a cold, bright blue. Like Heath's eyes when he was angry. Would he divorce her if she couldn't give him a child?

That was too terrible to contemplate. She did not want a divorce.

After Kiki's mother had gotten divorced, she'd rarely seen her father. They'd lost their beautiful house and gone to live in a tacky condominium with paper-thin walls and peel-and-stick linoleum tile floors. For three long humiliating years, while Kiki was in high school. She thought of it now as her season in hell. Then her mom had remarried a successful orthodontist and they were okay again.

But she'd never again felt completely secure. Until, that was, she married Heath. He was loving and generous and so patient with her mistakes.

Their happiness would be complete as soon as they had a baby, Kiki promised herself, gnawing away her lipstick as she worried at her bottom lip. Even though they could have signed up with an adoption agency years ago and gotten a baby by now, Heath didn't want to adopt. He said the baby would never be a Lucas, and thus would never be accepted by his grandmother.

Kiki took a mirror out of her purse and inspected her face. She was a wreck.

Poor innocent babies, she mused while applying fresh lipstick. How could anyone love them only for their bloodlines? Heath and his grandmother wouldn't know—by looking—that the baby was or wasn't a Lucas or a Salinger. They thought they could, but they were wrong. Look at Sophie's son. Grandmother Lucas had no idea.

Yet.

"Hello, Kiki." Dr. Cotter breezed into the room with a file folder in hand. She was a middle-aged woman with frizzy hair and a kind, homely face. "Sorry you had to wait. We had a small emergency on our hands."

"Grace McHenry? I was in the waiting room when she came in with her husband. She's gotten really big. Is she okay? And the baby?"

"I shouldn't comment on another patient." Dr. Cotter smiled. "But this is a small town, so I'm sure you'd hear anyway. Grace and the baby are doing just fine. We thought for a moment that labor was imminent, but not quite yet. I've sent them home for now."

Kiki shuddered. "They have a ranch way outside of town. I won't live so far from the hospital when I'm pregnant." A lump rose in her throat as she looked hopefully at the doctor. "Please. Will I ever be pregnant?"

"Kiki, dear, there's nothing new to report. We've done every infertility test in the book and you remain, as always, in the very pink of health." Dr. Cotter paged through the results as she spoke, then handed them to Kiki—proof in hard copy. "There's no reason for you not to get pregnant."

"Oh. Well. I'm relieved." Kiki clasped the sheaf of papers to her blouse, trying to look happy. Of course she was happy. Just not pregnant.

The doctor regarded her with sympathy, her eyes soft and comforting behind wire-frame lenses. "I've broached this possibility before, I know, but isn't there a way to persuade your husband to come in? The test is simple enough, nothing to be bashful about. It's your last option, other than patience. Or adoption."

Kiki shook her head. "I can't do that."

"Perhaps if I talked to him?"

"You don't understand," Kiki mumbled, her chin drooping. "Heath already knows he can have children. He, uh, impregnated a girlfriend." She laughed nervously. "Before we were married, of course."

"Oh, I see." The doctor frowned. "How long ago was this? There's a chance that in the meantime he's developed a—"

"No, no. I'm sure it's me. I'm the reason. I just can't have a baby." Tears formed in the corners of Kiki's eyes. She squeezed them shut, sniffling, awash with self-pity. She was a miserable failure, that's all. When Grandmother Lucas learned it was hopeless, she'd shake her head and call Heath into the study for a private conference. They'd decide to dump her like a—a—fallow heifer.

Dr. Cotter came around to sit on the edge of her desk with a box of tissues. "Now, Kiki, you mustn't blame yourself. There are times we simply don't know why this happens. You might get pregnant tomorrow."

Kiki's hand shook as she plucked a tissue from the box. "Can't you please give me fertility drugs?"

"That wouldn't be appropriate. Especially when you husband hasn't been tested. But there is another doctor I'd like to suggest…."

Kiki's hopes rose as Dr. Cotter reached across her desk. Another doctor? Of course. There had to be a specialist who could find and solve her problem. There had to be!

"This doctor is a colleague. Highly recommended." Kiki snatched the business card from Dr. Cotter's fingers. "You'd have to travel to see him, but I think it would do you some good to talk this out—"

Kiki blanched when she looked at the card. "A psychiatrist? That's ridiculous." She leaped up, scattering papers and tissues, dropping her purse. The mirror shattered on the hard floor, replicating the cracks that ran through her shrill voice. "I don't need a shrink, Dr. Cotter. I need a baby!"

THE THUNDERHEAD SALOON had been spiffed up since it had served as one of the Mustangs' hangouts. Years of cigarette smoke and fried food had been scrubbed away. New chairs and tables were in evidence, along with refinished floors and a jukebox that worked, all of it spick-and-span enough to eat off.

While they'd missed the heaviest lunchtime traffic, many of the tables and booths remained filled with loitering diners, half of whom wanted to say hello to Luke. His grandmother took him by the elbow and paraded him around the L-shaped room like a blue-ribbon steer. Heath soon grew tired of the friendly chitchat and the where-have-you-beens and went to get them a table.

He was sipping a beer by the time they joined him,

but jumped up to hold out their grandmother's chair before Luke could do it. Luke sat, thinking that at least the Thunderhead wasn't yet serving designer water. He checked to see if the menu had changed. It had. Salads and soups were listed on the fresh new inserts slipped into the plastic sleeve.

Punch Fiorelli came out of the kitchen, his midsection wrapped in an apron. "Maverick, my man! About time you dropped in." He greeted Heath and Mary, telling them to order extravagantly. Lunch was on the house.

Longtime waitress Ellen Molitor arrived next. She nodded around the table. "Mrs. Lucas, Heath. Luke… good to see you in here again."

He wrapped an arm around her hips and gave her a squeeze, bringing a look of pleasure to her plain face. "Ellie, my all-time favorite gal. You mean Punch still hasn't fired you for flirting with the customers?"

"Shoot, no. I'm the best waitress he's got. Better than Sophie was," she added, leaning down to speak in Luke's ear, "even though I gotta suspect she's still your *real* all-time favorite gal."

Luke lowered his voice. "Care to convince her of that?"

Ellen whispered, "I'm sure she knows."

"Not yet. But soon."

"We're ready to order," Heath announced. The waitress straightened, pad at the ready. Heath deferred to Mary, but she was speculating over Luke instead of the menu.

Luke met her interested stare. His grandmother had not approved of Sophie Ryan as his girlfriend. Too wild, too uneducated, too low-class. The bad upbringing showed, she'd claimed, ignoring in her stubbornness that it was Luke who'd led the way into trouble, not vice versa.

"I'll come back," Ellen said.

Mary gave Luke a little nod. "No, we'll order now." She snapped open the menu and asked for a steak sandwich and fries. Luke requested the same, distracted by the notion that his grandmother had just granted her approval of Sophie.

He could be wrong. And it wouldn't change his intentions, either way. But...

Wonders never ceased. Even his grandmother was capable of change.

Heath ordered a salmon salad, then changed his mind and asked for a steak sandwich, as if lunch was a game of one-upmanship. Luke had nearly forgotten how touchy his brother's pride could get, over nothing as well as over the big stuff.

As soon as Ellen left, Mary got straight to the point. "Lucas, look at me. Are you planning on taking up with Sophie Ryan again?"

"Yes."

Mary blinked at the blunt answer, but then she nodded. "Good. It's time."

Heath choked on his beer.

"It's past time," Luke said.

Mary wasn't ready to go that far. "No. The pair of you were too young and wild then. I was right to forbid the match. But I've been watching that young woman over the years. She started out bad, no denying it. But she's made something of herself, even with every disadvantage working against her. Don't get me wrong. She'll never be..."

"Worthy," said Heath, under his breath.

"A true lady," Mary said, overriding him. "But

she's got gumption. She's a worker. You could do worse than settling down with the likes of Sophie Ryan.''

Heath shrugged, raising his brows at Luke. *Grandmother's clueless,* was the unspoken message, an opinion they'd shared as boys when she'd stuck to various antiquated notions.

''Sophie was a mistake then and she's a mistake now,'' Heath said, speaking *sotto voce* to discourage eavesdroppers. ''Having Sheriff Warren put her on the police force doesn't make her an upstanding citizen, Grandmother. She still comes from white trash.''

A torrent of hot, frustrated fury filled Luke. Animosity at Heath for being so stuck-up and judgmental, anger with himself for being unthinking enough to listen. God, he'd been stupid and careless and wasteful!

He leaned across the table to address his brother. *''Stop. Talking. Now.''*

''It's the plain truth,'' Heath said, then saw that the expression on Luke's face had darkened with menace. He clamped his mouth shut.

Mary scanned the restaurant with her chin up, meeting each curious stare until it was turned away. ''Boys, boys. Take it down a notch. You're drawing attention.''

Heath picked up his beer, remaining silent.

Luke leaned back in his chair, arms crossed over his chest. This was a rare occasion—his grandmother favorably introducing Sophie into the conversation—but he wasn't ready to take advantage of it. He had to talk with her first, make his apologies. If there were secrets to tell and confessions to be made, this time it'd be done with him and Sophie face to face. No evasion. Only the truth—bare, blunt, possibly hurtful. They'd grown-up.

They were strong enough to take it. To tell it. Maybe even to forgive each other.

As usual, Mary Lucas operated according to her own agenda. She sipped water, waiting for all visible interest in their table to die down before she said, deceptively quiet, "Luke, you might be surprised to hear that Sophie has a son."

Heath became apoplectic. He sputtered, trying to speak, but Grandmother Lucas wouldn't let him into the conversation. Abruptly he left the table, taking his beer to the bar.

Luke noted the reaction. "So I've been told," he said carefully, wondering how much his grandmother suspected. Or if there was anything to suspect.

"Thirteen years old," she said.

The age riveted Luke. It wasn't entirely out of line with Heath's reports. But it also fit a scenario that made Luke the father. "Is that so?"

Mary nodded.

"You keep track of birthdays, do you?"

"In this case."

There was a strange unworldly roaring in Luke's ears. It wasn't like his grandmother to be circumspect. Was she waiting for him to ask outright if Joe Ryan was his son?

She went on. "A good-looking boy. Getting to be tall. Taller than the Ryans."

From across the room, Luke could feel Heath's stare burning into the back of his skull. An explanation for possible deception came to Luke in a thunderbolt. If Heath had suspected that Sophie was pregnant with Luke's child, his competitive pride would have been roused. The first grandchild was a valuable family commodity. In a perverse way, Heath would have counted it to his advantage to see that Luke stayed away.

"Tall as a Lucas or a Salinger," Mary continued.

"What are you saying, Grandmother?"

"Only that you might want to consider your options."

Luke was torn. If Joe Ryan was his son, he wanted to be a part of the boy's life, regardless of his relationship with Sophie. But the idea of claiming the boy because Mary Lucas was tired of waiting for a legitimate grandchild was distasteful. It brought back a churning gutful of resentments about his own parentage and the family matriarch's role in securing its secrecy.

"I'll do that, Grandmother." Luke met her challenging stare. The woman was a hard case. "Preferably with no interference from you or Heath."

She did the royal head incline. "I will trust you to take care of it."

Whatever that meant. With his grandmother, Luke couldn't be sure.

A scuffle broke out at the bar, accompanied by raised voices. "Lemme go," a man bellowed. "Iz my right t'say hello."

Luke stood. Heath was blocking the way of a tough little man with a grizzled face and oil-stained straw cowboy hat. He brought his arms up to shove at Heath. With a start, Luke saw the loose, knotted sleeve and recognized Sophie's dad.

"Go back to your drink, old man," Heath was saying, trying to prevent Archie's approach without actually touching him.

"You can keep the free beer, fancy pants." Archie gave Heath another push and stalked toward the Lucas table. He was puffed up like a bantam rooster. "All I'm doin' is sayin' hello to the *grand* lady."

Mary Lucas's mouth pinched with distaste. "Archie."

With Luke and Heath standing by, Archie swept off his hat and gave an absurd bob of a bow with his sparse gray hair sticking up in tufts. The sour scent of cheap beer rose off him. "Afternoon, Lady Lucas." The stocky little man's eyes glinted. "Out among the peasants?"

"Just having lunch with my grandsons, Archie. Thanks for dropping by." Mary turned her shoulder in dismissal.

Archie scowled. She didn't pay any attention. Belligerently, he eyed Heath, then Luke. The scowl deepened. "You."

"Hello again, Mr. Ryan."

"Back to cause trouble?" The old man's voice grated like a rusty nail yanked from concrete.

"Not planning on it," Luke said. He extended his hand.

Archie batted it away. "The Lucases already took my hand." A bark of a laugh. "'N never gave it back."

Mary's features drew tight. She gestured at Heath to take care of the nuisance.

Archie wrestled away from Heath's grip on his good arm. "Keep your hands off me, boy. I'll go when I'm good 'n ready."

Punch came out of the kitchen, wiping his hands on the apron, biceps bulging. "All right, Buzzsaw, you've said your hellos. Move along now. I don't want to have to ban you from the saloon."

The tough old man wobbled toward the door, grumbling. "In my day, a man could get prop'ly soused at the Thunderhead Saloon. Didn't have to put up with high-falutin' ladies eatin' their prissy lunches.'' He shot one more glare at Mary Lucas and her grandsons. "Them Lucases, takin' over the town…''

Punch shut the door behind Archie. The silenced patrons resumed their busy whispers.

Ellen arrived with their food.

Heath's face screwed up in distaste. "I have to go wash my hands.''

Luke took a plate from Ellen and set it at his place, then leaned down to say softly, "Excuse me a moment, Grandmother.''

"Don't bother,'' she said. "The only thing to do with Archie Ryan is to ignore him. The man's either always drunk or on his way there.''

"I want to be sure he gets home safely.''

So much for discretion. Every eye in the place followed Luke as he went after Sophie's father. The family was giving the gossips plenty of fodder for their rumor mill today.

Archie was standing beside the wagon-wheel walkway, working the brim of his straw cowboy hat before settling it on his head at a cockeyed angle. He gave a jolt of surprise when he realized Luke had joined him.

"Got a ride?''

"Pickup's outta commission.'' Archie's eyes narrowed. "What's it to ya?''

"It's a long walk into town.''

"I got nothin' but time.'' The old man started off, kicking up gravel.

Luke got into the Blazer, snagged the keys off the visor, and drove over to the exit where he waited for Archie to catch up. He reached across to leave the passenger-side door hanging open.

Buzzsaw cackled as he clambered in. "Yer'll be in trouble with old lady Lucas for delayin' lunch."

"She'll live." They didn't speak for a few minutes as the highway zipped past them. Treetop came up fast, and Luke took the main turnoff. "Where's your place?"

The former lumberjack gave him the street address. "Iz that what yer up to? Lookin' to drop in on Sophie?"

Not what Luke intended, but he wasn't averse. "Oh, do you live with your daughter?"

"Close by." Buzzsaw kept silent as they drove to the north end of town, passing residential streets with houses that hadn't changed for the past fifty years. "Turn here," he directed when Luke didn't speak either.

They pulled into the unpaved driveway of a white bungalow with trim painted plum and green. The front door was bright blue. There were flowers in the window boxes and a rocker and swing on the handkerchief-sized porch. It was modest, but cheerful. A homey little place, Luke thought, startled by how much it hurt—and, conversely, how proud it made him—to think that Sophie had accomplished all this without him. They'd talked about what it would be like to share their lives, to make a home between them as one should be made, without rancor or strain or distance. But when push had come to shove, Luke hadn't been there to help her.

His new admiration for her doubled. Regardless of where she'd begun, she'd ended up here, in the life they'd imagined. She was a heroine.

And he was pond scum.

"Looks like she's not home. Good thing." Buzzsaw stepped out of the truck. "Sophie doesn't need you in her life, Salinger," he said before slamming the door.

He shook a stubby fist. "So you can just stay away from us."

"You're welcome," Luke murmured, reversing out of the drive as the old guy traipsed around the side of the cottage, following a path worn into the seedy lawn. "But you're wrong."

Self-sufficient though she was, he was certain that some part of Sophie still needed him.

Nearly as much as I need her.

CHAPTER SEVEN

A COUPLE OF DAYS LATER, Sophie arrived home from doing the day's errands, her car filled with a passel of library books, a dry-cleaner's bag and four heavy sacks of groceries. No one came to help when she tooted.

Grumbling, she got out of the car. Buzzsaw was reliably unreliable, but Joey usually shot out of the house if food was involved. He'd rip open a package of cookies or chips right there at the car. When she protested that he should wait until the groceries were inside and unpacked, he'd turn on his most charming grin and insist that growing sherpas needed their strength. She'd shove a banana or apple in his mouth, dump an extra bag into his arms, and stand back to laugh while he staggered into the house.

Today, no Joe. Sophie wasn't pleased. He was supposed to come straight home from school so they could spend a little time together before her evening shift. Was that too much to ask? Probably, when an adolescent was involved. She was uneasy about Joe's recent quicksilver moods, how he glowered at her when he thought she wasn't looking. During the long, early morning hours in the patrol car, the guilt of what she'd done, the secrets she'd kept from him, gnawed at her.

Loaded with grocery sacks, she nudged the front door open with her elbow. It hadn't been closed all the way, a sure sign that her son was home. "Groceries, Joe! I need help. Have to make dinner and get ready for evening shift.''

Silence. No music or TV, even. Strange.

She set the groceries on the kitchen counter and pulled out a few of the frozen items. ''Joe?'' she hollered, closing the freezer door. ''You home?''

Still no answer. Worry niggled at her. Instead of getting the rest of the groceries, she went halfway up the attic stairs. The door at the top was closed. ''Joey, are you up here?'' Her voice came out shaky as a newborn foal.

Must be at Fletcher's. Sophie hesitated, but instinct made her double-check. She knocked loudly, in case he was using headphones, then opened the door.

Joe was lying flat on the bed, staring up at the ceiling until he turned his head to look at her. His brown eyes were iced over like a mud puddle after a frost.

She took a step. ''Joey? Are you sick?''

He rolled over onto his side, facing away from her. ''No.''

Sophie's insides squeezed into a painful knot. *He's heard the rumors. He knows, he knows, he knows....*

''I guess we have to talk.'' Even though there was no use in playing dumb, she had to force the words past her clenching throat. She sat on the end of the narrow twin bed, leaning against the old iron bedframe that she'd rescued from the dump, scoured and spray-painted cardinal red when Joey had outgrown his crib. He'd been sleeping in it ever since.

Sophie sat down on the end of the bed. Those had been hard years, but simple and clear. No time to worry about town gossip and guilty ramifications when you're working like a dog to make ends meet and raise your child properly. She'd never thought the day would come when she'd envy that life.

"Leave me alone," Joe mumbled, and she could tell his throat was as tight and painful as hers. He'd grown so tall so fast, and changed in other ways too, but there was still much about him that was a little boy. She wanted to hold him in her arms and promise everything would be okay. That she'd always take care of him, first and foremost and forever.

She touched the tip of his sock where it dangled off the end of his bony foot. A couple inches of his skinny shin showed where the leg of his jeans was rucked up. Her fingers crept upward. "Joey..."

He moved restlessly. "Don't call me that. I'm not a baby."

She withdrew her hand. Locked her fingers. "I know you're not, Joe. That's why it's time for us to talk. You're old enough to—" Deep breath. "To understand."

He jumped up. "It's too late, Mom."

His snarl made her recoil. She stared, the blood draining from her face. Joe was moody, sometimes surly, but he wasn't mean. He'd never before acted as though he hated her.

"Everyone's talking about me," Joe said. He picked up an open CD case, then slammed it down. His lean, live-wire body vibrated with pent-up emotions. Electric from the pillow, his hair stuck out in all directions, brushing the sloped ceiling as he paced the small room, rumpling the throw rugs. With a pang, Sophie realized he'd outgrown the room just as he'd outgrown his jeans and sneakers and acceptance of her simple explanations.

"They're all saying—they're saying—" He made a

sound of furious frustration and kicked over the waste-basket.

"Stop it, Joe!" Sophie went up on her knees on the bed. She extended an arm. "Please come sit with me. Don't be so angry."

"You shoulda warned me, Mom."

She sank back down. "I know, I know." Misery. "I thought the perfect time—" *the perfect way* "—would come and I'd know what to say...."

Joe stopped and stared accusingly. "I asked you."

When he was five, six, seven. And she'd told him that his father was someone she'd loved very much who had gone far away. One version of the truth. "You were too young then."

"I'm old enough now, and you didn't tell me." Joe's face crumpled. "How come everyone else knows?"

"They don't," Sophie insisted. She ached to soothe her son's pain, to stroke his cheek and exchange hugs and silly whispers the way they used to whenever he needed comfort. "It's all gossip."

Relief washed over Joe's face, transforming it for an instant before the suspicion returned. Her fault. She'd made her trusting son suspicious and resentful.

"It's not true, what Fletcher's mom said?"

"I—I don't know. It depends what—"

"I overheard her on the phone, saying that a guy named Salinger's my dad. She said he's a criminal, and a coward who ran away, and a Hells Angel, and you two used to ride around on motorcycles and break the law before you turned him in to the sheriff..." Joe ran out of breath and stood panting beside the bed, his hands clenched. He stared down at her with stunned disbelief, as if she'd grown horns.

Sophie swallowed. "Oh, Joe, I don't know what to say."

He flinched. "It's true."

"N-not exactly."

"My dad's a criminal."

"No! He was going to be arrested, but—"

Joe erupted like a meteor, tearing out of the room in a white hot blaze. She shouted after him, but he flew down the steps and out the house before she'd even hauled her numbed, shaking body off the bed. She was at the bottom of the steps when she heard the roar of the motorbike. "Joe!" she called in futility, running to a front window in time to see him speed across the lawn and down the driveway, skidding as he made a sharp turn onto the street in a shower of pebbles and dust. The motorbike blatted smoke and took off, her son hunched over the handlebars, his hair whipping in the wind.

"Oh please, God," Sophie said, her voice hoarse with fear. The hurtful accusations peeled away. All she cared about now was that her boy was in danger. He was speeding. No helmet. Fueled by anger.

He wouldn't watch himself. Or where he was going.

Reckless endangerment to others and himself. An accident waiting to happen.

Joey, Joey, she thought with a keening pain. She grabbed for her keys, stopping him the only thought in her mind. The anger and explanations would have to wait.

BY THE DRY metallic clacking and grinding, it was obvious to Luke that the engine wasn't going to start. Sophie tried it again anyway, and then again, rocking the car with her urgency as she put all her body language into each turn of the key. "Come on, come on, you stupid car!" She pounded the steering wheel.

"Hey, Soph." Luke hunkered down beside the car door and put one hand on the lowered window. "Cool your jets, girl. It can't be that important." There were two full grocery bags in the back seat, a pile of books and a plastic-shrouded deputy's uniform on the seat beside her.

She turned her hot, frantic gaze on him. *"Yes it is."*

Shocked by her expression, he was unprepared for her next abrupt move. She rammed him with the car door. He fell back on his butt in the dirt, a surprised, "Hey, now!" dying on his tongue when he realized that she hadn't intended to knock him down. She just hadn't noticed. Didn't care. All her attention was focused on the Harley he'd parked at the edge of her driveway.

She spun around. "Give me the keys."

Not when she was like this. He got to his feet. "First you have to tell me what's going on."

A cloud passed over Sophie's face even though the sky was a clear robin's-egg blue. "I need transportation, that's all. It's an emergency."

"You're in no shape to drive." She was pale and shaking.

She closed her eyes, taking a shuddering breath. "You're right. I have to calm down. Okay, there. I'm calm. Now give me the keys. Please."

Luke took her by the shoulders and was surprised by the way she leaned into his grip for support. Her face was stricken and she was wavering on her feet. "What is it, Sophie? Let me help."

Her eyes burned on his. "It's my son, Joe. We had an argument—" She stopped, biting back further explanation. "He took off on his motorbike. He's not licensed to drive on the street. And he doesn't have his helmet. I have to go after him—and, dammit, you're delaying me!'' She shook off his hands, purposeful and determined again. ''My car won't start. Give me the keys to your motorcycle. I'll bring it back in one piece.''

Luke shook his head. Did she really think his bike was what he cared about?

''I'll do it,'' he said. ''You don't have a helmet, so stay here and wait. If I don't find him, he'll come back on his own.''

Sophie sank her hands in wild, curly hair and pulled it back from her face, her teeth gritted. ''You don't understand. I *have* to go. I have to move.''

Luke looked at her for a long moment, then nodded in agreement. He understand better than she knew. ''But I'm driving.''

''I have Joe's helmet.'' She ran off toward a dilapidated shed, shouting something about her father over her shoulder. Snatching up the helmet, she banged it on the rust-pockmarked trailer parked in the backyard, yelling for Buzzsaw. He emerged in a wobbly haze and she gave him hasty instructions on what to do and who to call if she was late. ''If Joe comes back before we do, stop him. Wrestle him to the ground and sit on him if you have to, but get the keys to his motorbike and don't let him leave again.''

Buzzsaw squinted at Luke and burped. ''Watcha doin' with Salinger, girl? I told you to stay away from them no-good—''

''I don't have time for that.'' Sophie hurried back to Luke. ''Let's go.''

She clambered behind him as soon as he mounted the Harley. The bike's engine purred like a leashed wildcat.

His wasn't a roadhog like the big touring bikes—it was designed for agility and speed.

"Hold on tight," he said to Sophie. As if she wouldn't remember, he thought while they moved off at a quick clip along Granite Street. He was stung by the familiarity of having her snugged up close behind him on the saddle of the bike. Her arms hugged his ribs, but it wasn't a sexual contact. She was yelling directions, telling him to cruise up and down several of the residential streets.

They drew a few interested stares along the way, but Sophie was beyond caring. "I was hoping he'd gone to a friend's house," she said when they were idling at a stop sign. For a moment, her shoulders slumped, her arms went lax. He thought she might let out a sob, but she recovered quickly. Her fingers closed over his elbow like a vise. "Let's head out of town. There's a dirt bike course out by the fairgrounds. If he's not there, try the Jackpine Lake campground. We used to go there all the time."

They took off again, picking up speed on the highway outside of town. The road was flat and open; Luke was able to think. It was as if Sophie's words had made time collapse. *We used to go there all the time.* She could have been talking about him and her. And the Mustangs. They'd cruised the countryside, impressed with how wicked cool they must look. There'd been lots of big talk, far-flung dreams, and all of it had come to naught.

He'd gone away, chased by betrayals both real and presumed, while Sophie had stayed put to become both an upholder of the law and a single mom with the weight of the world on her shoulders. The best he could do was share her burden. If she'd let him.

They cruised past the empty fairgrounds, a motley

collection of sheds and barns and fences, closed down for the winter. Sophie pointed over his shoulder, directing him toward a new motocross course. A charge went through her body and into his as they drew close enough to see activity. Several bikes raced up and down the dirt hills, wheeling around the tight curves.

Luke slowed his bike to a crawl. Sophie flipped up her visor to examine the course, then turned away. She pressed her face into his shirt, the hard edge of the helmet grinding against his shoulder blade. Her mouth moved. He couldn't hear her over the buzz of the bikes, but he didn't have to. The meaning was clear. *No. He's not here.*

Luke's chest constricted. It didn't matter if Joe Ryan was his son or not. The boy was alone and angry—he needed help.

He put his hand over Sophie's tense fist where she clutched the front of his shirt. "We'll find him." *We'll help him.*

They drove back to the highway turnoff and continued on to Jackpine Lake, cruising past the empty public campsites, continuing around the large, sprawling lake. There were several hiking trails that Joe might have taken. Motorbikes were forbidden, but he might not have cared. Hikers were sparse this time of year.

Luke stopped in a clearing at the north end of the lake and shut off the bike so they could listen for signs of Joe. The silence was complete in the moment after the engine quit. Then softer sounds became audible again—the rasp of the scrawny jackpines ringing the lake, the chatter of birds and squirrels, the lap of water among the rustling reeds.

"We'd hear his bike if he'd taken one of these trails," Luke said. "Where now? The switchback?"

Sophie stepped off the bike, her shoes crunching a small circle in the thick layer of rusty pine needles while she pried off the helmet. Her curly hair sprang free, sticking out in all directions. She pushed it off her face, eyes closed as she angled her head toward the hiking trails.

The raw vulnerability in her face went straight to Luke's battered conscience. His fingertips bit into the handgrips. He hated this. Feeling impotent. Unsure. If it were possible, he'd solve all of Sophie's problems in one fell swoop.

But he didn't think she was looking for that, especially not from a man known as Maverick, the unlikeliest white knight of them all.

"I don't know." Sophie dropped the helmet to the ground and sat on it. She put her head in her hands, her fingers tugging at her untamed waves. "I was counting on him getting off the highway as soon as he could." She squinted at the rippled surface of the blue water. "Sound carries well across this lake. He's probably not here, unless he's gone so far into the hills we can't hear—" She stopped. "Oh, I don't know. I don't know."

Luke said, "There are a hundred back-country roads he could have taken."

"Yeah." She was bleak at the prospect.

"We'd better get going if we want to search them all."

She shot him a grateful look, the first time she'd met his eyes since they stopped. The exchange quickly became intense; she blinked and blushed pink and fussily pushed up her sleeve to check her wristwatch. "I'm supposed to be at work in twenty minutes. I told my dad to call if I didn't get back in time, but…'' She shook her head. ''Do you have a cell phone?''

''Nope. But we can stop at the Thunderhead. You can make your calls and I'll ask around, find out if anyone's seen Joe.''

Her features froze. ''It would be better if I did that.''

He nodded easily. Now wasn't the time to push for explanations in that regard. ''Fine.''

''Fine,'' she repeated, clipping the word. ''Let's go.''

Under less strained circumstances, he would have enjoyed their subsequent tour of the countryside. They drove all around rural Sweetwater County, paying special attention to unpaved, back-country locations where a young boy might go to get away. Luke's years away didn't matter; he remembered feeling the same way himself and knew all the places to search.

In the woods, they flushed out a group of teenagers who hurriedly stamped their funky cigarettes into the ground when they recognized Sophie. At the closed-for-the-season drive-in, they ran across a couple—married, but not to each other—who were canoodling in the back row. Sophie stopped twice along the way to call home. Another deputy, Nick Hardin, had agreed to take her shift, but she hadn't asked him to look for her son while on patrol, explaining to Luke that the gung-ho Deputy Hardin was as likely to arrest Joe as to rescue him.

As the sun dipped lower in the sky, they descended the switchback in its rosy glow, outgunning the shadows stretching long across the pavement. Lookout Point, at the top of the switchback, had been their last resort. Now Sophie drooped against Luke, exhausted. Little wonder. She'd run on nervous energy for the last hour, meeting each disappointment with a wearying mixture of relief and frustration. He had reassured her that Joe was old enough to take care of himself, but as daylight grew short with no sign of Joe, Luke knew she was imagining crashes, blood, broken bones.

They reached the turn onto the highway, the same spot where he'd first asked about her son while he sat handcuffed in the back seat of her patrol car. A week ago, Luke thought. A lifetime ago.

He shouted over his shoulder. "I'm taking you home."

She lifted her helmeted head, hesitated, then shook it in denial.

"Yes," Luke said.

She pushed tight against his body, her thighs flexing around his hips as she rose up to reach his ear. He heard her clearly. Two words that went through him like a bolt of pure electricity:

"Hidden Lake."

The air, blue with dusk, suddenly crackled with awareness. Sophie tightened her arms around his abdomen, squeezing the tightly wound control out of him in shocking bursts of memories. Hidden Lake had been *their* place, a blue diamond tucked away from view in the mountains, as secret and precious to Luke as the private intimacies of his girl's sweet naked body. That Sophie had shared the place with her son—*their* son, his churning gut insisted—was cataclysmic. It was revealing—revealing right down to the bone.

He gunned the engine, letting the vibrations carry through them for a long moment of shared anticipation, until finally Sophie shouted, "Go!"

They did. Shooting toward their past at sixty miles per hour.

"HE'S NOT HERE."

Sophie frowned, knotting her brow to stop up the

tears welling in her eyes. She knew it had been a mistake to come to Hidden Lake, but something in her wouldn't give up the search for Joe until every rock was overturned.

All sorts of creepy-crawlies were lurking beneath this one, slithering and scurrying into the light of day.

She couldn't look at Luke.

The lake was visible only in narrow slivers, slate blue in the waning sun. Jackpine and spindly spruce surrounded it, packed tightly trunk to trunk so that little light got through to the spongy ground layered thickly with rust-colored forest debris. She and Luke had once made a path through the trees, tucked away behind the brambly bushes so that it wouldn't be visible to the casual observer. A steep wall of rock rose high on one side. If you climbed to the top, there was a flat stone where you could sit and watch the lake, the sky, the early mountain sunset.

The memories were a heartache.

"I wonder if the path is still there," Luke said, swinging his leg over the bike. He tipped his helmet onto the seat and thrust a hand through his hair.

Sophie shut her eyes. "Overgrown. It's been fourteen years."

"You've been here since then." His voice was quiet. And he was staring at her, she could sense it. His gaze was on her face like the sun. Damn if she didn't feel what was tight and closed inside her begin to open up to him.

She tossed her head, eyes wide, almost defiant. "Only a couple of times."

"With Joe."

"Yeah. But not for several years."

"Still, you think he'd remember the place?"

"A shot in the dark. That's all." She'd brought Joey here many times as a baby and toddler, then had stopped when real life caught up to them and her time was too crunched for sentimental journeys. Joey wouldn't remember those times, but they'd camped here one weekend when he was seven, and once or twice after that. Her son had loved the idea that the lake was hidden, a secret he must keep from outsiders. He'd seemed to sense that each visit was a rare, valued occasion.

"Let's climb the rock," Luke said.

She refused. "No. It's too dark. I have to go home."

"Sophie," he coaxed. "C'mon. We'll watch the sunset."

She shook her head. "We're not here to sightsee. And, besides, the sun's gone down." *On our relationship.*

"It'll give us a minute to sit and talk. Or is that what you're afraid of?"

She shook her head even harder. "Luke Salinger, we can talk till the cows come home, and that's not going to bring my son back to me. There's only one thing I care about right now—and it's not explaining myself to you."

"Who said anything about explaining yourself?"

"Right, like you wanted just to chitchat." She wrapped her arms around her midriff and walked quickly in the other direction, through the long buffalo grass and brittle goldenrod to the edge of the forest.

He followed her. "I'm not so ruthless, Sophie. I can see that now isn't the time to—" His voice cut off, as sharply as a knife.

A deep, goading apprehension inched through her

bloodstream. There would be relief in getting all her secrets out in the open, but...

Don't say it, Luke.

He came up behind her. Slid his hands over her arms with a rush of prickling sensation, until his arms had crossed over hers and she was held in his embrace. His chin rested on the top of her head. The wind sighed through the trees. For a long moment, she felt warm, safe, cherished, loved. After fourteen years without it.

The moment passed. Only an insidiously misleading chemical reaction to his closeness, she told herself, even though she didn't try to move away. She and Luke had loved each other once—a bright, shiny love, as flimsy and easily torn as a piece of tinfoil. What she wanted now was the kind of love that was built on bedrock and would last forever.

That Luke's body felt solid and strong and infinitely supportive didn't matter in the least.

"Now isn't the time for *this,* either," he said, loosening his embrace. She thought he meant to let her go. Instead, before she could react either way, he turned her in his arms and dropped a kiss upon her lips.

Sophie's body rose to meet it. The kiss lingered, sweetly poignant. Like a memory, she thought. Revisited.

Time to put this particular memory in a lock box.

She'd allow the kiss for another second. Maybe two. *Starting now.* But such a lovely sensation shot through her, she couldn't make herself break away until the tip of his tongue touched the inside of her parted lips. The questioning flicker of heat scared her as much as it drew her, as though she was a child playing with fire.

I know better than to touch the flame again.

She jerked backward out of Luke's arms. "What are

you doing? Are you crazy?'' His kiss, simple though it'd been, burned on her lips. She couldn't afford the distraction. Didn't want it. ''Stay away from me!''

Luke was dogged. ''Don't deny us, Sophie.''

''I'm here to look for my son,'' she said, shaking inside but outwardly calm. ''He's all that matters.''

''Your son is…'' Luke's throat worked in silence, as if the words were too big to fit. The dying light had turned his eyes a flat silvery blue—the calm before the storm. ''Joe's as much a part of us as the rest of it.''

A part of *us*. He'd said it out loud.

Time didn't simply stop—it petrified. This was the moment she'd been both dreading and wanting for fourteen years.

Her body was frozen. She literally could not move. But her mind raced for an exit.

Deny it.

''I know he's my son, Sophie.''

''Ha-how?'' One word, and her voice fractured it.

''How?'' Luke was quizzical. ''That's all you have to say? How?''

She gave her head a little shake. ''Who told you?''

''I didn't have to be told. It's become obvious. His age, his looks. Your reactions.''

''Looks can be deceiving.''

A heavy silence grew between them.

''You're denying that he's a Salinger?'' Luke finally said, filled with reproach.

''I can't,'' she blurted, stricken by the thought of hacking through the impossible Gordian knot of Joe's parentage. She didn't know which way to turn when the truth was sure to harm at least one of them. *Take the easiest route,* a large part of her said. *Give Joey the father he deserves.*

Did she dare? Could she allow Luke to believe that he had a son when it was far more likely that Joey was...his *nephew?*

CHAPTER EIGHT

THE EXPRESSION on Luke's face split a fresh crack through the center of Sophie's heart. *He wants Joe to be his son.*

"Joe's a Salinger," Luke repeated. Wonder lit his face like a paper lantern glowing in the dusk. He took a step toward her, reaching out a hand. "Aw, hell, Sophie, if I'd known…"

A hot burst of anger shot through her frozen limbs. "Don't you dare, Luke. You have no right. It takes more than shared genes to make a father." Her fists clenched. "By all the deeds that matter, Joey doesn't have a father!"

She whirled away from him and ran blindly into the pine trees, crashing through the network of spindly lower branches where sunlight didn't reach. Twigs snapped. Others bent, lashing her as she pushed past, scratching her face and hands. She barely noticed—her focus was on the lake. More importantly, on getting away from Luke.

"Sophie!" He was coming after her.

She emerged at the very edge of the water. Mud sucked at her shoes. Dried-out husks of cattails rattled in the breeze. Nowhere to go but in the lake itself. Part of her would have welcomed the cold shock that would chase everything except survival out of her mind. But she wasn't that desperate.

Having no choice, she dashed at her tears, then turned to confront Luke.

He stopped an arm's length away, one boot propped on a hillock. "Don't look so scared, Soph. I haven't been a father to Joe, I know that. But it's not all my fault. I never knew about him—about me being his father—so how—"

"You didn't know because you didn't stay. Not my fault either!"

His smile was sad. "We sound like children arguing over a broken toy."

"I don't remember what it's like to be a child. I grew up real fast after you left Treetop, Luke. There was no other choice, because when my dad found out I was pregnant he threw me out of the trailer."

Luke winced. "I'm sorry."

"I'm not. It turned out to be the best thing that ever happened to me. Lettice Bellew offered me a room at her boardinghouse. She was one of only a few people in town who were willing to help out an angry, poverty-stricken, knocked-up teenager with a bad reputation and a chip the size of a mountain on her shoulder." Sophie couldn't stop; the story was pouring out of her in a hot flood of words. "Miss Bellew helped me stay in school by giving me room and board in exchange for housekeeping. I was able to get my high-school diploma."

She stopped to take a breath. Her chin stayed up. "But I didn't go to the ceremony. I wasn't invited. The principal told me that they don't make graduation gowns for girls who are eight-plus months pregnant."

"Sophie, if I'd known…"

The surge of energy was abating. "I would have told you, Luke. It was your right to know about the baby." Heat crawled up her neck. *His right to know what the odds were, you mean.* "I even swallowed my pride and asked after you. But your family wasn't eager to share your whereabouts."

"The only one who knew was Heath. And even he didn't know exactly, until I called. I was on the road, going nowhere special. Just trying to outrun the mess I'd made of my life."

Sophie's hair lifted in the breeze. Her discomfort had eased by a tiny degree. Maybe they could come to a civilized agreement to keep on as they were. Luke would eventually leave town. Joey would adjust. She'd mothball her romantic dreams, just as she'd done before.

She sighed. "I guess we both screwed up pretty bad."

"Not you," Luke said. "You were innocent."

Her eyes narrowed. Something in his tone was off the mark. "Innocent? You know that Heath, among others, thought I was a snitch. He blamed me for turning you and the Mustangs in to the sheriff. Probably still does." She remembered their conversation in the patrol car. "And so do you."

Luke squared his shoulders. "Heath was wrong. *I* was wrong."

She gritted her teeth, ridden with other guilts. "You're sure of that, huh?"

"It wasn't up to you to protect the Mustangs." He glanced across the lake, its water a deep gray-blue corrugated by wind. "It's late. We can talk elsewhere. Let's get out of this muck before it's too dark to see."

She didn't want to see his eyes. They would reach straight into her soul and she'd never be able to keep up the construction of pretenses that were as shaky as a house of cards.

Her feet squelched in the mud when she moved. "Give me your hand."

"I'm all right." She teetered atop a hillock.

He stepped one foot into the wet sludge and stretched an arm around her waist to swing her onto dry land. The contact was entirely impersonal, yet she shivered from it, too caught up in old memories not to react.

Fourteen years ago, it had been she who was unabashedly hands-on with Luke. She hadn't known about physical closeness until then, so once she'd acquired the feel for it she'd itched to put her hands on him whenever he was near—smoothing his hair, locking fingers, hugging, kissing. Kissing all the time.

She was shameless, but it wasn't about sex as much as it was about the warmth of human contact. Her father wasn't demonstrative, and her mother had died before Sophie had formed strong memories of her. After years as a neglected daughter and lonesome foster child, the intimacy and trust that had grown between her and Luke had been a revelation. No wonder she'd craved him even after he was gone. No wonder she'd given all of her love and affection to her sweet baby boy, determined that he would have what she lacked.

Except that Joey had grown up deprived in another way. Sophie winced. She should have set aside her own desires and found a stepfather for her son.

"You're scowling," said Luke.

"I'm worried."

"He's probably home by now."

Please. "I hope so."

"Are you going to tell him about me?"

She brushed past Luke and picked a path among the pines. The dark, arrow-straight trunks looked like the bars of a cage. Luke had flown away from Treetop.

She'd wanted to, but she'd stayed—through humiliation and triumph. He had no right to return one day and expect to step back into their lives the next.

Luke stayed on her heels, reaching past her to snap off twiggy branches so she wouldn't acquire any more scratches. "You're making assumptions," she said, keeping her voice husky so it wouldn't catch. His assumptions were those a big part of her wanted him to make. The situation would be much easier if she could say for sure that Luke was Joey's father.

She felt Luke stop in surprise behind her, but she kept going. After a moment, he caught up. They emerged from the forest as an eagle swooped low across the darkened sky. Narrow red and gold threads of light draped across the cloudy blue-gray horizon were all that was left of the sun.

"I'm making assumptions because you haven't answered my question directly." Luke's voice reached through the twilight, sending vibrations that danced across her nerve endings. "Look at me, Sophie."

She wound her arms around her ribs and turned.

He held her gaze through sheer willpower. "Is Joe my son?"

A rushing sensation filled Sophie's ears. It was as if he'd turned her world upside down and was shaking out all the nasty little bits that she'd swept into the darkest corners. Her actions in the first days after Luke had gone away were her deepest shame.

The break-in at the law office had been a Treetop scandal. Talk had spread about Ed Warren's visit with Sophie and his subsequent arrest of several members of the motorcycle gang. The Mustangs scorned her for being a traitor. Townsfolk had shaken their heads over her, whispering that they'd known all along she'd come to no good.

Sophie might have been able to stand being an outcast—she'd been one most of her life—but Luke's abandonment had scorched her so badly she hadn't cared what she did, or what people said. For a few weeks, she'd lost herself in the oblivion of hard partying and late nights out with the few friends she had left. Nothing mattered. Might as well live up to her bad reputation.

"Answer me, Sophie," Luke said, pulling her back to the present. "Is Joe my son?"

She held herself tighter. Her nails bit into her arms. When she couldn't stand it anymore, she tipped back her head and opened her mouth and let the truth fly out of her. A wail of lament. "I don't know, Luke. I am so sorry, but I *don't know.*"

The red-hot shame of it came roaring back, strong as a wildfire. Luke would hate her. Joey would never forget. Mary Lucas would be scandalized. And how could Sophie blame them? Even she couldn't forgive herself.

"What do you mean?" Luke asked carefully.

A cold calm settled over her, detaching her from the burning shame. "It's pretty simple. I don't know who fathered my child."

At first he seemed angry. Jealous, maybe, but not altogether shocked. Then his shoulders slumped. The longest minute of Sophie's life passed before Luke said with bitter acceptance, "How many?"

She kept her teeth clenched. "Two."

"Besides me, or counting me?"

"Counting you."

"That's something." His laugh was mirthless, and it

sliced right through the hide she thought was tough enough to take any cut. "I've got a fifty-fifty chance."

"I g-guess so."

Luke came closer, brooding with his hands shoved in the pockets of his jeans. "I hear he looks like a Lucas."

Who'd told him that? Sophie couldn't make herself respond when all questions led to giving the secret away.

"We can take blood tests," he said. "Or match DNA."

"No!" She was frightened at the prospect of what the tests would reveal. "Look, I just—I can't think about that right now." She wanted to be struck down by a thunderbolt. She wanted to fly far away from here. "I have to deal with my son first."

Luke nodded. "I'll bring you home," he said, "but don't think I'm dropping this."

Sophie slipped on her helmet and snapped the visor into place. She didn't want Luke to get a close look at her face as they climbed onto the motorcycle. He kicked over the engine. Its roar blasted a hole into their tension. She was able to touch him, curling her fingers around his belt loops.

Turning, the bike bumped over rough ground. She had to press closer, close enough to feel the heat of his body, part and parcel of the fervor that had once been his trademark.

A tear leaked along the side of her nose. If only she could confess how, barely a week after Luke's departure, Heath had shown up one night at their Jackpine Lake hangout, sat and talked with her for a while, and then offered to drive her home. He'd been so concerned and gentle, looking and speaking and even smelling enough like his brother that it was almost as if Luke was with her again. They'd parked—to talk—and drank a few more beers. Sophie had become maudlin, then brash. Somehow, she'd found herself in Heath's arms, submitting to his kisses. With her eyes closed, she'd almost been able to fool herself that he was Luke.

Take a little comfort, she'd told herself at the time. *Just for the moment.* She hadn't been in any shape to understand that one weak moment of carelessness could result in an infinite regret.

Her blame, her shame.

Her innocent, beloved son, branded forever by his mother's mistake.

Sophie's heavy heart knocked in her chest when she saw that the lights were on and that Joey's motorbike had been tipped over into the bushes by the corner of the porch. Luke insisted on waiting in the driveway while she went inside to see if the boy was all right—physically.

Her junker sat abandoned with the groceries still in the back seat. The hood was up. Three opened beer cans balanced atop the radiator. Sophie went right on by. Let Buzzsaw clean it up, for once.

Her father was in the living room, watching TV. "Upstairs," he said when she asked about Joey. "Came in all dirty. Didn't say a word." Archie huffed. "Didn't even stop to eat."

She hesitated in the hallway, listening for sounds of life from her son's room before going to wave at Luke on his motorcycle. But he'd come to stand at the bottom of the porch steps, an odd light—was it yearning?—in his eyes. The two remaining grocery sacks had been set on the floor by the door, the garment bag draped across the stack of books. For one instant, she thought of inviting Luke inside for supper, but that would be insane. More trouble she did not need.

"Joe's home," she said.

Luke nodded solemnly. "That's good."

"We'll see." She rolled her bottom lip. "Um, thank you. For getting my stuff. And...helping me look for Joe. It was very kind and I appreciate—"

He interrupted. "Don't brush me off with platitudes, Sophie."

She plopped onto the top step like a shovelful of wet cement, the adrenaline that had kept her going suddenly drained away, leaving her chilled and bereft. "I know how terrible this is for you, Luke. A major shock. I'm really sorry you were never told. There were reasons, but they don't matter now." She rocked, hugging her knees. "We're too late for excuses."

"It's not only your fault to bear."

She glanced back at the house before lifting her gaze to meet his. "I was in love with you, Luke," she whispered. Her chest ached. "And I cheated—I had sex with another man."

His eyes were bleak. "You can't cheat on a boyfriend who left you without a word of explanation."

"Yes, you can. In your heart, distance makes no difference." Her chin drooped to touch her knees. "In *my* heart."

Luke's mouth gave a token quirk. "We're arguing the wrong sides." He slipped his fingertips beneath her chin, lifting it higher, tilting her face toward the light from the windows. "Your cheeks are scratched. I want you to go inside and clean up. Take a little time to think all of this through. Make some kind of peace with your son. I'll talk to you tomorrow, when things have settled down."

She made a quiet sound of assent even though she knew that tomorrow would be as turbulent as today. There was no running away from the coming confrontations.

"It'll be okay, Soph." Luke touched a gentle kiss to her mouth, catching her by surprise. "We'll work it out."

Even with his kiss lingering on her lips, she couldn't stop a brief flare of fear. Did he intend to work it out?

Or to stake a claim?

She turned her face away. "Just go."

Luke backed off. "This isn't over."

That's what she was afraid of. Arms crisscrossed on her knees, she watched him drive away. He hadn't changed as much as she'd believed when she'd first confronted those cold steel eyes up on the switchback.

But was that good or bad? As drawn as she'd been to Luke when he was eighteen, she'd recognized that there were complicated reasons for his rebellion against his family, beyond their expectations that he'd take a position with one of the logging or mining operations that he abhorred. He'd never completely opened up to her about those problems. She'd always suspected that they were connected to his reasons for breaking into the law office—which not coincidentally happened to be the office of the Lucas family's attorney—because as reckless as he could be, she'd never known him to be completely lawless.

Now she was beginning to put together a few of the missing pieces. Going on tonight's revelations, it must have been Heath who told Luke that she'd turned him in.

Yet Heath had kept the larger secret. For his own selfish reasons, most likely. But how long would that hold up if Kiki and he couldn't provide Mary with the next generation, as expected?

Sophie shuddered. One way or another, the Lucases would be coming to claim her son.

Joe was only thirteen. Too young for her to be brutally honest about the circumstances of his conception. But she couldn't see any way to get around it.

Tiredly, she took the groceries inside to the kitchen and made a thick roast beef sandwich with three slices of sharp cheddar and lots of horseradish. The way Joe liked it. She pulled a package of cookies from the brown paper sack, groaning when she peered inside. A pint of melted sherbet got thrown out, but she stuck a few of the other perishables in the fridge to see if they could be saved. She took out a carton of orange juice, set it on the tray, found a paper napkin, every motion rote. She knew what her son was going through. It was nourishment he needed, yes, but not food alone. She had to give him love and understanding and space to talk. She had to give him the truth.

Feeling like Marie Antoinette on her way to the guillotine, Sophie took the tray upstairs.

Luke. *Maverick.* Why hadn't he stayed away?

The names spoke inside her head with each of her footfalls on the attic steps. Maverick. *Luke.* Maverick. *Luke.*

Absurdly, she imagined them as a happy family. Luke and Sophie Salinger and their son, Joe. Even now, it could have happened—if she'd been able to maintain a lie.

Don't kid yourself, Soph. Luke did not come back for you.

She knocked on Joe's door. No answer.

She called to him without response. Tried the knob. Locked.

She had a key, but was loath to use it. A teenager's space should be sacrosanct, another little lesson she'd learned as a girl with very little she could call her own.

Balancing the tray on her hip, she put a palm to the door as if testing for a heartbeat. "Joe, you know you're going to have to face me sooner or later."

Utter quiet. She asked herself—again—when her cuddly chatterbox had become so stubborn and withdrawn. She could blame the timing on Luke, but not the rest of it. It was probably the way of most adolescents. She'd been no Suzy Sunshine herself. Naturally Joe was going to want answers to the questions she'd been able to avoid when he was younger. She only wished it hadn't happened so harshly.

"You must be hungry. I have a sandwich."

Still nothing. "I'm putting the tray on the floor outside your door. But I'm not going away until you give me a sign that you're..." Not okay. She couldn't say *okay*, because he wasn't.

She took a breath. "That you're still breathing."

A muffled thud. She figured that he'd stamped a foot on the floor. Then came a blast of the radio. Her son was the Wolfman Jack of communicators.

"All right for now," she whispered. Even though she'd intended to confiscate the motorbike keys and give him a lecture about illegal driving, that could wait. Lord knew, her role as a deputy sheriff was the furthest thing from all their minds.

Oh, hell. That was another problem she'd have to contend with. When—if—the truth came out, the respect she'd fought so hard to earn over the past decade would be wiped away. She'd be Sophie Ryan again, wild child, rowdy teenage punk, lost in a world without understanding.

But she'd get past all that. The deepest pain, the one she couldn't forget, was that they truly could have been a family, her and Luke and Joe. The three of them, together and happy.

Instead the triangle was only ironic. Joe didn't want his long-lost father to be Luke, the town's maverick black sheep.

Whereas she wished with all her heart that he was.

SATURDAY MORNING, and Sophie's stomach was in knots. Joey was still upstairs, pretending to sleep. She'd gone in and sat on his bed, waiting for a sign, but he'd pulled the covers up to his nose and kept his head buried in the pillow. In a way, that made it easier. She didn't have to see the accusation and blame in his eyes as she made her confession.

She'd given him the straight dope on her teenage years, her attraction to Luke and thus the Mustangs. She'd revealed as much as she knew about the break-in and vandalism of the law office. But she'd fudged on the vital question.

"Luke Salinger may be your father," was all she said, watching the top of Joey's head as he pushed his face deeper into the pillow. "It's very possible." She paused. "And I want you to know, despite what happened fourteen years ago, despite the rumors that you've heard, Luke is essentially a good person." *Are you a hundred percent sure of that?* "You can be proud...if he's your dad."

Her son was smart; he'd figure out the implications of the ifs and maybes. When he'd adjusted to the idea, after he'd grown-up a little more, she'd tell him the whole story.

Meantime, there was Luke to deal with.

Hence the knots. Big ones, tying up her appetite.

Sophie leaned against the broom she'd been using. To keep up her strength, she'd tried to eat breakfast, but emotional turmoil didn't go well with eggs and toast. Sitting alone at the kitchen table didn't help either. She wasn't used to that.

A sharp rap at the screen door made it rattle on its loose hinges. Sophie's stomach clenched, but then Kiki was calling, "Hello? Sophie?" and she stopped worrying over Luke's reaction and started in on Kiki's.

There was no hiding. The front door was open to the sunny September day. "In the kitchen," she called, putting the broom aside to grab the shed key off the table. First thing that morning, she'd wheeled the mower out of the shed and the motorbike in. But where to hide the key?

Kiki entered, dressed smartly in high-heeled boots, hip-hugging skirt and a fitted soft wool turtleneck, soft blue against the dark elegance of her smooth hair and careful eye makeup. She always made Sophie feel like a frump.

"That's what I call service," Kiki said, gesturing toward the front yard. Her laugh sparkled. "Keep them at your beck and call is my motto."

"What?" Sophie went over to the dining room window. Luke was outside, hunched under the open hood of her car. She'd been in such deep thought, she hadn't heard him drive up.

Kiki peered over Sophie's shoulder. "I suppose this means you two are picking up where you left off."

Sophie blinked. "Why would you say that?"

"Men don't randomly fix women's cars. When they get under that hood—" Kiki pointed outside "—it means they want to get under this hood." She waved at the front of Sophie's "Property of the Treetop Sheriff's Department Size S" T-shirt. Ed Warren had special-ordered the Size S, making another of his jabs about the lady deputy not filling out her uniform in the proper areas.

Sophie backed away from the window. She couldn't refute the statement, so it was better to ignore it.

"What's that?" Kiki asked, looking at the key in Sophie's hand.

"Just the key to the shed. Joe's grounded. No motor bike." Sophie saw her sewing basket on the sideboard and dropped the key into it. Joe wouldn't look through her embroidery floss. "Um, how about coffee?"

Kiki sighed. "Oh, why not?" She'd been limiting her caffeine for years, preparing for pregnancy. Whenever she came over for a good gab session over a few cups of coffee, Sophie knew another barren month had gone by.

"I'll go see if Luke wants some." Sophie slid quickly out the screen door, checking the house as she approached Luke. Kiki watched from the dining room window; no sign from the small four-paned square in the peak of the eaves.

Sophie cleared her throat. "Morning."

Luke straightened, his shoulders immense in a charcoal-colored denim shirt. His sleeves were rolled up over strong forearms and competent hands already stained with oil from the engine. Her knots loosened, thinking of the way he'd watched out for her last night. She'd felt so safe, even on the back of a speeding motorcycle, when Luke was with her. Working with her, but not taking charge.

"Good morning," he said.

She slid nervous hands down the outside of her hips. "Maybe for you."

"Joe's still angry?"

"He won't talk to me."

"Then you haven't told him." They both kept their voices low.

"I told him that you might be his father. It seems best to leave it at that for the time being. Joe will know what I meant. No need to grind his nose in it."

Luke's hands dropped. The wrench clanged against metal. "How am I supposed to get to know him under those circumstances?

Sophie sucked in a shallow breath. "Who said you were?"

He met her eyes. "I'm not looking for permission."

She stepped backward, shaking her head. "It's too soon. And—and—" She gulped air. "*I'm* in charge of my son's welfare. *I* get to say who he sees and where he goes. Don't you forget it."

She whirled and slammed back into the house, having forgotten all about offers of coffee and gratitude with Luke's accusing eyes burning holes in her conscience.

Kiki trailed Sophie into the kitchen and watched in silence while she took out their usual colorful ceramic mugs. She set them on the kitchen table and went to get the carafe, but had to stop to clench and unclench her hands. They were shaking. She didn't want her "friend" to see.

Plastering on a careless smile, Sophie turned and poured. Kiki was too observant. After every seemingly casual visit, Sophie was left wondering if Heath had sent his wife to gather intelligence information in the opposing camp. What she'd never quite been able to figure out was whether Heath had told Kiki of the possibilities regarding Joe. She thought no. But if Kiki knew, she was very skilled at concealing it.

"Luke didn't want coffee?" Kiki stirred a sugar cube into her mug.

"Not right now."

A saucy grin. "He's busy tinkering under your hood."

"It's not like that." Sophie sat. From the small kitchen window, she could see both the shed where she'd locked up Joe's motorbike and most of the backyard. In the other direction, a portion of the front hall was visible. Her son wasn't going to be sneaking out until he'd spoken at least a few words to her. That was important. Vitally important.

"There has to be a reason he's hanging around," Kiki went on, smiling as if she weren't fishing.

"You know what the judge said. I'm responsible. I have to keep an eye on Luke." And on Joe. Her father. Heath. Sheriff Ed Warren, the other deputies. The Mustangs.

She was surrounded by troublesome men who needed watching.

"Grandmother Lucas isn't happy about that."

Sophie started. "Me and Luke, you mean?"

Kiki tilted her small pointed chin. Her red lips pursed. "I really don't understand why she disapproves so vehemently."

Even after all these years, Sophie thought sadly. Well, if that was so, it would take a miracle to get Mary Lucas to accept Joe as her great-grandson. Which should have been a relief.

And, strangely, wasn't.

What—did you expect a happy ending?

"I'm trailer trash," Sophie said, trying to act like it didn't hurt. "Caused the downfall of her grandson. Loose, immoral, low-class. Take your pick."

Kiki patted Sophie's hand. "But you're a deputy now."

She let out a groan of a laugh. Kiki was pampered in her position as Heath's wife. Even at twenty-six, she was young and sometimes thoughtless. Then there were the other times, when Sophie glimpsed a needy insecurity in the other woman's eyes that reminded her of her own, not that long ago.

"Oh dear." Kiki giggled. "What I meant was that Grandmother Lucas respects the law."

"Up to a point." The point at which it intersected with her rule of her family. Sophie frowned. Was she being any different, refusing Luke the right to get to know Joe simply because legally he wasn't named as the boy's father?

But I don't know for sure and that makes all the difference in the world.

Or did it?

"You seem worried," Kiki said.

Keen observation. Sophie shrugged. "I didn't get much sleep."

"Did Luke stay over?"

Sophie's mouth hung open. "Of course not! Where did you— Why did you— How—"

Kiki wrapped her fingers around the emerald mug and lifted it to her mouth. "He wasn't home at all last evening, and then wasn't there for breakfast either. When I saw him out front, naturally I assumed..." She winked and took a sip.

"Luke was absolutely not here overnight," Sophie said stonily.

"I apologize. It's just that there's been so much talk about the two of you." Kiki tittered. "I think everyone in town is waiting for you two to set off some kind of explosion, one way or another."

Sophie closed her eyes and drew in a calming breath. She didn't need for the gossip to be reaching Joe's ears. He'd be listening closely, now.

Speak of the devil. She heard stealthy sounds coming from the hall, and then Joe appeared, heading for the door. "Joe," Sophie said, and he stopped. "Don't say anything," Sophie whispered quickly to Kiki before raising her voice again. "Want some breakfast?"

His chin was planted on his chest. "No."

"You're grounded, so you might as well come and eat something."

His head shot up. "I'm grounded?"

Sophie glanced at Kiki. "For taking the motorbike out without a helmet or the proper license." She went to Joe and grabbed onto his shoulders to make him look into her eyes. His lashes fluttered before he stared defiantly, a flush staining his cheeks. "I love you, Joey. Remember that. It's the most important thing."

He ducked his head and said in a gravelly voice, "I know, Mom."

She hugged him. He let out a suffering sigh. She gripped tighter. After a few seconds, he relaxed his stiffened shoulders and patted her on the back with one hand. "Okay, Mom. Jeez. You can let go now."

"Don't ever run away again," she whispered fiercely in his ear. "I was scared out of my head." She landed a quick kiss on his jaw before pulling back. "You're still grounded. I have to work a double shift this weekend and I want to know where you are, so no wandering away.''

He rolled his eyes. ''That's not fair! What am I gonna do all day?''

''You can—'' Sophie's voice cut off. She'd looked past Joe's shoulder, directly at Luke, who'd been standing near the porch steps watching them as they hugged. His expression was revealing—filled with longing and regret. Her heart went out to him, but instinct made her want to protect Joey.

''You can clean the shed—no, scratch that. I've locked it. You can mow the lawn and rake out the vegetable garden.'' She gave him a light slap to get him going. ''Wait in the kitchen with Kiki. I'll make you a good hot breakfast.''

Joe went without seeing Luke. Sophie hesitated, staring out at him through the screen door. The sunshine glanced off the top of his dark hair. He was tall and rugged and slightly dangerous looking. He'd taken a bandanna out of his pocket and was wiping his hands, occasionally glancing at her from beneath his brow. She wanted to ask him inside, but froze up at the thought of undergoing such a painfully awkward encounter under Kiki's watchful gaze.

Sophie stepped forward.

Eyes brightening, Luke bounded up the steps.

Hating herself, she shut the door. In his face.

CHAPTER NINE

KIKI LEFT THE HOUSE several minutes later and stopped to say hello to Luke. Oozing good cheer, she blinked big eyes at him, her mouth forming an arch three-cornered smile. "Aren't you a honey, fixing Sophie's car?"

"I sure am," he agreed, giving away nothing. However friendly Kiki made herself, she was in cahoots with her husband, and by now it was clear that Heath was not to be trusted. This disillusioned Luke, since Heath had been his main family contact for so many years. Another mistake in judgment.

Kiki was thinking. Luke could almost see the various calculations spinning like pinwheels in her bright green eyes.

"I suppose you're hoping to get a look at Joe?" she nudged.

Luke bent over the engine. One glimpse of the boy had about torn his heart out.

"Grandmother Lucas shouldn't be pushing him on you. She doesn't realize that you're bound to be disappointed."

Luke stood up so fast he almost bonked his head on the hood. "What do you know that I don't?"

Kiki maintained her coy smile. "Enough."

Luke scoffed. "Heath's version."

"Sophie's been my friend ever since I moved to Treetop. We've exchanged many confidences."

"Uh-huh."

"She's had a rough time of it, living down the old scandal—her association with you and the Mustangs, being a single mother. You coming back to town is..." Kiki shrugged.

Doing her no good, Luke thought, as he was supposed to. The sticking point was that, even though he suspected Heath and Kiki were trying to manipulate the situation to their own best advantage, they were right. He was causing trouble for Sophie. Distressing her.

But it was too late to retreat, now that he'd seen her again and knew about Joe. This time, he was completely aware of what he'd be giving up by quitting too fast.

"Can I give you a ride back to the ranch?" Kiki offered.

"No, thanks. I have my bike."

"Oh." Frowning, Kiki looked for the Harley he'd parked off to the side at the end of the short pebbled driveway. "All righty then. But you'd better finish up fast. Sophie has to go to work."

"I'm almost done."

Still stalling, Kiki looked over the ancient Honda hatchback with obvious distaste. "Sophie should get a new car. Something with a little style."

"Maybe you can mention that to her, since you two are so tight." So tight she couldn't figure out that Sophie couldn't afford the payments.

"Maybe!" Missing his sarcasm—or ignoring it— Kiki smiled brilliantly and walked over to her own vehicle, a red sports car that was as glossy and striking as she. Her trim little figure slipped behind the wheel. With a jaunty wave, she pulled out from her parking spot on

Granite Street without checking for traffic, neatly swerving around a kid on a bike who was approaching from the opposite direction.

Luke watched until she'd zipped around the corner. He turned to find Sophie standing nearby. Her expression was solemn. Despite an instinctive leap of joy, he schooled his own features, hardening himself against further rejection.

"I'm sorry," she said, pleading. "I had to wait until Kiki left. This is too important." She hitched her shoulders. "Will you please come inside and have breakfast with me and Joe?"

"Are you sure he's ready for that?"

"I'm not sure that *I'm* ready. But Joe...I told him you were out here working on the car and he's curious. Not necessarily friendly, you understand. I can't be sure what he'll say." Her short laugh carried an uncharacteristic warble—the edge of hysteria. "Consider yourself forewarned. If you'd rather wait..."

"For what? The blood tests that you've refused?" Luke was sorry he'd spoken so quickly when she sobered as if he'd thrown a bucket of cold water in her face. He reached out to touch her, then stopped. His hands were dirty.

But the day was bright, sunny, exploding with possibility. Chickadees twittered in the trees and somewhere down the street a lawn mower roared. Children laughed as they played, their shouts carrying along the row of humble homes.

The question was loud and important in his head, but Luke spoke it quietly. "Sophie, do you think he's my son?"

She was hesitant. "Well, um, since you and I always used condoms—"

"They're not foolproof. But I don't want odds or statistics. I want to know what you feel in your heart."

She swiped her fingers across her eyes, then looked off into the distance, her gaze focused beyond the tops of the elm trees. "With all my heart, I want Joe to be your son."

For a man who'd prided himself on staying unemotional, Luke's feelings had been on an elevator ride to hell and back in the past ten minutes. Now he felt as if the elevator had smashed through the top of his skull and fireworks were shooting out in glorious celebration. It almost didn't matter whether or not he was the boy's biological father, as long as Sophie had *wished* that he was.

She continued. "I've always wanted that, since the day I found out I was pregnant. It didn't matter to me that you were gone, that I was too young, that I'd be solely responsible for the baby. I still loved you. I wanted your child."

"I hate that I wasn't here with you."

She shook her head, compressing her lips when her chin trembled.

"Heath told me you'd had a baby."

Surprise flickered across her face. *"You knew?"*

"Long after the fact. Either Heath wasn't aware of the timing, or he purposely misled me so I wouldn't begin to question whether the baby was mine. I did wonder about the father. Hated him, in fact, whoever he was. All I knew—from Heath—was that there'd been plenty of—" Luke cleared his throat "—possible candidates."

Sophie was ghostly pale, but her eyes snapped with outrage. "Plenty, huh? He said that, straight out? That I was a tramp?"

Was it all lies? "He said that after I left you got sort of wild and crazy..."

"That much is true. And it's also true that I did something stupid. Very stupid and very wrong and very regrettable. But with only one other man, not a troop of them." She clenched her jaw, kept her shoulders defiantly square, and pivoted on her heel to go back into the house. "Look, now's not the time to rehash this. Joe's waiting inside, if you still want to meet the illegitimate son of the town trollop."

Luke's gut wrenched. Her plucky bearing got to him even more than the caustic acceptance of the slur. He knew the real Sophie, knew how much she'd been shamed by sneers and put-downs in the past, and yet he'd let himself believe Heath's condemnations. Unforgivable. "God, Sophie, I'm sorry I doubted you. I should have looked deeper into Heath's motivations."

She kept her head turned away, looking at him only from the corners of her eyes. Fiery spots of pink had ignited in her pale cheeks. "No apology is due on that account. I gave you reason, didn't I? Even if you'd asked around, you would have heard the same thing from Punch or Skooch or...or...just about *anyone*." She shuddered. They'd all been quick to believe the worst of her.

"We both made mistakes," Luke said. "Let's not keep going back and forth over which was the worst and who's to blame for what."

She flicked her fingers. "Sweep it all away? Just like that?"

"No. It's not so simple. I might want to sweep away the thought of you with another man, but I can't."

"That's what I was afraid of. I didn't want to tell you."

"You had to."

"But now I'm not—" Her mouth twisted. "I'm not the sweet young innocent you left behind, am I? I'm...*used goods.*"

"Don't say that about yourself."

"Why not? Everyone else does."

"Not me."

"You believed Heath's lies about me."

"I was mistaken."

She winced. "Back to our many mistakes again. Do you think you'll ever be able to completely forgive me for mine?"

"Can you forgive me?"

"You left fourteen years ago. I've had a long time to get over it."

"And to get over me." Luke slammed the hood and placed the socket wrench on top of it, careful not to mar the finish even though the car was one big collection of dents, dings and scratches. "I tried to get over you, but it didn't work." Dejected, he leaned his weight on the hood. The metal was hot beneath his palms.

Suddenly Sophie was there, placing her hand atop his. His heart skipped a beat. "I didn't forget you, either," she whispered, holding her face against his shoulder. The wispy ends of her hair brushed his cheek. Her fragrance, his surge of emotion, the sudden awareness— all of it was too tantalizing to resist. "How could I?"

The warm air seemed to coalesce around them in a bubble. Time slowed. He picked up her hand, turned it over between his. Caressed it. She didn't have soft, pretty hands. She was tough, his girl. Generous, too.

He gazed into her eyes. "Then it's not too late for us?"

She made an O with her mouth.

"Tell me it's not too late for us."

"You ask too much." Her lashes lowered. "Too soon."

"Can't help myself." His voice was rough with the longing that had been withheld for too many years. "I've wasted enough time."

Sophie slid her hand away, visibly bristling, giving a short, sharp laugh that pierced the bubble. "When Judge Entwhistle told me to stay close to you, I don't think she meant like this."

The Sophie Ryan Porcupine Act. He remembered it well.

"Are you sure? That judge was one sharp cookie." *Just like you.*

Sophie turned and walked away, saying over her shoulder, "You'll find there are plenty of interested by-standers left in Treetop. Their memories are as long as the winters, and we're the hottest gossip since the Triple Eight counterfeiting scandal and Demon's last arrest for drunken brawling at the Thunderhead." She thrust her hands into the front pockets of her jeans, pulling the denim distractingly tight across her rear end as she stumped up the porch steps.

"From what Punch said, Demon's arrests are too frequent to be big news."

"It's mostly been penny ante stuff. So far."

"Oh?"

Sophie paused with her hand on the screen door. "Don't ask for details. I can't say more."

"Must be strange for you, tangling with the Mustangs from the other side of the law."

"It's not like I went over to the dark side, Luke." She shrugged. "Even though I do sometimes feel as if I've landed between a rock and a hard place."

"Which is Ed Warren?"

"Definitely the rock. His attitude comes straight from the Stone Age." Sophie peered inside her house. "Well. Joe's waiting. You ready?"

Luke flexed his fingers, imagining shaking hands for the first time with the tall, skinny boy who might be his son. A momentous occasion. "I need to wash up first, if that's all right."

"Of course." They stepped inside and she directed him to the bathroom at the end of the hall. He went swiftly, catching glimpses of bright color from the other rooms. In the bath, the towels and fixtures were all white, but the walls were a deep watermelon pink that made him smile, wondering when Sophie had developed a penchant for such vibrant shades. She'd been a black Megadeth T-shirt and jeans girl when he knew her.

Ah, there was the obvious explanation: *When he knew her.*

He had a thousand details—a whole lifetime—to catch up on.

His gaze traveled around the room while he washed his hands. Sophie and Joe must share the bath—a grimy-soled athletic sock had missed the hamper and there were two toothbrushes in a cup, one purple and black, one neon pink. He touched the head of the pink one with a wet fingertip, then laughed at himself and briskly dried his hands.

The tropical-fish shower curtain was half open. He took down a bottle of discount-store shampoo, papaya-coconut scented, flipped up the lid and sniffed. Sophie's hair smelled like this. Nice, but it used to smell like the sun and the wind.

Luke put the plastic bottle back. What was he doing, sniffing shampoo? Hadn't he wasted enough time?

Joe Ryan was waiting.

His son. Had to be his son.

The scene in the kitchen was homey. Almost normal. Luke focused on the room for a moment because if he looked at Joe he'd stare. And stare. And maybe even shed a tear. A fine impression that would make.

Swallowing the lump in his throat, Luke took in the sight of Sophie at the stove with a spatula, flipping French toast. The room was a little messy, but cheerful. The cabinets were yellow, the walls golden brown. There were ancient appliances and black-and-white checkerboard linoleum, towels and curtains. They'd lived and laughed and fought in this kitchen. All without him.

"Luke," Sophie said. Her smile was tremulous as she set a plate of steaming slices on the table. She looked nearly as nervous as he felt.

"This is my—this is Joe." Her hand curved around the boy's elbow, urging him to shove back his chair and stand for the introduction.

Joe was taller than his mother by an inch and gangly like a colt in baggy jeans and a T-shirt, Luke saw, still going for the overall picture. Details were harder. Details like the familiar shape of the boys face, his pinched mouth, his stormy eyes. Brown eyes, Luke realized with a start. He'd thought they'd be blue, like the rest of the Lucas men.

"Joe, this is Luke Salinger." Sophie took a breath as if she meant to go on, but then stopped right there. What else could she say?

Luke extended his hand. "Good to meet you, Joe."

They shook—very briefly. Joe pulled his hand away.

"Yeah," he muttered, averting his face while he twisted and pulled at the bottom of his shirt. Still a young boy, Luke thought. "You too, uh, Mr. Salinger."

"Call me Luke. I hope we can…get to know each other."

"Sure." Joe glanced at Luke, looking mutinous. Sophie scowled a warning at her son and he dutifully produced a smile that, even though forced, hinted at what it might be like to share his good favor.

Take it slow. Luke tore his gaze away from the boy's face even though his gnawing hunger for familiarity wasn't nearly satisfied.

"We should eat while the food's still hot," Sophie said, breaking up their frozen tableau.

They took seats at a table shoved up to a windowsill lined with glossy-leafed begonias. Pouring juice and milk, passing syrup and butter took up a few minutes. Luke snared quick glances at Joe whenever he dared. Now and then their gazes intercepted and their eyes would clash for a split second before Joe blinked or looked away, fiddling in his seat. He seemed fractious, pent-up, ready to bust. Luke remembered how it felt to be a teenager. Speed had been his antidote—fast horses, fast motorcycles, fast talk, fast temper.

Sophie, on the other hand, sat very still with her feet and ankles wound around the legs of her chair. She looked only at her plate, her flashing utensils, but Luke could feel the nervous energy thrumming through her veins. "You have to work today?" he said, as if everything was normal. Maybe Joe would relax if the focus was off him.

She nodded. "I'm pulling a double shift this weekend. To make up for switching with Deputy Hardin last night."

Joe's cheeks grew ruddy. "I was gonna come home. You didn't have to drive around looking for me like I was a stupid little runaway kid."

"Sorry, but that's a mother's job. Next time tell me where you're going and I won't have to worry. It'll be a lot easier on both of us."

"How could I *know*—" Joe shut up fast when he glanced at Luke.

"Now that you're a young man, you have to learn to control yourself even under trying circumstances," Sophie said. "Don't go off half-cocked."

Joe rolled his eyes. "Jeez, Mom."

Luke was almost able to stifle his snort of amusement.

"What?" Sophie raised an innocent face, looking from one to the other. "What did I say? Half-cocked?"

Joe dropped his fork. "Not again."

Sophie smiled. "But it's a perfectly acceptable expression. It means—"

"I know what it means," Joe said quickly.

"It's not the meaning," Luke said, "it's the Bobbitized image that the phrase conjures up."

Sophie's smile was growing a little too self-satisfied. "Oh, don't be such weenies."

Joe squirmed in embarrassment.

Luke laughed. "You definitely said that one on purpose."

She winked at him. He cut another few squares of the French toast, feeling damn good inside. The shared joke had eased them past the worst of the introductory awkwardness. Although not a word about Luke's reason for being here had been expressed, that was okay. Getting to know Joe as a person should come before the stress of verbal acknowledgements of his role as a father.

Luke addressed the boy directly. "What will you do while your mother's at work?"

Joe shoveled a forkful of food into his mouth. "Mmph."

"He's staying home and doing chores," Sophie said. She got up, scraped her plate and started running water into a dishpan.

Joe glowered at her back.

She squirted soap into the pan. "Isn't that right?"

"Whatever."

Sophie came back to the table, making a stern face. "Joe, you know I don't like for you to talk to me like that."

The boy's eyes skipped across Luke's face, as if expecting backup. Luke raised an eyebrow. Joe gulped and said, "Sorry, Mom." He stood. "May I be excused?"

Sophie held his face firmly between her palms. "You may go. But remember. You will stay home."

Joe's "Yes" was grudging.

"I mean it. I'll be calling to check up on you." Sophie smoothed his hair. "Okay. Go on. Why don't you start on the lawn?"

Joe ran a hand through his hair, re-tousling it. He grabbed a banana from a fruit bowl and in several loping strides was halfway through the adjacent dining room. "See ya," he called, moving even faster. The screen door slammed.

"Was that meant for me?" Luke said.

"I guess so." Sophie sighed. "Sorry about that. Joe wasn't at his best. He's usually more friendly, but you know adolescence. Moods come and go like quicksilver.''

''It wasn't so bad, considering. We even exchanged a few words.''

Sophie leaned against the edge of the sink. ''I wish I could stay home today, to keep him company even if he won't talk about all this, but…''

''Do you think he'll take off again once you're gone?''

''Not on the motorbike. It's locked in the shed and I hid the key in my sewing basket, just in case. Joe's usually good about behaving when he's on his own.'' She dropped her head to peer out the window, watching her son amble aimlessly around the backyard, whipping the bushes with his banana peel. ''But he's never had to deal with so much all at once.''

''It's hard.'' Luke identified. He'd been seventeen when he'd first learned of the chance that the man he'd called Dad was not his biological father. Several years passed before he'd been able to acquire irrefutable proof of who was, and he'd still been freaked by seeing the truth in black and white. ''Joe's only thirteen.''

''Right. Boone's going to drop off the cruiser at the end of his shift. I'll make sure my Dad's up and moving before I leave for work. He'll keep an eye on Joe, more or less.''

''Hey.'' Luke stood. ''Why don't I do it?''

Sophie stared.

He walked toward her, his palms up. ''I'll hang out here for a while, tune up the car, help Joe with the yard work. Maybe he'll talk to me, maybe not. At least you won't have to worry about what he's up to.''

''That's pushing it, Luke. Joe might react badly. Or

he could come out with questions that I'd rather be here to answer."

"I won't force the subject. I won't even bring it up. All I want is the chance to get to know him."

"I'm not sure that's wise," she said, troubled. "We should give him more time."

"Sophie, I've been in Joe's shoes. He doesn't need distance. Too much thinking and worrying on the subject and hell get as crazy as I did when I broke into that law office fourteen years ago. After my mother's death, I was so mixed up inside, I began to believe that the ends justified the means."

Concern shone from her eyes. "Why *did* you do it? I've always wondered."

Luke shook his head. "Proof's what I told myself. But now I think it was to force a confrontation. My family's very good at keeping secrets buried."

Sophie touched his cheek, almost the way she'd done with her son, except that when Luke reacted by stepping closer she snatched her hand away again and gripped the edge of the countertop instead. "I knew you had personal problems. What was it? Did you learn you were adopted?"

"No." Luke's throat twisted. "Adoption messes up the bloodlines."

"What does that mean?"

"It's complicated."

"Tell me."

Luke placed his hands on the kitchen counter on either side of her and leaned in close enough to see the tiny flecks of gold in her eyes. "I can't tell you. If you knew how bad the Lucases and Salingers are messed up, you wouldn't let any of us near Joe."

"You think that hasn't occurred to me? The kicker's that my own family's just as dysfunctional."

"You've done a great job on your own. You've made a really nice home for Joe."

She tipped back her head to watch him through narrowed eyes. "Yes, I have. You see why your return is so troublesome."

He brushed his thumb over her knuckles, gratified to see her lashes widen. "Maybe this time the ends *will* justify the means."

"I've stopped believing in happy-ever-afters."

"Did you ever believe in them?" His voice was husky.

She made a small sound in her throat when she swallowed. "For a short time."

"When?"

"You know when."

His fingertips grazed across the soft cloud of her hair. "Tell me anyway."

"When I was with you." She squeezed her eyes shut, then blinked them open, her lashes sparkling. "But I was young and foolish. Now I'm more cynical."

"That's only the hard candy shell. Inside you're still as soft and sweet as a marshmallow."

"Phooey. Marshmallows are sickening."

Luke angled closer.

She crooked her elbows, tilting away from him. "They rot your teeth."

He was inches away. Breathing her breath.

"They go stale once the bag's opened," she whispered.

His lips slid sidelong over hers, a tingling horizontal tease of a kiss. His mouth hovered near her ear. "Not always."

She'd arched her back to move another few millimeters away from him, but all that did was draw his hands up to her breasts. He cupped them gently. She let out a shivering breath that he caught in his mouth as he swooped in to kiss her again. It was their first real kiss—a thoroughly serious, utterly captivating kiss. Offered like a promise. Taken as a gift.

Suddenly Sophie was welcoming. They moved together in perfect harmony, as if the knowledge of how to please the other had been bred in their bones and needed no time for adjustment. She slanted her face, parting her lips. He made short strokes with his tongue, softly biting and sucking at her mouth until desire burned so hot in him that he had to pull away, knowing somewhere at the back of his swirling mind that they needed more privacy to continue.

"No," Sophie said, and reached up for him. Her hands slid through his hair, urging his mouth closer to hers. "Kiss me," she breathed, sweet as maple sugar, "again and again and again."

"What about Joe?"

She licked at Luke's mouth, making him groan and circle his palms over her breasts. "It's okay." A shudder moved through her, head to toe. "I have mother radar. He's still outside."

It seemed strange to talk about the boy while they were engaged in decidedly indecorous kitchen activities. But Luke was finding that Sophie was a natural as a mother—accepting her in the role was easy for him. It had even deepened his admiration.

And, apparently, attraction. Her tongue was warm velvet, dancing against his, and her breasts were round and soft, more generous than he remembered, the nipples diamond-tipped even through her clothing. "Nope, you haven't gone stale," he whispered against her neck. "You're too soft for that." He tweaked her nipple. "Except here."

"And here." Boldly she pressed her hips into his, rocking slightly against the evidence of his arousal.

"Umm." He swept his hand across her lower belly. "No, you're soft there too." And hot as a furnace.

She pulled air through her teeth. "I guess we'd better stop before this goes too far."

"Too late."

Her voice dropped an octave. "I know."

He held her in his arms. "I want us to be together again, Sophie. Not only like this..." He nudged up her chin and kissed her so deeply he nearly forgot he was speaking. "We should be...together...in other ways too. As a couple. I've missed so much. I've missed you, and our son—"

She thrust him away from her. He gave her six inches of space. "Is that what this is? You know that if you want Joey you have to take me in the bargain?"

"Don't be ridiculous. Can't you tell—"

"Yeah, I know—we've always had chemistry. That part wouldn't be a hardship for you." Her expression was torn between desire and resentment and fear. Although she presented a strong, take-charge, adult persona to the outside world, he suspected there were parts of her that were still dealing with feelings of inadequacy. She'd had such a rough childhood that there was no way to completely heal the damage. Overcome it, yes. She'd already proved that.

"Don't sell yourself short, darlin'."

She blinked. "I'm not. Joe, either."

The emotional elevator was dropping again. "Do I look like a buyer?"

"You said—" Sophie stopped and bit her lip, avoiding him with her eyes. "You said adoption would mess up the bloodlines."

"You're mistaking me for the rest of my family."

"Maybe you're looking to please them."

He made a sound of disbelief. "You and Joe are the only people it's vital for me to please. I'll do anything to be accepted as his father."

Sophie grimaced. "Don't say that. Don't—" She shook her head. "You can't come charging in, taking over, making wild promises that aren't—" She stared him in the eye. A bitter challenge. "Promises that won't last. You just can't."

Desperation raced inside him. He held her by the shoulders. She twisted her head away. "I can. I will. You'll see." Hell. He couldn't talk, let alone explain himself.

"You don't even know if he's your son!"

"He is. He has to be. He looks like me."

"Maybe. Maybe not."

"He's my son, Sophie. You might as well admit it, because I'm not going away." His palms slid down her bare arms. She made a small sound of protest, but let him hold her hands. "I'll do right by both of you. That's a promise you can count on."

Sophie sniffed. Her face was wretched—which put a cold shock into him. "You shouldn't make such promises until you know all the facts."

"Then tell me." *Who's the other guy?*

She refused. Turned her back and started washing dishes, scrubbing at plates with stiff, jerky motions as if they needed deep scouring.

Outside, the lawn mower roared to life and it occurred to Luke that Sophie was only protecting her son.

Eventually he'd prove himself to her and she'd understand that he wasn't a threat. But for now...

Luke let it be.

EVEN THOUGH Kiki Salinger was driving west, she didn't particularly want to return to the ranch. She just couldn't think of anywhere else to go after spending all day away. There was nowhere left to shop in Treetop—or the whole of Sweetwater County, for that matter. She'd seen it all, found it lacking. These people thought fancy yokes and pearl-button snaps were the height of fashion.

The car edged up to seventy miles per hour. Kiki's mind raced equally fast. She could call up a friend to go out for an early dinner, but then she'd have to talk. She didn't want to talk. She *couldn't* talk. One sympathetic gesture or probing question, and she'd open her mouth and not be able to stop. A torrent of self-pity would gush out.

She was on the edge of panic, barely hanging on. None of this was fair.

She'd been working as a teller at a Laramie bank when she'd caught Heath's eye. After he'd proposed, she'd been so sure that her life would become perfect. And it had been, for a while. Then they'd started having trouble conceiving. Naively, she'd asked Heath to be tested early on, but he'd refused. Finally, during one of her emotional meltdowns, he'd blurted out the truth about Sophie.

How she'd lured him into a one-night stand.

How, when she'd turned up pregnant, Heath had waited and watched. And counted. He was so sorry to tell Kiki this, but he was sure the baby was his.

All of Treetop thought Joe Ryan was Luke's son. Only Heath and Sophie knew the truth.

And Kiki. The secret was lodged like a pool of acid in the pit of her stomach, eating away at her as months, then years, passed without her becoming pregnant.

She pressed the gas pedal. *Seventy-five.*

After Heath had confessed, she'd made a point to become friendly with Sophie. It was smart to keep your enemies close. But in the years since, never a single word had passed Sophie's lips about how she'd once slept with Kiki's husband and had a thirteen-year-old son to show for it. Kiki had encouraged confidences by sharing her own, but by now there were times when even she forgot. She'd catch herself thinking of Sophie as a true friend, when they were only adversaries.

Kiki clenched her jaw. Pounded the steering wheel. She had to have a baby soon. If she didn't, Heath worried that Grandmother Lucas might give up on them and go ahead and accept Joe Ryan as her heir. Kiki didn't give a fig about who inherited the ranch—as long as she was taken care of—but Heath did. He was the eldest son, he said. He deserved it. All of it.

If Mary Lucas acknowledged Joe, then Heath also would. To keep his place. And Kiki could be shoved out in the cold.

Eighty.

Heath swore he wasn't interested in Sophie Ryan *that way,* but he certainly was eager to get the inside dope whenever Kiki had been visiting at the Ryans'. So far, Sophie had seemed satisfied to keep out of their way. She hadn't even asked for money. But now that Luke was back, thinking *he* had a son....

Heath said they had to be on guard. They had to make sure that Luke and Sophie didn't get too close.

The countryside was a blur. Kiki dashed at her wet eyes.

She wasn't sure that she agreed with her husband, but of course she couldn't tell him that. The way she saw it, if Luke married Sophie, then at least Kiki could be sure that Heath wouldn't just dump her and hitch up with Sophie so he could claim a convenient heir.

Dammit. Kiki made a fist and pressed the knuckles into her stomach. Why wasn't she pregnant? Dr. Cotter was wrong about Heath, so it had to be all *her* fault. And Heath was a perfectionist. How long would he keep an inadequate wife?

The sound of a siren cut into Kiki's intense worries. She glanced at the rearview mirror. *Not another speeding ticket!*

She eased up on the gas, silently berating herself for going so fast. She'd have to hide the ticket from Heath till she had a little extra cash to pay it. She couldn't put another one on her credit card so soon. He'd go ballistic.

The patrol car pulled up behind her. Kiki smoothed her hair. She checked the mirror to see if tears were glistening attractively in her eyes. If it was Deputy Hardin or that goofy Boone Barzinski who'd stopped her, she had a good shot at talking herself out of trouble. Sophie, despite their friendship, wasn't as susceptible to being charmed.

Except when it came to Heath, Kiki thought. Then she'd been charmed right out of her pants.

"DON'T TRY THIS at home," Luke said with a laugh.

Joe studied the diagram drawn in the dirt. Small stones had been placed here and there to represent various obstacles. Luke had traced the bike's route with a stick. "How about at the dirt-bike track?"

"Not there, either. Your mother would kill me."

"I know I could do it," the boy boasted. "Just maybe not so fast. At least the first time."

Luke winced. Sophie *would* kill him if she knew he'd merely introduced the idea. "Don't even think about it, Joe." He dragged his foot through the scratchings. Dumb move, boasting on his motorcycle stunts. But he'd been trying to get the boy to talk.

"Listen up, Joe. Stunts like that are dangerous at any speed. Remember, I planned the route, calculated the speeds and had every possible safety precaution in place. Even then, the stunt looks nothing like what you see up on the screen. The films been enhanced with F/X, cut and edited in split-second flashes. The finished stunt is superhuman. Impossible to duplicate."

Joe squinted, measuring the words, halfway back to resentful.

"End of lecture," Luke said easily.

The boy's face cleared. "Yeah, sure, but it's still killer cool."

"Yeah." They shared a grin.

"I could show you a few tricks," Luke said off-handedly. "Safe tricks. At the track, under the proper conditions."

Enthusiasm lit Joe's eyes. "That would be so—" He stopped, pulling back in. "Uh, I guess that would be okay."

"We'll have to get permission from your mother first."

"Jeez. She won't even let me ride without a helmet."

"Then she's a wise woman. You be sure to listen to her."

"Tom Cruise didn't wear a helmet in *MI-2*."

"Only because he had to show off his pretty face."

Joe guffawed.

"You don't need to do that. Even when your girl-friends are watching."

"I don't have a girlfriend."

"Then who was the girl who biked past the house six times this afternoon while we were working on the car?"

Joe turned bashful. He covered his face with a hand. "Just this dumb girl who lives down the street."

"Pretty cute."

"She's okay," Joe muttered, then added hastily, "But I don't like her, or anything."

"Too bad. She likes you."

"How can you tell?"

"She wasn't cruising *me*."

Joe shifted on the porch step, looking down at his hands dangling between his knees. "She coulda been. You're, like, this big deal."

Luke frowned.

"They're *all* talking about you. Cause you're a—a—*fugitive*."

There was a responsible, fatherly image for you. "That's not exactly how it is, Joe."

"My mom told me all about it this morning. She said Ed Warren was after you, man. He was comin' with the handcuffs. And you made a fast getaway on your motorcycle, just ahead of the law."

Great. Joe was showing some animation, but about the wrong thing. "Sophie said that?"

Joe blinked. "Well, sorta."

"What else did she tell you?"

"Just stuff." The boy shot off the step, thrusting his hands in his pockets while he scuffed up the dirt and pebbles, obliterating all traces of the diagram for Luke's *Maximum Velocity III* stunt.

"Like...?"

Joe's voice dropped, then rose to a question. "Like maybe you're my dad?"

Luke nodded. "Maybe."

Joe flushed.

"Would that be okay with you?"

"I dunno." Joe edged away, stepping backward through the freshly mown grass. "Maybe." He whipped around and ran off, slamming the corner of the house with an outstretched hand as he cut past it.

Maybe.

In one huge exhale, Luke let go of a days worth of tension.

Last night, he'd thought *maybe* was a terrible thing for Sophie to say.

But right now it was the most beautiful word he'd ever heard.

CHAPTER TEN

A TYPICAL SATURDAY NIGHT night at the Thunderhead, Sophie told herself as she eased inside the dark wood doors. No reason to be nervous.

The lights were dim and the air was thick with smoke and the sour scent of beer. The noise was an assault. To one side of the room, a local band played a second-hand version of contemporary country on a small platform stage. Dancers shuffled in the space created by jamming the tables so tightly together you couldn't pass through without sucking in your stomach and knocking off a few cowboy hats along the way.

On the other side, in the hook of the L-shaped space, was the bar, packed with milling customers. Bystanders loitered around the pool tables, jeering the players' skills. Over in the farthest corner were the flashing lights and virtual violence of the video games. Dark figures hunched in the glow of the animated screens, swaying in synch with their joysticks.

Sophie was a familiar face at the Thunderhead. Usually she was in uniform, called in to ferry home a booze hound or cool off hotheaded customers on the verge of fisticuffs. Occasionally she made an arrest for vandalism or public disturbance. More often lately, since Theresa had taken charge and wanted every broken ashtray accounted for. Punch was the lenient type, especially as the culprits were often Mustangs. Or relatives of Mustangs. Or friends of Mustangs. Sometimes, or so it seemed to Sophie, the brotherhood extended to include half the population of Treetop.

She went right ahead and did her job, either way. The lawbreakers would just have to deal with it.

Kiki Salinger was waving from the table she'd secured on the edge of the dance floor. A case in point. Even though Kiki hadn't been happy about the citation Sophie had written her a week ago, she hadn't held a grudge. In fact, she'd been friendlier than ever, insisting that Sophie join the girls' night out she was putting together for a few of her friends.

"Where's the uniform, Deputy?" one of the local jokers called as she squirmed her way toward the table. He belly-laughed. "Look, fellas. Sophie's got legs! And they shure are puuurdy!"

Another man caught her arm. "You gonna dance with me, Deputy?" He smooched at her. "If I said you had a beautiful body would you hold it against me?"

"Get yourself a new line, Cliff. Plagiarism is an ugly thing." She pulled his felt cowboy hat down over his face and continued on, leaving the men sniggering into their beer mugs.

"Why, Sophie. Look at you!" Kiki hopped up for a hug. "I've never seen you so dressed up."

"I wear dresses for weddings and funerals and church," Sophie pointed out. Maybe she'd gone to a little extra trouble with the makeup—if you defined that as wearing *any* at all—but her dress wasn't so very unusual. A flirty floral thing she'd pulled from the back of the closet and topped with a short angora sweater. Somewhat on the sheer side, but the length was modest.

"The local guys have no social graces," said Gen Richards, a single woman of a certain age who worked at the bank and had developed a habit of pinched concentration and tight, quick movements. "They need to learn how to treat a lady."

"That's just it," Sophie said, wedging a chair out from the table. She swiveled her hips sideways and sat. Exhale. "I'm usually in uniform, so they don't think of me as a woman."

"I wear pants or jeans around the ranch all the time, but it doesn't confuse Raleigh." Molly Tate chuckled. Dark-haired and comfortably rounded, she owned and operated the Triple Eight dude ranch with her husband, a former Secret Service agent. A year and a half ago, they'd uncovered a counterfeiting operation run by a bunch of bumbling crooks. Sophie had been in on the arrest—the most excitement Treetop had seen in eons.

"You're newlyweds," Gen said.

"Mmm, five months and counting." Molly raised her voice to be heard over the chaos. "Does that still qualify?"

Sophie nodded. Molly had been the prettiest spring bride she'd ever seen, all rosy cheeks, shy eyes and antique Chantilly lace. It had given Sophie a pang to realize that she'd never be that kind of bride herself, even if she were to marry. She'd grown too cynical about love.

"What about you and Heath?" Gen said to Kiki, pinch-faced. "Four years, no kids to hold you down. Are you still living it up like newlyweds?"

Kiki smiled inscrutably, her eyes narrowing beneath the smooth fringe of her bangs. "Heath is a prince among men. He's fab-u-lous in the bedroom." Her gaze cut to Sophie. "And you? What do you think?"

Sophie stuttered in shock. "Wha-what—?"

Kiki watched Sophie for a moment before giving a

deliberate blink. She leaned closer. "Is Luke as good as you remember?"

Heat shot to Sophie's face. "Kiki, I already *told* you—"

"What'll it be, girls?" Ellen Molitor paused at the table with her order pad, looking harried.

Sophie stood, glad for the interruption. "You go take care of another table, Ellie. I'll get our drinks at the bar."

Ellen threw her a grateful look as she backed off into the crowd. "Thanks, Soph. I'm running my feet off tonight."

Sophie caught up. "Any sign of Luke?" she asked, putting her mouth to the waitress's ear so she didn't have to shout as loud.

"You need him for anything in particular?"

"Just keeping an eye out, the way the judge said."

"Yeah, sure." Grinning as she eyed Sophie's dress, Ellen shoved a pencil through her damp hair, itching her perspiring scalp. "He's dropped by a few times, but I haven't seen him yet tonight. A coupla Mustangs are here, though, hassling the pool players." Ellen plunged into the crush, yelling over her shoulder, "I'll give you a holler if Luke shows up."

Sophie made her way to the bar to relay the drink orders. When she stood on her toes and leaned over the bar to grab a handful of napkins and paper coasters, a pair of strong male hands wrapped themselves around her hips and snugged her rear end into intimate alignment with a hard groin.

Sophie gasped. A spurt of shame flashed through her, followed by anger that Luke would be so bold with her in public. She wrenched herself away, realizing almost instantly that it wasn't Luke.

"Oh, sweet thing, you do me right," her accoster crooned.

Sophie blanched, recognizing the voice even before she saw the grinning face. *Damon "Demon" Bradshaw.*

She reacted on instinct, flinging the napkins and coasters in his face to distract him. She kicked out the back of his knee, catching his arm simultaneously and wrenching it behind his back as she spun him around.

The crowd fell back. *Wham.* She slammed Demon's face into the pool table, sending colored balls spinning off in all directions. One dropped into a pocket with a thud.

Demon struggled. Luckily he wasn't a large man, more the wiry type, and Sophie was able to hold him down and press his twisted arm to the breaking point. She bent over his prone figure. "Never touch me."

Demon was breathing heavily through the pain. But he still managed to waggle his hips against hers. "Yeah, baby, that feels so good." He'd always fancied himself a smooth talker.

Sophie jerked on his arm till he let out a keening howl of pain. "Don't mistake me, Demon." She was nearly spitting in her fury. "I may not be in uniform, but I can still arrest you for assaulting an officer." Damn, she wished she had her handcuffs.

Demon was the type who hated to concede, but he was in no position to argue. "It was just a friendly squeeze," he panted. "For—for one of our old ladies."

She sank her nails into his wrist, exerting enough pressure to grind his bones. "What did you say?"

He let out a whistling grunt. "S-sorry."

"I was *never* your old lady," she seethed. "And if you ever touch me again I'll see you in jail for good. That's a promise."

To a smattering of applause, she released him, every sense alert to his response as she stepped back. But Demon only sagged against the pool table with a groan before gathering himself enough to push up off the green felt. He cradled his arm against his abdomen, looking at Sophie through slitted eyes.

She stared him down, her fists clenched, her heartbeat going like mad.

Demon's mouth twisted with a silent oath.

"Mustangs like their women flat on their backs anyhow," he said, turning away. The boast was hollow, but a few of the guys laughed in compliance, shooting wary glances at Sophie as they shuffled around the table, resetting the game.

She backed up to the bar, bumping into another patron.

"I'd have given you a hand, but it looked unnecessary, seeing as you already had Demon's."

Sophie's head whipped around. *Luke.*

"I didn't see you."

"Just arrived," he said. He glanced at Demon, his eyes cold steel. "Trouble?"

"No more than usual."

Demon had spotted Luke. He gave a slight nod of his whiskered chin, his grease-rimmed fingers curling and uncurling around a pool stick. Luke didn't respond— his expression was as frozen as a mountain peak.

Sophie looked from one to the other, trying to gauge the situation as hackles of apprehension rose at the back of her neck. Were they still comrades of sorts, in the way of gang members? And did Luke not want her to know?

One of the other men hailed Luke. Snake Carson,

another old Mustang. "C'mon over and play a game for old times' sake, Mav."

Luke put him off with a wave.

"Old home week," Sophie said, sliding drink glasses together with a clink as the bartender set them up. Whether it was her cop instincts or a more personal involvement, her every sense was aroused—and she didn't like it. "Are you planning to pick up with the Mustangs where you left off, *Mav?*"

Luke took Gen's piña colada from Sophie, letting his fingertips brush over her knuckles. "A ragtag gang of thirtysomethings with nothing better to do than relive their glory days? Now that would be a sorry sight." His gaze drifted to the pool tables.

"Then keep away," she urged. "Judge Entwhistle would call them an unsavory element."

Luke's eyes shifted to her face. She felt sweaty and disheveled, not what she'd intended when she'd dressed up for him. "You're here in a professional capacity?"

"Bottled beer," said the bartender. "And your diet cola, Sophie."

"On the wagon?" Luke asked her.

"I haven't drunk alcohol since—" She stopped herself abruptly, then filled the awkward pause by paying the bartender and gathering up the drinks and napkins. "I'm here with a couple girlfriends," she told Luke, nodding in the opposite direction. "We're over there, by the dance floor."

Luke picked up Molly's beer with his other hand. "I'll stop and say hello."

"Suit yourself."

Sophie's apprehension had eased, but the shivery tingles continued playing across the surface of her skin as they walked to the table. "Drinks are served," she said, swallowing hard when her voice came out girlishly high-pitched. You'd think a woman who could throw one hundred sixty pounds of Mustang across a pool table could control her reactions better than this. And why was it that the tattoo on her behind seemed to burn as hot as if it were newly inscribed into her flesh?

Guilt, she answered.

No, said another part of her. *Sexual awareness.* Their interlude in the kitchen had cranked up her body temperature. She was no longer simmering. This was full boil.

"Luke!" Kiki twisted around in her chair, tilting her head back to stare up at her brother-in-law. "What are you doing here? Weren't you and Heath going over the ranch books with Gilley?"

He shrugged. "That's no way to spend a Saturday night."

She pouted. "But Heath promised me he'd be kept busy while I was having my girls' night out."

"One evening on his own won't kill the guy," Gen said distractedly. She was eyeing Luke, who looked very good in jeans, a tooled leather belt with a silver buckle and a plain long-sleeved T-shirt that seemed tailored to fit every contour of his honed physique. There was such an aura of virility about him that Sophie could sense female hormones stirring in all corners of the vast room. Every woman in the vicinity was perking up, taking lingering glances, laughing and talking with a bit more animation.

Sophie introduced the group, keeping it brief, first names only, since it was a strain to hear over so much noise. Yep, that was why. She wasn't jealous that other women found Luke as attractive as she did. She certainly did not have visions of keeping him only to herself. Entertaining a fantasy about chaining him to her bed would be ridiculous.

Sophie smiled to herself. Damn, now she *really* wished she had her handcuffs.

Luke exchanged a few pleasantries with Gen and Molly, stroked a finger under Sophie's chin in parting, and headed back toward the pool tables.

"Woohooo," Gen whistled. "So that's Luke Salinger."

"I can see why everyone's been talking about him," Molly said, tilting her head as she watched him walk away. Her appreciative smile carved dimples in her cheeks. "Or should I say, him and Sophie."

Sophie sat tall, craning her neck, trying to keep Luke in her sights. "Folks ought to be worrying about expanding their horizons if I'm a fascinating subject in their lives." She didn't have to look to know the women were exchanging grins. "There's nothing happening between me and Luke." *That you need to know.*

"Why not?" Molly said. "If I wasn't married..."

"Luke and I were teenage sweethearts," Sophie explained, "but that was fourteen years ago. Nobody carries a torch for fourteen years, except in movies or books."

She sank lower in her chair. Luke was playing pool with Snake, but Demon was hovering nearby. Seeing the Mustangs together brought back the uneasy feeling, full force. Which meant that she still didn't trust Luke. Without trust, how could she be so attracted to him? Was it only a matter of chemistry? Was she that shallow?

"I like to think I'd wait fourteen years for Raleigh." Molly put her chin in her hand. "Although, to be honest, maintaining a long-distance relationship for even a matter of months was excruciating."

"You see?" Sophie murmured.

"But then again, who says you had to have lived in suspended animation all that time? You didn't, did you?"

Sophie shook her head. "I've done things with my life. I haven't been hankering for him to return. So I wish everyone would stop assuming I'm going to immediately jump into his arms just because he's back for a visit."

"It's not a visit," Kiki said. She'd been brooding. "He's planning to stay and run the ranch."

Sophie's heart leaped. "I didn't know that."

"He didn't tell you?" Kiki's brows arched. "You've been together often enough the past week."

"Oh, really?" said Gen, her smile a bit snide.

Sophie scowled. "It's just…you know." Luke had been by the house several times, it was true. But she couldn't tell them it was to see Joe, not her. The two of them had gone out to the motocross track, then fishing, which became dinner. A family dinner, was how she thought of it, even though her father refused to join them. Considering the complications, it wasn't much easier for her to focus on Luke's interest in Joe than on his interest in her. But it certainly was less vexing to her libido.

Gen and Kiki looked ready to pounce on the rumors and bandy them about, but Molly took pity on Sophie and changed the subject. "What happened over there between you and the Bradshaw guy? He's a bad character."

"Demon has a problem with showing me the proper respect."

"I didn't know you're so strong, Sophie," Gen said. "It was quite a takedown."

Molly chuckled. "That'll teach him."

"He's not a bad-looking guy," Gen mused. "If he was cleaned up some."

Kiki screwed up her face. "But what about the vulgar, low-class tattoos? Ick. Those don't wash off."

Sophie shifted, reminded again of her own revealing tattoo and her similarly low-class roots. Kiki had a knack for making her feel that way, even though she'd figured out long ago that Heath's wife had her own hang-ups about money and status. Kiki wasn't putting Sophie down as much as she was reassuring herself about her position. Unfortunately, the effect was the same.

Sophie purposefully switched her thoughts to Demon, who was shaggy and unkempt, but might have a certain hard-bitten renegade appeal if you considered him objectively, an option she found difficult to stomach. Girls *had* fallen all over him in their younger days, before his bad habits and attitude had become too obvious to overlook. At least as far as Sophie was concerned. There was no accounting for taste.

A guy with a bottlebrush moustache came over and asked if any of the women wanted to dance. Kiki and Molly flashed their wedding rings, leaving Sophie to gladly concede to Gen. The remaining three chuckled over the singer's bad impression of Tim McGraw, until Molly excused herself to go to the ladies' room. Kiki soon followed.

Sophie was left to stare into her soft drink. Most of the ice had melted. Too warm. She took off her sweater, rubbed a hand across her perspiring upper chest. The back of her neck was damp, so she lifted her hair off it with both hands, hoping that a cool night breeze would drift past the mass of humanity between her and the open doors.

A sudden puff of air on her nape made her flinch. "Stop it, Luke," she said, glancing back at him. Her heart lifted. "You're being childish." She let the mass of her hair drop to cover the gooseflesh he'd aroused.

"Come outside with me," he said into her ear, tracing a pinkie over her nape. "It's an Indian summer night. Warm and mellow. There's magic in the air."

"No."

He slid into a chair. "Why not?"

She caught her lip between her teeth. "It wouldn't look right."

"All this time, and you're still worrying about how things look? I thought you were more independent than that."

"With a family like yours, it's easy to be reckless. *I* have to be diligent about my behavior."

"Of course. I forgot." He nodded. "Because of your job."

"That, and…" Sophie tore a corner off her napkin. Luke leaned closer to hear her. "My situation as a single mother. I take one wrong step and the gossips will gear up, dragging every old skeleton bone out of my closet." *As if they hadn't already,* she silently mocked. Why worry about what people would say when they would say it no matter what? For some people, nearly a decade and a half of quiet, decent living obviously hadn't been enough to overcome her past.

The song ended, lowering the decibel level considerably. Sophie took a breath of the hot, moist air, feeling nearly claustrophobic. The singer announced the band was on break. Immediately someone pumped quarters into the jukebox.

Before the second wave of throbbing sound broke, Sophie brought her mouth near Luke's ear. "I'll meet you outside in five minutes."

MOLLY HAD GONE back to the table, but Kiki made an excuse to linger behind, hovering outside the rest room doors. Amid the traffic, she'd overheard an interesting tidbit—Luke's name. Nearby was a niche lined with coat hooks, and she slipped into it, pretending that she meant to hang her smart Gucci jacket among the blue-light specials. As if.

Men's voices. "Now Maverick's home, he's gonna—"

The shrieking laughter of a group of girls heading into the ladies' room drowned out the rest of the comment. Kiki turned deeper into the coatroom, gnashing her teeth in frustration. Heath would be *very* pleased if she could learn details about Luke's activities, particularly if they were the illegal sort.

"He was hanging out at your place a couple days ago, wasn't he, looking over the guns?" a different man said. She thought he might be one of the Mustangs, but she couldn't say which one. She didn't pay attention to that type of lowlife.

The other guy jeered. "You mean Deputy Sophie let him wiggle outta those handcuffs she's got him wearing?"

A menacing chuckle. "Shit, I'd like to get that bitch in a pair of cuffs."

Demon Bradshaw, Kiki identified with a shudder. She hated the way his blatant stare crawled over her body whenever he came within range.

"I got no worries," Demon continued after another round of lewd comments. "Luke's the same as always. I know how to get him to—"

A group of women passed. The Mustangs made crude remarks, jostling them about. "Back off, you creeps!" one of the women said, slamming past the rest room door.

The men laughed. "Let's wait for her to come out," one of them said, "and show her who's boss." They moved closer to the coatroom niche.

Kiki flattened herself against the wall, hoping the outerwear would shield her position. For a few moments she was too frightened to concentrate on the conversation, but when she tuned back in they were talking about Luke again.

"Next time, Salinger better leave that fancy rifle at home," Demon was saying. "I got me an old faithful Remington that'll do the job just fine."

Kiki gripped the front of her jacket so tightly one of the buttons popped off and rolled across the wooden floor. She cringed against the wall, but the men had their backs turned and didn't notice. They were comparing gauges and scopes.

One of them scoffed. "Rifles are no good, what with ballistics and all. What you want to use is—" The rest of the sentence was lost in the noise.

The turn in the conversation had stunned Kiki. Luke had been back for ten or so days and already he was involved in a potential crime. Maybe another break-in? She hadn't expected to learn *that*. All she really wanted to know was how much Sophie had told him about Joey and what Luke's intentions were. Heath knew his brother had been going over to Sophie's place all week, and he was getting antsy, particularly since Luke had mentioned inviting Sophie and her son to the family reunion barbecue planned for next weekend.

"Hey-ah, look," one of the Mustangs said. "Sharleen's dancing in a T-shirt. And I swear she's not wearing any bra."

The trio forgot all else. "Hell, yeah," Demon hollered. "Jiggle 'em, sweetheart!"

Kiki panted in relief as the men moved away. She waited another minute, then slithered out of the niche and lost herself in the crowd surrounding the dance floor. Part of her was scared about what she'd overheard, but in another section of her brain she was already working over how she could use the knowledge to her advantage.

And wondering how much she should tell Heath.

FROM OUTSIDE, the Thunderhead seemed to hunker low in the gravel, as solid and squat as a fat cat with a full belly. The neon roadhouse sign glowed amber and red at the front of the dark wooden building. Music pulsed in the warm night air, the refracted light from a row of small glass-block windows shifting and wavering, extending only a few feet into the darkness of the parking lot.

Luke's boots crunched on pebbles. "Sophie?" he said softly. There were others around, loitering here and there, subdued voices and laughter lifting on the breeze. Occasionally a deep laugh would ring out or a car door slam, as loud as a thunderclap.

"Sophie?"

"I'm here," she said. He followed her voice.

She was at the edge of the back corner of the lot, nearly standing in the ragged patch of weeds that separated it from a dark crop of pine trees. In the opposite direction was the highway, a silvery ribbon reflecting the neon lights of the Thunderhead.

Luke's breath caught. Sophie's light-brown hair tumbled across her shoulders, framing her face like a dimmed halo. The uneven hem of her dress fluttered against her legs, sheer enough to reveal the shapely silhouette of her thighs. She stood quite still, yet the gentle bow of her body and the shifting shadows of her skirt and loose hair made her look as if she were moving—like the figure on the prow of a ship, gliding through the warm, sweet air.

"What are you doing back here?" His chest constricted. "Don't want to be seen with me, hmm?"

She made a sound of amusement. "As if the entire town doesn't already know how often you've been by my house."

"But that was during daylight hours." He touched her elbow, just her elbow, and a familiar awareness leaped between them. "This is different."

Her voice was a sable-soft murmur, brushing against his senses. "Trouble's trouble, no matter the time of day."

"And I'm trouble?"

"Yes, you are."

"Are you sure of that?" He breathed in the tropical scent of her hair. "Maybe I'm the solution, not the problem."

"Don't say that." But she leaned slightly toward him, her head down. He took a step closer and put his arms around her, listening for her sigh of surrender, of welcome, of faith.

Instead her lips smacked as she tilted her face up. Her eyes were wide and dark. "My life isn't wrong. I don't need a solution, Luke."

No, it was *his* life that had gone wrong, from the moment he'd decided to leave town without Sophie.

He stroked her upper arms. "Then what do you need?"

"From you?" She closed her eyes for a brief moment, taking in an audible breath. "Nothing."

"Liar."

"You should know better by now. Haven't I told you the truth, even though it hurt us both?"

"Yeah," he conceded. "So let me put this another way." He held his lips near hers—a whisper of a touch that seemed more intimate than a kiss. "Hey, brown-eyed girl…" Their breath mingled; their heartbeats matched. His voice sighed on the wind. *"What do you need?"*

Sophie's answer was unnecessary. Her need was there in the eagerness of her parting lips, in the stroke of her tongue as the kiss deepened into passion, the strength of her arms as she wound them around his body, the sexy moan, the womanly shift of her breasts, the animal nip of her teeth on his lip—and, finally, the frantic gulp of air she took when headlights suddenly swept across their corner of the lot and she tore herself away, the back of her hand pressed to her mouth.

"Oh, God," she said, blinking blindly into the dense black that returned as the lights switched off.

The car had parked not far away. A group of young people barreled out of it, slamming doors and yelling back and forth, giving no notice to the couple who'd been making out at the edge of the grass.

Seconds later, the doors to the Thunderhead were thrown open, letting out a blast of noise and the pungent miasma of smoke, beer and fried food. People came and went, exchanging greetings or farewells, the gravel grinding beneath their footsteps.

Luke drew Sophie toward him again. "Let's get out of here."

She nodded easily enough, taking his hand as they hurried past the rows of vehicles. A couple of motorcycles were parked nearby and she slowed, squinting at them in the dark, but he tugged her past them, saying, "I've got the Blazer. Over here."

Raucous laughter erupted close by. Luke and Sophie quickly ducked into the black shadow thrown by the bulky vehicle. He put his arm around her.

"Should we drive up to the lake and check it out?" a man asked.

"Naw. Not tonight." Demon Bradshaw walked by with his buddies, doing a clenched-fist, hip-thrusting motion. "I'm gonna go wake up the old lady and give her the boom-she-bang-she-boom." He cackled.

Snake Carson disagreed with those priorities. "We should go tonight. 'Cause at least we know for sure that Deputy Sophie's occupied."

Demon's ugly laugh rang out even louder. "Yeah, Maverick's always good for *that*."

Sophie didn't look at Luke, but her shoulders had gone hard as stone beneath the drape of his arm. He touched his palm to her cheek, silently soothing her. She didn't react, keeping preternaturally still as Demon and the unidentified man mounted their bikes and stepped down hard on the ignition pedals. Snake moved off toward a rusty red Trans Am with flames painted along the side.

"Lets follow them," Sophie said, as soon as her voice was covered by the sound of their engines. Once all three had taken off, she pulled open the door to the

Blazer and climbed behind the wheel, tucking her dress between her thighs. "Give me the keys."

"You're not driving." Luke nudged her over.

Her forehead creased with the stubborn Buzzsaw scowl, but there wasn't time to argue. She climbed over the console to the passenger side, flashing flimsily covered hindquarters.

Luke tried not to notice. "Why do you want to follow them? Demon's going home."

She gripped the dash, watching as the bikes turned onto the highway. Snake's car went toward town, where he lived with his wife and daughter. "Follow him anyway. Just in case."

"Demon?"

She threw Luke an indecipherable glance. Her face had closed down into cool professional detachment. "He's the leader, isn't he?" Special emphasis on the *isn't he.*

"Who else?" Luke followed her direction at the highway turn-off.

She faced straight ahead, looking for motorcycle taillights. "Used to be you."

"And you're wondering if I'm getting roped in again?"

"That's my job."

He bit down on his molars. "Then ask me straight out, Deputy."

She didn't hesitate. "Are you involved in any way with Demon Bradshaw's illegal activities?"

"No."

"I see them," Sophie said. "Slow down a little. They might recognize your truck."

"They're turning in at Demon's place," Luke said as the taillights blinked.

"Keep going. Drive by at a regular speed." She ducked low as they passed Demon's bike shop. The motorcycles had stopped in back, by the cabin, but only Demon was dismounting. "Do you know the other guy?"

"Nope. Never seen him in my life."

"I have, several times. His name's Larry Dryzewiecz. They call him Drizz. He appears in town every month or so. I'm thinking the bike's a loaner from Demon, because Drizz usually drives a pickup truck."

"And you've run the plates. Arrest record?" Luke said. The wheels of the Blazer hummed on the highway.

"Petty crimes, mostly. One possession of illegal substances." Sophie looked toward the front again. "Let's double back, find a spot with some cover and pull over. I want to see if Demon's really in for the night."

"What about Drizz?" Luke asked, making an illegal U-turn since the road was empty.

"He usually stays at the Hideaway rental cabins. You know the ones. I'll check up on him on my way home."

"What's up? Drugs? Guns? Stolen goods?"

"Maybe." Sophie opened her window. "This is good, right here. If you can drive over the rise and park behind the trees, we'll be hidden but still have a clear view of the highway. And we're close enough to hear the bike, if Demon makes a move in another direction."

The Blazer's undercarriage got bumped a little, negotiating the uneven terrain, but they were soon situated in an advantageous position. *You can say that again,* Luke thought, aware of the irony of parking with Sophie—but not *parking* with Sophie—as the silence of the countryside settled upon them. A vehicle passed, traveling slowly, but it wasn't a motorcycle so he didn't pay much attention. The tension in the truck's cab grew more dense with every passing second. Neither one of them spoke.

Sophie played with the hem of her sheer flowery dress, inadvertently giving him flirty glimpses of her crossed legs, silky smooth in panty hose. He couldn't remember ever seeing her wear panty hose before. Nor a dress, come to think of it. Jeans and shorts and swimsuits had made up her wardrobe when she was seventeen.

He thought of her previously coltish legs, opening shyly to him as they lay together in the fresh green grass. She had more of a shape now. When she parted her thighs for him this time, it would be with the sensual knowledge of a grown woman. She would know exactly how to wrap them around his hips, how to rock with him, when to speed up, when to tighten around him in a wet velvet glove of heat...

"Are you sick?"

Luke blinked, focusing on Sophie's curious face. "Was I making noises?"

"Yeah. You were moaning, under your breath."

He shifted behind the wheel. "Oh. Well, uh, I was just wondering..."

"What?" she prodded.

"How long does it take to boom-she-bang-she-boom?"

Sophie snorted laughter. "I don't know." She tilted her head in the direction of Demon's cabin. "You'd have to ask Ricky Martin, back there."

Luke laughed, but it wasn't exactly a subject that would ease the sexual tension. Especially when Sophie was twisting around, folding her legs up beside her on the plush seat. She rested her cheek against the open window. There must be wetlands nearby—the bullfrogs were chorusing like crazy in basso profundo, deep counterpoint to the crickets' soprano chirps.

"I have another question," he ventured.

"Yes?"

"Back there, when I said no, I wasn't involved..."

Sophie's lashes flicked. She looked at him from the corners of her eyes, her cheeks tinted pale rose.

"Did you believe me?"

CHAPTER ELEVEN

"I CAN'T— THAT'S—" Sophie's tongue stumbled over the words. She pushed at the door latch, falling out into the dry stalks of goldenrod that filled the clearing. Deep breath. "Luke," she said, turning to peer into the vehicle, where he sat behind the wheel, his head pulled down and forward to keep her in sight.

She gulped more oxygen. His eyes. They were burned into her soul, as permanent as the tattoo on her derriere. "You—you know it's not black-and-white," she told him, feeling stupid and inadequate. The door thunked as she carefully pushed it shut.

She walked away from the truck, her head thrown back in silent appeal to the heavens. *Help me do what's right for all of us.* The stars glittered back at her, hard and bright and silent.

The deep putter of a motorcycle broke the countryside's hush. A light flashed on inside the vehicle as Luke opened his door. "Close it, quick," she said, rushing over.

"Wait. I saw some binoculars in the back seat." He fished them out. She pressed the door shut as quietly as possible.

They moved closer to observe the silent stretch of highway, hunching behind the natural rise in the land as the motorcycle's headlight grew brighter. Luke gave Sophie the binoculars. "It's only Dryzewiecz," she said, as the motorcyclist passed in a blur. "Heading to the cabins."

"You're sure? He was wearing a helmet."

"No doubt. He's got that ponytail and scraggly blond beard." She fingered her chin in demonstration, then trained the glasses in the direction of Demon's homeplace. A small, faint light shone through the trees. Porch light, maybe.

"How long are we going to wait here?" Luke asked after a few minutes, lowering himself to his knees.

She tried for a light laugh. "You've got something better to do?"

"Nope. In fact, I can't think of anywhere I'd rather be than tumbling around in the long grass with my brown-eyed girl."

"I don't tumble," she said, shooting him a pretend-haughty look over her shoulder.

"You're a regular saint, I hear."

Her stomach muscles tightened. She dangled the binoculars on their twisted cord. "Ironic, isn't it?"

A crackling sound in the bushes nearby gave her a moment's pause, but suddenly Luke caught her around the waist and pulled her down in a tangle of limbs. He held her above him for a moment, grinning at her surprised laugh, and then he was rolling her over onto her back, crushing the grass flat. Her dress was up around her thighs but all she could concentrate on was Luke's face—stripped to bare emotion. She lost the binoculars. She lost her cool, professional composure. She lost her resolve to be noble.

Such longing, she thought, studying his face. Luke's beliefs and desires had always been that way. Burning as bright and hard as the stars. She'd felt cherished when she was one of them. Bereft when she was not.

So dangerous, that was. Hinging her happiness on his shifting convictions.

"Ironic how?" he said, plucking broken bits of goldenrod out of her hair.

"You know." She arched her back against the weight of him. Kept her gaze direct. "Considering the circumstances of Joey's conception."

A wince. "Let's make a deal." He smoothed his hand along the outside of her cheek, a touch so loving it reached deeper than he knew. "I'll forgive you for that bad decision if you forgive me for mine."

Her heart sang with hope. "And yours was?"

"Not believing in you. Leaving you."

She'd forgiven him a long time ago. But she said, "Deal," her voice dry in her sandy throat.

"And maybe, one day…" He nuzzled beneath her chin. "One day soon, you'll believe in me again."

"I want to."

"Mm-hmmm," he purred, stroking her face with his tongue, making tracings of shivery sensation. "What else do you want?"

"I want…" She couldn't stop herself, the words slipped right out. "I want your hand on my breast."

Frowning with concentration, he parted the front of her sweater. Smoothed wrinkles out of her chiffon dress so it was drawn taut over the swell of one breast. Then, with another little humming noise, he scooped his hand around her breast, finding her nipple through the thin fabric and teasing it until it was drawn into a tight, aching bud and she was squirming restlessly beneath him, her body riding waves of pleasure.

"What else?" he said.

"Your tongue in my mouth." She wanted his kiss more than she wanted her next breath.

"Then open your lips."

Her eyes narrowed. After an instant of hesitation, she parted her lips—just a sliver. Her tongue flicked out, then curled defensively against her teeth. It was strange, but she felt vulnerable following his direction, as if...

As if a kiss required an enormous amount of trust.

It can, when you're not sure.

Luke's tongue dipped into her mouth, catching her sigh as her lips opened wide. She *felt* sure. Or as sure as she could be when her pulse was as erratic as an amateur drummer and her head was lost in the swirl and spin of uncontrolled desire.

He kissed her for a long time—sweet, luxurious kisses that pattered like fat raindrops against her lips and face, her throat and breasts, dripping and spreading and washing her in warm, wet pleasure. They moved together in the dry grasses, golden dust powdering their clothes and skin. It was wonderful, and heedless. As instinctive and spontaneous as when they were young.

"Tell me what you want," Luke whispered. "Tell me all of it."

"I want you inside me, all the way inside me," she said, slipping her hands beneath his shirt, running them over the hair-roughened layers of hard muscle. His skin twitched at her touch. She remembered that. How his skin reacted as a separate living thing to her every stroke and kiss and caress.

"That's what I want too."

She kissed him.

"But not here by the side of the road like crazy teenagers."

"What road?" she said dreamily, licking her bee-stung lips.

"Don't look at me that way." He got to his feet with

a guttural moan, bent at the waist like an old man with a crick in his back. She smiled. The crick wasn't in his back.

He extended a hand. She took it, and he pulled her up, winding their arms around behind her back so she was brought firmly up against his chest. She put her chin on his shoulder. "Just like Fred Astaire and Ginger Rogers."

"I knew I'd persuade you to dance with me."

They swayed. "If you want to call it dancing…"

"Vertical or horizontal," he murmured, stepping them toward the Blazer, "doesn't matter to me."

She closed her eyes, giving herself up to pleasure even as she wondered if she was making a mistake, or if she dared to go for it anyway. "Um, FYI. Joey is sleeping over at a friend's."

Luke laughed. He dropped the tailgate of the Blazer, hoisted her up onto it, and started kissing her again, all over her face. "Why didn't you say so sooner?"

She nipped at his bottom lip, then soothed it with a broad swipe of her tongue. "Because I'm a saint."

His hands skated over her legs to bracket the back of her knees. He lifted them, parted them. Stepped between them. Her heels caught on the edge of the tailgate as she scooted in closer, driven by dark, primal urges. In some ways—*this way,* she thought, brushing against his blatant arousal—it was as if no time had passed at all. He was still the one man in the world who ignited her. Every part of her.

"Starlight becomes you," he murmured, gentling his kisses.

She was glowing, but it wasn't a reaction to heavenly bodies. Her desires were strictly of the earthy variety. Tilting back on her arms, she wrapped her legs around

his hips and drew him toward her, laughing at his be-
mused expression. She didn't want gentle.

"Roadside sex becomes *you*." Oh, yes, she dared!

His lower body was hard against her now. A sweet,
aching pressure. She closed her eyes, catching her lip
between her teeth with a languid "Mmmm." She rolled
her shoulders, wanting him to see her breasts, put his
hands on them.

And *he* was looking at her face. "Sophie Ryan,
you've changed."

She flexed against him, belly to belly. "Figured that
out, have you?"

"I don't know what to make of it."

Something in his tone chilled her. "You're wondering how many men I've been with." Her legs dropped,
dangling off the tailgate. "I could relate my entire sexual history to you. If it matters."

"That's not what I—"

"You say you've forgiven me, but you can't get it
out of your mind." She wasn't accusatory, merely accepting. Sad. What had she been thinking? Or *not* thinking?

She wasn't seventeen. Time *had* passed. A lifetime
of it. She knew the consequences. They'd be even
greater this time around.

"Sophie, sweetheart." Luke held her face in his
hands. "You're wrong. I was only taken aback for a
moment. It's not the other men, not really. It's not how
you kiss or the way you know exactly how to turn me
on—you've always known that, even when you were
less…adept."

He smiled, but his was sad, too. "It's realizing that
I've wasted so much time. Years of it. Years when I
could have been with you—intimately, yeah, but espe-

cially in other ways." His hands tightened on her cheeks, smooshing them a little, making her lips pucker. "It hurts that you're a stranger to me. But so familiar, which hurts even more. How do we make up for that? Is making love all it takes?"

She peeled his hands off her face. Squeezed them. "I don't know, Luke. I'm a lot smarter than I was at seventeen, but I still don't have all the answers. Most days, it seems like I make up my life as I go along. And us...this..." She blinked up at him, clasping his hands between her breasts. "This seems like a chance at happiness. Can't we just...hope for the best?" She knew that was wrong, even before she said it. With a son to think about, a son who was already mixed up enough as it was, she had to *know* she was making the right choice—for all of them.

Luke said, "You deserve a lot better than that."

"What about you?"

He shook his head. "You and Joe are all that matters. I don't think that—" He grimaced and pulled away from her to sit hunched over on the tailgate, his arms propped on his knees, elbows locked.

She waited, swollen with suspense, dread, desire.

The night had turned his tousled hair jet black. She wanted to brush the chaff off his shoulders, but felt she shouldn't touch him. He was inhaling, exhaling. Struggling.

Finally he spoke. "Despite your willingness tonight, I don't think you're ready to give me your heart, Sophie. And that's what I want, even more than your body." His eyes had a startling silvery sheen when he looked straight at her, even though most of his face was in shadow. "Make no mistake about it."

She couldn't answer.

"I know." He smiled faintly. "What right do I have to ask for so much?"

"As much right as anyone."

He gazed toward the highway when a car flashed by, wheels singing on the pavement. His nobility touched her. He was a man who would sacrifice momentary pleasure for a greater goal. It didn't seem right that she could doubt him, but she had to admit that she did. Call it injured feelings or stubborn pride, but she did.

"We all deserve happiness," she said.

"Even me, the man who abandoned his pregnant girl-friend?"

She rearranged her dress, shifting uneasily. "That's a debatable issue."

He ignored the out. "You must have hated me."

"I had my moments. Mainly when I was as big as a whale and couldn't go out without encountering half a dozen scornful stares. It seemed so unfair that I had to bear it all alone."

He reached for her hand. "Yeah, it was."

"After Joey was born, it got better for me. People find it tougher to resist a sweet, cuddly baby, y'know?" Luke nodded. She patted his hand, sorry for all that he'd missed. "As Joey grew older, I got busy, channeling my emotions into work. I was determined to have a real home. We lived at Miss Bellew's for three years. Then several different apartments. When I got the job with the sheriff's department, I was finally able to buy a house."

"Is Miss Bellew still around? Someday I'd like to thank her."

"Yeah. She's running the boardinghouse and doing sewing on the side, same as ever. Joey and I have Sunday dinner with her, at least once a month."

"I missed so much by not being here with you. If only I'd known there was a chance the baby was mine."

"I'm surprised you weren't told," she admitted. "Even though Heath claimed not to know where you were in the early days, I always figured you'd be in touch with your family eventually and one of them would tell you. About me and Joey."

"Did you want that? Were you waiting for me?"

"I guess…" She sighed. It was hard to admit. "Yes, I was. In the early days," she echoed. "When it finally got through to me that you weren't coming back, I gave up hoping for a happy ending. I decided that I'd do the best I could on my own."

"The other man was never an option?"

"No," she said immediately.

A silence welled between them, but Luke didn't ask for the explanation she dreaded.

"Heath deliberately misled me," he said.

Sophie could hardly speak. Her small "How?" came out all raspy.

"About all of it—you turning me in to the cops, your supposed wild behavior and bad reputation in the town—"

Impelled by honesty, she said, "That's not completely a lie."

Luke shook his head. "Heath led me to believe your baby was born a year or more after I left, not nine months. I thought you'd forgotten me immediately and found someone else. I felt betrayed, when it was really *me* who abandoned *you*…" He stopped, too choked up to continue.

"Shhh." Sophie hugged him. "It was a complete mess. Both our faults, and neither of our faults. But it's done with. We can't change the past."

Luke lifted his head. "Only the future."

The words were significant enough to take her breath away. She wouldn't have been surprised if he asked her to marry him, right then. But would the proposal come out of nobility, or true love? And how could she want to marry a man she wasn't sure she trusted?

"I don't know about that," she whispered, held in place by his magnetic eyes. Her voice grew stronger. "It might be a good idea to hold off on the future for a while. Let's concentrate on the present. We have a lot of reacquainting to do."

"You always did have a practical streak, little Soph."

"I've been taking care of myself for a long time."

"And others too." He stroked the back of her hand, sending shivers up her arm. "You need to be taken care of."

"Sounds like you're planning a hit," she joked, knowing she had to pull back before they wandered too deep into dangerous territory. A second time.

"My family's bad, but they won't go quite that far."

"Huh. Why do you think, um, Heath lied to you?" She had to force Heath's name out. As much as she didn't want to bring him up, she had to know what he was conniving. She hated that he had power over the direction her life would take. And that she'd given it to him through her own thoughtless, careless actions.

"I'm guessing he didn't want me to come back." Luke shrugged. "There's more to it, but that's the simplistic version."

Lots more to it, she thought, wishing with a physical ache that she could just blurt out the truth and be done with it. But there was so much at stake; she had to be more careful than that. If the new relationship between her and Luke continued to grow as it was, she'd have to find a way to rip out the weeds without killing the blossom.

But she was a cop, not a gardener. She didn't have a delicate touch.

NO BINOCULARS, THIS TIME. Only crawling around in the bushes, attacked by bloodthirsty mosquitoes, trying to get a glimpse of what the two of them were up to now. Sophie Ryan wasn't much of a deputy. She couldn't even trail a suspect without being spotted. It had been easy enough to double back when they did, even though skulking in the thick undergrowth was a major pain in the ass.

The watcher stopped, crouching, peering. Close enough.

The shiny roof of the indigo Chevy Blazer was visible, parked at the bottom of a slope. But where were Sophie and Luke?

A soft laugh floated by on the night air. Forget the Mustangs. She was busy sexing Luke up, by the sound of it. *The woman's a slut. What did you expect?*

The pair of them were kneeling close together in the grass on the hillside. The lurker raised up to get a better look. The dry brush crackled as it parted, and for a moment it appeared that Sophie and Luke had heard. But they settled back in the grass soon enough, going at each other like animals.

Easily distracted by the ants in their pants. That's good. I can use that to my advantage. If Luke's only thinking about taking up where he left off, he won't notice what's going on elsewhere. And neither will Deputy Sophie.

Once the mustangs were gotten rid of for good, it wouldn't be difficult to break Luke and Sophie up.

A few choice words about who the tramp's son belongs to ought to take care of that. Given a choice between her precious Joey and Luke, Sophie will do exactly what I want her to.

WHEN SOPHIE WAS A GIRL, shuffled between foster homes and stays with her dad, meeting Luke had been a saving grace. Her times with him had been what sustained her through Archie's days-long benders and black morning hangovers. Through living in poverty. Through her inauspicious high-school career. Fearful that she'd be sent away at any time, always feeling out of step with classmates from normal families, she'd been too withdrawn and sullen to make many friends. In her police work and college studies, she'd learned that many families had some form of hidden dysfunction, even the law-abiding, church-going outwardly picture-perfect ones. It was human nature to struggle with personal issues. She wasn't so very different from the rest of the world after all.

Reaching that understanding, and learning from the kindness of others, had made her feel less alone. Bit by bit, she'd opened herself to accept help and friendship. First from the generous spinster Miss Lettice Bellew, who was as good as a grandmother to Joe, then with Ellen Molitor and a couple of the other waitresses she'd worked with. Then Kiki Salinger and Boone Barzinski, who was a cheerful guy, welcoming when the sheriff and other deputies were not.

But she'd never again experienced the kind of unalloyed, heart-lifting joy that Luke had given her for a few brief years. She'd nearly convinced herself that had been the splendor of first love, never to be repeated. Now that he was back she knew it was more.

It was him. And her. Together.

Fourteen years later, Luke was changing her life again. While she could never be as naive as she was as a starry-eyed teenager, suddenly her future seemed brighter than ever before. Because Luke might be in it. Every hour of every day was burnished to a glow. Because Luke would be there at the end of it. Even her nights were less lonely. Because of the anticipation of spending them with Luke.

For the past week, they'd seen each other frequently, in a casual way. He dropped by with a carton of vanilla ice cream and a ten-pound sack of Granny Smith apples, hinting for her to make pies. She came home from work to find him and Joe painting the shed while Archie scowled in grudging approval from a sagging aluminum lawn chair. One afternoon, Luke whisked Joe off to the mountains, bragging that they were going on a men-only motorbike adventure, too rugged for the likes of Sophie. More often than not, she invited him or he invited himself to dinner and they'd wind down the day in the porch swing, watching the sunset, with Joe lounging nearby on the steps, his wariness about Luke gradually turning to hero-worship.

Though Sophie tried to temper her growing hopes with reminders of the complications, it was a near-impossible task. She was falling in love with Luke all over again. Not with the boy she'd idolized, either. With the man he was now.

A complicated, flawed, proud, radiant, giving man.

Her light o' love, she thought in her more rhapsodic moments, after Joe had gone in and she and Luke had been kissing in the moonlight till their lips were puffy and sore. Doing more wasn't an option with Joe in the house, so she felt safe from her ignited passions. She knew they couldn't go on this way forever, but for now it was…bliss. Bright, burning bliss.

"HEY, GORGEOUS," Luke called from the open window of the Blazer.

Even though Sophie was dog-tired, she did her best Robert DeNiro. "You talkin' to me?"

"Yeah, you. I love a woman in uniform."

She cocked a hip and posed with one hand resting on her heavily weighted equipment belt. The wide leather belt and poly-blend uniform slacks weren't items designed to streamline a woman's measurements. "Is it the billy club or the handcuffs that do it for you?"

Luke leaned both arms on the open window and rested his chin on them, giving her a blatantly appreciative once-over. "I've tried the cuffs. Let's skip the billy and go directly to the club. How about joining me for a Friday-night fish fry at the 601 Club?"

Whew. No denying it, that would be a date. A very public one, at that. Attendance was high at the fish fry, particularly by the seniors who took the majority of their all-you-can-eat dinners home in doggie bags. "I'm kinda tired," she said. "And I'm not dressed for it."

"Go home and change, catch your second wind. I'll pick you up in half an hour."

She squinted beneath her hat brim. "Are you sure you know what you're letting yourself in for?"

"I'm game if you are."

"We could get carry-out. Eat at home." She liked the way that sounded. Her and Luke, *at home.*

Luke clucked like a chicken. "You wearing feathers under that uniform?"

"Of course not."

"How about if I let you bring me in handcuffs? That would make you feel more professional about it."

She made a face at him. "What about Joey? Is he invited?"

"Nope. He was moping because you wouldn't let him go on the camp-out, so I gave him money to go to the movies with a bunch of classmates. He'll be staying over at Fletch's house." Luke flashed a brilliant smile. "Hope that's okay with you."

She wasn't sure it was—his familiarity with their lives was striking—but could think of no reason to complain. She'd been nervous about the boys camping anywhere close to the area where the mustang carcasses had been found, even though there'd been no further incidents and no real progress in her investigation.

"Buzzsaw's holed up with a pay-per-view wrestling event," Luke added.

And probably a bottle of whiskey to put him out like a light.

"So it's just you and me, way too much greasy food, and a condom with our names on it."

Sophie gasped. "Luke!" She glanced up and down the street. "Hush your mouth."

He gave a hearty laugh. "What do you say, Deputy?"

Her adrenaline was pumping something fierce. "Could any girl turn down such a romantic invitation?" she called out, too busy flipping off her hat, ripping away the heavy belt and hurrying to her car to look for his response. Luke's tune-up had rejuvenated the little hatchback's undependable engine and she was able to peel out of her employee parking space with a tire squeal worthy of the Mustangs at their wildest. Luke tooted at her, but she just waved out the window at him and gunned it for home. She had a date!

Her hair was still damp underneath when he rang the doorbell. She shut off the hair dryer and fluffed at her wild curls, wondering with an unusual excitement if she should restrain them in a ponytail, if she should make more of a concession to femininity than one squirt of perfume and a dab of mascara, if she ought to unbutton one more button on her blouse to offer a glimpse of her lace-edged tank top. Her black jeans and gray brushed-cotton shirt were not exactly tools of seduction, but she really was not skilled at this girly stuff. Besides, they were going on their first public outing as a couple. She needed for Luke to behave.

"You are going to behave, aren't you?" she said as soon as they were on their way. Even though he'd cut his hair, he still looked the teensiest bit disreputable in his leather vest with his Mustang tattoo showing below the pushed-up sleeve of a green T-shirt. "I've attained a certain standing in this community. People have to be able to trust me."

His brows went up. "I won't embarrass you."

"Fancy a Salinger embarrassing a Ryan," she mused. Her dad was known for belligerent, drunken confrontations with just about anyone who represented the Lucas Ranch. She'd been frequently shamed by his behavior.

"We've become opposites, you and I. The deputy and the maverick." Luke sneaked a quick look at her before returning his attention to the bumpy blacktop road. "Think we've got a chance in hell of making a go of it?"

Heat tinted her cheeks. "There's a lot to overcome."

He placed a hand on her arm, below her rolled-up cuff. "A lot to forgive."

And still they were doing it. This past week was proof. There'd been no grand declarations or group hugs. But her son was smiling and laughing and even talking to her again. A lot of that might have been because his friends had been quick to tell him that Luke Salinger would make a way cool dad. After fretting over that, Sophie had decided she could live with the assumption even if it made her uncomfortable. She'd begun to believe that the three of them could accept each other as a family of the heart, if not the blood. Because wasn't that what really mattered?

"We're not so different, you know. I've obviously got a lot of maverick in me. And you—black sheep or not, you're one of the Lucases. You can't get more upstanding than that."

Luke turned the vehicle into the parking lot of the 601 Club, a dinner club that had been named after the county road of its address. "But what if I don't really fit in with the Lucases?"

The question distracted her from the butterfly flutters in her stomach. "What do you mean?"

"Would it matter to you if—" He shook his head, answering himself. "Nope, I know it wouldn't."

"I don't get you."

He cut the engine and sat in silence for a moment, restlessly running the heel of his thumb around the edge of the steering wheel. "I shouldn't have brought that up." He sighed. "Someday soon I'll explain, Soph. But for now, let's go get dinner like an ordinary couple."

"Not possible." Her shy smile flickered like a firefly. "You see, I don't feel ordinary when I'm with you."

Luke's eyes took on a deep glow. "You'd better

douse that smile of yours, Deputy, or people are liable
to say we're in love.''

AFTER THAT, Sophie pretty well floated through dinner.
The restaurant was crowded and noisy, but they didn't
seem to draw an inordinate amount of attention. There
might have been a few whispers and hurried retellings
of the old story, but Sophie was too happy to look for
snubs. A few friendly souls came by the table to welcome Luke back to Treetop and josh Sophie about frat-
ernizing with her ''prisoner.'' Indeed, they seemed
more interested in asking about Luke's experiences on
Hollywood movie sets than in fishing for clues about
Joe Ryan's parentage.

Maybe, Sophie thought, she'd become hypersensitive
about the issue because of a handful of cruel comments
early on. What if she'd never been as much of an outcast as she'd imagined? It could be her *own* shame that
she needed to confront.

She declined dessert. Luke followed suit, despite his
sweet tooth. ''Not to rush you,'' he said, ''but are you
ready to go?''

She leaned over the cluttered table top. ''All the
way?''

''Only if that's what you want.''

''I'm thinking about it,'' she said, teasing him. Her
mind was made up on that count. She'd been careful
for too long. Luke was worth taking a chance on.

On their way out, they ran into Boone Barzinski and
Polly Childress, holding hands. ''Oh, no, you caught
us!'' Polly giggled and batted her lashes at Boone,
which made the tall, skinny deputy blush and stammer
and shuffle his feet. Ed Warren was in the process of
drafting a No Fraternization policy, mainly because

he'd realized that he had no chance of dating either Sophie or Polly himself.

Sophie grinned, thrilled that Polly had chosen the nice guy over Deputy Hard-on. "Hi, you two. Does the sheriff know about this?"

"Uh, well, the dating ban's not in effect yet," Boone said, "and Polly wanted to go out for fish, so I thought it would be okay—"

"You don't have to explain, Boone. I was only joking. Luke and I won't tell if you don't." She gestured over her shoulder. "But I can't promise about the rest of them."

Worry lines webbed Boone's pale forehead. "Maybe we better not go in...."

"Don't be such a scaredy-cat," Polly said, pulling him past the threshold.

Boone halted. "Say, Sophie, I almost forgot. We were trying to get in touch with you. Nick said he'd handle the situation, but I thought you should know. There was another mustang killing. Fresh, this time. Nick caught the call fifteen minutes into his shift. Same area as the last."

Sophie blinked. "What?"

"There was another mustang killing," Boone began repeating.

"Right. I got you. I'm just shocked." She looked at Luke, hoping he'd understand what she had to do. His face was grim. "I'm sorry, but I have to—"

"Of course," he said. "Let's go."

Sophie was climbing into the truck when she remembered her son. "My gosh. Joey wanted to camp in the mountains this weekend. If I hadn't said no, he'd have been up there when it happened...."

"Don't worry. He's safe." Luke indicated the car

phone installed in the Blazers console. "Go ahead and call Fletcher's house. Reassure yourself."

Sophie made the call while they sped toward the hills west of town. She spoke to Fletcher's dad, who'd driven the boys directly to the movie theater to meet their friends. He was due to pick them up in another hour. "He should be fine," she told Luke after hanging up. "Unless they did something stupid like sneak out the back of the cinema…"

"Don't even think it," Luke said, because that was just the kind of stunt he'd have pulled at thirteen.

"He wasn't happy with me for saying no."

Luke didn't respond immediately. It wouldn't help Sophie to hear that while she was at work, Joe had tried to persuade Luke into giving him permission for the camp-out, playing on Luke's desire to please the boy. Thank heaven he'd realized that acting in such a fatherly capacity would be overstepping. Joe had seemed satisfied with the movie option, especially when the cute neighbor girl decided to go along.

"Tell you what. After I drop you off, I'll go and check up on Joe myself."

Sophie was gripping the dash, using body language to make the truck go faster, but she shot a grateful look Luke's way. "Thank you. I'd appreciate it."

"It's the least I can do." After missing the first thirteen years of his son's life, sharing her worry was little enough to ask. There was no making up for all that he'd lost, but he was doing what he could to prove to her that he was here for her.

The rest of the drive, Sophie didn't want to talk much. She'd switched over to her Deputy Ryan persona, efficient and controlled. Seeing her in that capacity made Luke realize again how much time had passed, and how she'd matured. From her mother's early death to the instability of her upbringing, there'd been so many negatives for her to surmount. He was downright proud of her. But just a little worried. He couldn't help it. She was his woman again and naturally he wanted to protect her.

He'd been working on it, in his own way, ever since she'd mentioned the ongoing investigation of Demon and the mustang killings. Sophie probably wouldn't appreciate his interference, so he'd kept quiet about how he'd hung out at the bike shop so he could check what rifles might be on hand.

He slowed the Blazer as the blacktop ended. The engine churned, dust rising from beneath the wheels as they climbed in elevation. Pebbles pinged off the undercarriage. The turnoff to Hidden Lake was well concealed in the underbrush. Not many people knew about the isolated lake, and even fewer made the trek when there were other, more accessible waterways in the vicinity.

"Keep going," Sophie said. "Nick must be around here somewhere."

The sky was a deep, bruised blue by the time they reached the spot where he'd come upon Sophie using her binoculars. A large parcel of Lucas land bordered the road along this stretch, the piece he'd once intended to persuade his grandmother to deem a protected refuge for the band of mustangs that roamed the hills. Another of his failures that he'd never been able to chase out of his mind.

"There," Sophie said, spotting the lights of a patrol car. A pickup truck with a rusted-out bed was also parked nearby. "Harve Buchanon," she explained. "I told him to keep an eye out for me."

The sour scent of death hung in the air. Sophie kept her lips tightly compressed as they walked toward the two men who stood overlooking the bleak sight of the dark, rounded humps of the dead mustangs. "How many?" she asked, sounding ill.

"Four, at least. I haven't secured the perimeter. There may be more." The deputy in charge waved at Luke, who was approaching one of the carcasses. "Careful, there, fella. This may be a crime scene."

"*May* be?" Sophie said.

"They weren't shot like the last ones. Harve thinks they might have gotten into some bad grass. Toxic. Like poison."

"Maybe bracken," said Harve. "I seen it happen."

Luke and Sophie exchanged a glance. "Let's string up the crime tape all the same," she said. "Get out a camera too, before the rest of the light goes. Luke? You can go. I'll get a ride back with Nick."

He'd seen enough to make him sick. These animals had suffered. "Are you sure you won't need help? There's a lot of land to cover."

"Nick and I can handle it." She walked him back toward the vehicles. "What do you think?"

"Might be poison."

She nodded. "That was my first thought. I guess a rifle wasn't efficient enough."

Luke eyed Deputy Studly-Do-Right, whose thickest muscle appeared to be located between his ears. "Are you sure? I hate to leave you. It's a gruesome scene."

"I have to do my job." She looked him square in the eyes. "Do you have any ideas on who wants to get rid of these mustangs? There's got to be a reason, but I'm not seeing it. Who profits?"

"You're asking me because this is happening near Lucas land?"

"I realize that could be a coincidence."

"Could be."

"Did you ever look for that rifle I mentioned? The Steen Scout? It's quite distinctive."

He nodded. "I did. No dice."

"Fair enough." She paused. "You'll check on Joe, then?"

"I will."

"I am sorry about our...you know. Our plans." For a brief moment, she let her guard down and he saw the regret—and female yearning—in her eyes. Then she blinked, shuttering her emotions to prepare her for the job ahead. "Right. I'd better get started." Luke's heart swelled with an immense respect as she took a deep breath and turned to confront the carnage.

CHAPTER TWELVE

IT WAS PAST MIDNIGHT by the time Sophie got home. She'd expected the house to be dark, but there was a light burning on the porch and another couple inside. She blinked, double checking for Luke's truck or bike—her hopes taking a leap at the thought that he'd waited for her—but the only vehicle parked in the driveway was her own. Her shoulders drooped again.

She paused at the window of the patrol car, tiredly sliding her hands into the back pockets of her jeans. They'd called in the Feds from the BLM and then had waited quite a while for them to arrive, so naturally Luke was long gone. She hadn't expected otherwise, but all the same this was not how she'd wanted the evening to end. "Thanks for the ride, Nick."

Nick Hardin looked up at her from behind the wheel, his gaze lingering at the region he and Ed called "breastesess" when they were being sophomoric idiots. She quickly crossed her arms. His tongue flicked at his lips. "Say, Sophie, if you wanted I could come in and—"

"Nope, I'm fine from here." Whatever he was going to say, she didn't want to hear it. He'd been putting the moves on her ever since they'd become colleagues, too brontosaurus-brained to register her no-thank-yous for longer than one shift. His doggedness was helpful in police work, but hell on personal relations.

"The Feds will be in bright and early tomorrow

morning to go over the case, so make sure you file the proper reports at the end of the shift,'' she said, waving goodbye. She'd already checked in the evidence they'd collected, wanting to be sure it was done correctly. For all his loyalty to the badge and by-the-books enthusiasm, Nick was under Ed Warren's thumb. He'd slough off the mustang investigation if that was what Ed wanted him to do. Which meant that Sophie must ride herd, because after tonight nothing was going to impede her investigation.

She would see the horse killer caught and punished even if that meant spending the next three weeks up on the mountain on a stakeout.

She climbed the steps and let herself inside. Nights like this, she appreciated her little house with a depth that was almost soulful. The comfort of this home was all she'd had for a long time. That it seemed lacking without Luke in it was something she'd have to deal with.

There was a faint hint of cinnamon in the air. The scent momentarily lifted her dragging spirits. Must be the leftover pie. Archie had probably snuck over and warmed up a piece in the microwave.

Sophie dropped her handbag on the hall table and was heading toward the kitchen when Luke appeared, silhouetted, his broad shoulders filling the doorway.

Such a mix of emotions hit her, she couldn't tell which was which. All she knew was that she'd never been so grateful to see a man in her life. She took a shaky step. ''Oh, Luke…''

In two strides he was there, holding her close. ''Sophie, sweetheart. I hope you don't mind that I let myself in—''

''M-mind?'' she repeated in disbelief. She melted

into him, greedy for his warmth and solidity. He smelled so good. So clean and masculine. She wanted to hold on forever.

Her face was pressed to his chest; she *felt* his voice when he said, "I knew you'd be heartsick."

She nodded, burrowing deeper, letting his presence push the night's horrors out of her mind.

He kissed her hair.

She gave a start, but still clung to him, reluctant to step away. "Ugh, I must stink of—of it. Disgusting. I have to go take a shower."

"Go ahead. I'm fixing you hot chocolate and apple pie."

"How domestic." She wanted to kiss him, but wouldn't let herself with the taint of the evening's work fouling the moment. Such filth mustn't touch what was still fresh and new between her and Luke.

She took as hot a shower as she could stand, soaping herself over and over again until her skin was nearly raw. She put her hair up in a towel turban and wrapped her body in a terry-cloth robe. Luke was waiting in the bedroom. Not only was there pie and a steaming mug of chocolate on a breakfast tray, he'd made an extravagant pile of the pillows and turned down the bed. The only illumination in the room came from a small ceramic jug lamp on the nightstand.

"This is nice," she said, feeling shy as she climbed into bed. Luke sat at her feet and put the tray over her lap. "But I can't get over you, being Mr. Housewife. If the Mustangs could see you now…"

He chuckled, not bothered in the least. "Or Judge Entwhistle."

She pierced a syrupy chunk of apple with the tines

of her fork and lifted it to his mouth. "Does this mean I've successfully tamed you?"

He gave a low growl before snapping up the tidbit. "I wouldn't count on it."

"But I can count on you."

"Yes. You can."

"You're sure?"

His head tilted. "What are you asking?"

"What if I have to question—and maybe even arrest—a member of your family? Would you stand by me then?"

"If you were in the right, I would."

She frowned. "If."

"Who do you suspect?"

"It seems obvious." She held the mug in both hands, dropping her face toward the steam as she said in a low voice, "Heath."

"How so?"

"There was talk in town about mineralogists or geologists—I'm not sure which—working on the Lucas land where the mustangs sometimes run. What if they discovered a profitable source of, say, coal or natural gas, and the only way Heath can get permission for further exploration is to drive off the mustangs? That land is registered under the Wildlife Preservation Act, you know."

Luke seemed surprised. "It is?"

"Has been for years."

"But I—" He raked his hand through his hair. "I'd asked my grandmother to do that, years and years ago, but I never knew... She must have seen to it after I left the ranch." He hesitated. "Isn't the designation irrevocable?"

"Not necessarily. It's still Lucas land, and Mary is a shrewd businesswoman."

Luke was subdued, thinking it over. Sophie nibbled at the pie. Eventually he said, "And the rifle you've mentioned..."

"It's distinctive. The proverbial smoking gun."

"What about tonight? Was it poison?"

"Very likely. I found some sweet feed spilled on the ground. We'll be sending samples to the lab for analysis, and we've got a vet who will examine the carcasses to determine cause of death." She leaned over the side of the bed to put the breakfast tray on the floor, prompting her turban to unwind. "I can't think of any other reason to kill the wild horses," she said, lifting off the damp towel. Her hair fell across her face in a tangle. She pushed it back. "Some ranchers consider them troublesome, but there are none in that area to complain, other than Shane McHenry at Goldstream, and he's not the type. It's too remote for anyone to be bothered, or to bother, which is why the band keeps returning to the same location."

"There's another possibility," Luke said, his face grave as he studied her face.

A sense of disquiet tickled her nerve endings. "If you have a theory, I'd like to hear it."

"What if the culprit is someone who has it in for the Lucases? Wants to create trouble for us?"

Sophie's stomach swooped. "You're accusing my father?" She clenched her hands on the towel in her lap. "That's absurd. I know he has it in for your family, but he wouldn't—he wouldn't hurt—"

She broke off, suddenly remembering the kitten. She'd been ten or eleven. Her father had found a job and swore to the court and social workers that he'd cleaned up his act, so she'd been lifted out of her latest foster home and sent back to the trailer. The tiny kitten had been a going-away present from her foster mother, one of the good ones. The first time Archie had come home drunk, the kitten had gotten in his way and he'd boosted it out the door on the toe of his boot. She still remembered its pitiful cry and how she'd scrambled after it in the dark wearing only her pajamas, and sat cradling it to her chest on the steps for at least an hour before Archie had fallen asleep and she'd dared to creep back inside. The kitten hadn't been hurt, but she'd known that next time might be worse. So she'd given it away to a girl who lived in a yellow house with a picket fence.

No. She shook her head, her hair dampening her cheeks. "You're wrong, Luke. Archie wouldn't do that. The plan's too convoluted, for one thing. He's all bluster. He never actually *accomplishes* anything."

"The possibility occurred to me, that's all. I realize it's far-fetched."

"Well, thanks for putting *that* image in my head." She squeezed her eyes shut and rolled to her side, moving her legs restlessly beneath the covers until she'd kicked them away. "He doesn't have a rifle at all, let alone such a fancy one."

Luke shifted. "I'm sorry. I shouldn't have mentioned it."

"No, I asked. And it's an avenue to explore. Revenge, I mean."

"What about Demon and his buddy, Drizz? Remember what we overheard them say—about me distracting you?"

"I remember." She'd even wondered if they'd purposely sent Luke to distract her.

"Obviously they're up to no good."

"Nothing new about that." She rested her head on her arms, her fingers sinking into her hair. "I have to get up and comb my hair or it'll be one big snarl in the morning."

"Let me," Luke said, the mattress shifting as he went to find a comb.

Sophie grimaced to herself. It was bad enough having to suspect Luke, but her *father?* She couldn't accept that.

Then Luke was back, winding an arm around her waist. "Sit up," he said as if to a child. She felt like one, trembling and defenseless. She hadn't been defenseless since she was six.

"I was thoughtless, pressing you like that about your dad," Luke murmured, crouching behind her and running his fingers through her tangles. "Forgive me."

"I'm a grown-up. I can take it."

"You shouldn't have to, not tonight."

His fingertips massaged her scalp. She sighed and slumped against him, surrendering to the rare pleasure of being taken care of. "I cannot comprehend such a thing."

"Of course not." He was backed up against the pine headboard, his chest and thighs supporting her reclining figure. It was both tantalizing and relaxing. Her eyes were closed, but her senses were alert. She anticipated every move he made, combing out the tangled hanks of hair with only the occasional small tug at her scalp, his chest expanding and contracting beneath her shoulders, the muscles in his thighs flexing against her arms and back when he reached forward. She was lost in the pattern of his breathing, his soft, soothing words, his steady heartbeat. The connection was almost supernatural.

She knew he was aroused before his body did. He'd prodded her to move slightly so he could comb out the rest of her hair, and when he tilted her head forward, she saw that her robe was beginning to gape, but was too lazy to reach up and close it. It was only a breast. Half a breast. But she felt the quickening in Luke when he tilted her head back again and saw the deep gap that had opened.

He didn't say anything. Neither did she. There was a small click as he set aside the comb. A quiet hitch in his breath and *thunk* of his skull as he relaxed against the headboard.

Sophie stretched her legs, the robe falling away from their length as she clenched her calf muscles and curled and uncurled her toes. She rolled her head against his flat stomach, laying a hand beneath her cheek. One fingertip worked its way between the buttons of his shirt to stroke his ridged abdominal muscles. His body was so warm and hard. Growing harder. Divine.

"I didn't stay here for this," he said.

"I know."

"I stayed because you needed me—or someone—"

"You," she said, "Definitely you." She freed a button and pressed a small kiss beneath the open flap. His stomach muscles jumped.

"After I checked on Joe, I went home to the ranch, but I kept thinking about you, coming back to an empty house, and I couldn't stand it. So I..." He moaned. She'd slid the flat of her hand inside his shirt and was making small circles over his ribs. "I drove back here...parked the bike in the shed...where no one will..."

"See," she said, squirming to her side and inching higher against him, the motion dragging the robe off her shoulders. She tilted her face, taking in his guardedly wondering expression. "You know what I see? I see a man who came home for a reason. A man who cares as much as he ever did but is too damn good at hiding his feelings beneath a stone facade. A man who is learning how to love again." She kissed him on the lips, the chin, the throat, nuzzling her face into his chest with a sigh. "I see a man I'm falling in love with all over again," she whispered.

His arms curved around her, tendrils of desire coiling in their wake. "When did you get so brave, Sophie?"

"I'm not the one who drives motorcycles through fire for a living. I've been hearing about your exploits from Joey, you know."

"My risks are only physical. Your kind takes more courage. You're not the timid girl I used to know."

"She's still inside me. I'm scared all the time, even when I won't let myself acknowledge it." Afraid that her life would always be a struggle, that she'd never have a partner, but afraid for Joey—losing Joey to the moneyed Lucas lifestyle—most of all. Luke didn't know how big a risk she was taking, being with him.

"You know what they say. It's not courage if you're not afraid." His hands had strayed from her waist to her lapels.

Leaning against him, she settled her hands over his and guided them to open the robe. "I know this. Even though my feelings for you scare me, I'm brave enough to make love." She placed his palm on her naked breast. The sensation was direct, pure, almost a relief. "Are you?"

He reached both hands around her breasts, lifting them, his fingers spreading the delicious shivery warmth with languid ease. Held flat, his thumbs rubbed across her nipples and pebbled aureoles, circling back and forth until she was making soft grunting sounds, her upper body taking up the sensual rhythm. Soon his shoulders rolled in sync with hers, matching the motion. Together they swayed, slow dancing in bed. No music. Only sweet harmony.

Sophie pushed herself up on her arms and turned face to face, slithering nakedly against his chest. "Are you brave enough? Are you man enough?" She knew the answer, of course. But she wanted him to know it too. To say it out loud. For both of them.

He cupped her face. "I swear I'll never let you down again."

She smiled. "And will you love me forever?"

No hesitation. "Until the end of time."

He kissed her, openmouthed, her springy hair bunched in his hands. The kiss felt good and strong, and then he put his hands beneath her robe on her naked behind and held her against his erection and the kiss became deep and wet and searchingly intimate. Extravagant.

Oh, yes! Tearing off his shirt, she was equally extravagant with her caresses, her passion. The pressure inside her was dense, lush, demanding—as she wanted it. Luke would know without a doubt she wasn't his timid brown-eyed girl. She was a woman. He was making love with a woman. An equal.

"Yes," she said. "Like that." His mouth was on her breasts, his tongue first stiff and raspy-rough and then soft and moist as he sucked, pulling hard the way she needed it, pleasure rushing in a hot stream through the center of her body.

She ran her trembling hands over his chest, down to the snap on his jeans. Her fingers fumbled, jerking at the tab of the zipper. He caught her hands, pried them away with a wince that made her laugh out loud. "Out of practice," she gasped while he undid his fly himself, both of them rising up on their knees, shedding the last of their clothing, which in her case meant merely unknotting the strip of terry cloth at her waist and letting the robe fall away.

A momentary hesitation came over her. She'd had a baby, and kept fifteen pounds and a few faded stretch marks from the experience. But she was in good shape and she was darn proud of her body. It had taken her this far, and if Luke couldn't—

He could. In his luminescent eyes, she saw all the respect and reverence one ordinary woman could ever need. He knelt before her, his fingertips grazing across her skin from shoulders to thighs, barely touching, yet reaching all the way inside to her heart. "How is it possible that you've grown more beautiful?" he asked, breathing hard.

"It's not me. It's you. How you look at me."

"Ah. Let's test out this theory." He looked again, his gaze moving slowly along her body.

With an effort, she held herself still. "What do you see?"

"You're very pretty, but very pink."

"I scrubbed myself raw."

His radiance clouded. "Aw, Soph."

"Let's not think of that." She sank so she was sitting on her heels. "In fact, let's not think at all. Let's only feel."

"Sounds like a plan." He glanced down. "Right now, I feel hard." He stroked the slight curve of her belly. "And now I feel soft."

She reached for him, laughing, equally entranced

with her vision of his body. He'd changed too. He was all hard, hairy muscle, crisscrossed with several new bumps and scars, his skin browner than she remembered, his erection far more…flagrant. An absurd giggle rose inside her. She leaned her arms on his shoulders and studied his eyes, tickling the back of his neck, playing with the ends of his newly shorn hair. "I feel happy."

He pushed her backward onto the bed and fitted himself between her open thighs, his mouth descending upon hers. Their kiss tasted of sugar and sex and too many years apart. When Luke drew back, she didn't want to let him go until he said, his voice hoarse with emotion, "I feel love," and then she understood that it was okay. It wasn't sex that would bind them. It was love.

This time, they were wise enough to know there was a difference.

His fingers dipped between her legs. She arched into the caress, her skin prickling in response. Electric. Like a lightning storm. She swore her hair stood on end. Sort of like him, she thought, most wickedly, kissing him long and hard as her hands reached down to draw him in to the center of her, where she ached to feel him deep inside.

"Wait, wait," he said, reaching for the jeans he'd thrown off the side of the bed.

She squirmed beneath him, wrapping her legs around his hips. "Don't say that. I can't wait."

Mylar tore. "Good. Because I'm not going to last very long."

"Me, neither." She was so responsive, her climax was on a hair trigger. "One touch and I'll go off," she warned. "So you'd better make it a good one."

His smile was more of a grimace, but his eyes were hot and direct, his body built to please her every request. "That's pressure."

"Mmm, no, this is." She reached for him again, but not only with her hands. She used her entire body, her voice, her lips, her thighs, her spirit, all welcoming him deep into the heart of her. He filled her and she filled him, both of them surrendering to the great surge of pleasure and promise that came over them like a tidal wave. It was potent. Poetic. Profound.

Sophie saw her love mirrored in Luke's eyes and it took her breath away. He was stroking inside her, their bodies molten in the heat, the coursing satisfaction. She held on tight to his flexing shoulders, letting him take her down from the starry heights to the reality of her warm bed in her cozy bedroom in her humble little home.

She held him close, cherishing his weight. He murmured soft words about how beautiful she was, how brilliant and brave, how much she'd pleased him, and all the while he kept kissing her, small kisses peppered across her flushed cheeks and shoulders and tender pink breasts. The intimacy was sweet and sentimental and a little bit giddy, the way it was supposed to be.

After a while, they moved apart, fluffing pillows, reaching for tissues, regaining most of their equilibrium. Luke leaned over the side of the bed and scooped up the rest of the pie in his fingers and ate it in one big gulp that reminded her so much of Joey she had to stifle a laugh by biting down on the quilt she'd drawn up to her chin.

Luke's arms encircled her. He nuzzled the back of her neck, kissed his way to her mouth. "Pie breath," she said.

"You know you like it."

"Umm. I like it, I love it," she singsonged.

He picked up the tune. "Got to have the girl…"

She squinted one eye, made a move to peer under the comforter. "Again? So soon?"

"Won't be long now."

"Won't be *short* now," she countered.

"You've acquired quite the sassy tongue, woman."

She stuck it out.

He caught it with a juicy, slobbering kiss.

"Yuck," she said, laughing and wiping her face where he'd swiped it with his tongue.

They settled deeper among the pillows, spooning. The low-wattage lamp gave the parchment-painted walls a warm yellow glow. There was little in the room—a pine dresser, a big banana palm, a rag rug and the queen-sized bed covered with a tea-stained, rose-patterned quilt. "This is nice," Luke said. "Kind of girly, but I'm willing to overlook that. Can I stay and never leave?"

"Sure. As long as you know how to make the night last forever." Sophie sighed with contentment. "I might miss sunshine though."

"Waffles drenched in maple syrup."

"The wind in my hair."

He squeezed her. "And mine."

"Sunset in the Rockies. The smell of new-mown grass."

"Playing basketball with Joe."

"Oh—Joe." Suddenly needing darkness, she reached over and flicked off the light, then waited until her eyes had adjusted. "We have to talk about Joe, and how we're going to handle the situation."

"What situation?"

"You know. I have to think about setting an example, proper behavior, and all that. You can't stay overnight with him in the house. I probably shouldn't even have you here now…"

She felt Luke's chest grow tight with tension. "I told you—I put my bike in the shed. No one will call you a scarlet woman."

"That's not so much my concern as what Joey will think." She waited, but Luke didn't relax. Curious. "Umm, is something else bothering you?" Maybe she'd pushed too hard, asking if he'd love her forever. The women's magazines probably advised against being so audacious about your needs. Well, jeez, that was just too bad.

He didn't speak, so she filled the awkward silence. "It's not only how this will *look,* it's how Joe will feel about us being together. I'd rather he didn't know until…" She ran out of steam because there was nowhere to go. How was she ever going to solve the predicament of which brother had fathered her child? How could she and Luke stay together forever when there was still a lie—of omission, true, but a rather large omission—between them?

"We don't have to make explanations," Luke said. "If you and Joe will have me, I'm willing to accept him as my son, and you as my wife. Let the busybodies go hang."

"Oh." The small sound floated out of Sophie's mouth without her realizing it. She was trying get her mind around the possibility of the kind of happy-ever-after she'd rarely let herself imagine over the years. She'd already told Luke she didn't believe in fairy tales. Did he really have to come back home and flip all her steady, workable beliefs on end by acting so princely?

He nudged her. "What about it?"

What about you and the Mustangs? What about Heath? What about trust?

She cleared her throat. "What would your family say?"

"Maybe it's time we found out. The Lucas family reunion is this weekend. Saturday night's the stuffy formal dinner for the important bigwigs Heath and Grandmother want to impress. I wouldn't ask that of you. But why don't you and Joe come as my guests to the Sunday barbecue?"

After so many years of keeping a careful distance, the very thought was frightening. "Oh, no, we couldn't do that."

"Why not?"

"We're not family. At least I'm not."

"We're together as a couple. That's close enough."

Too close for comfort. "It would be terribly uncomfortable for all of us. I can't imagine what your grandmother would say."

"I already mentioned it to her. She's all for it."

Sophie went up on one elbow. "All for it? You're kidding. She's never given me the time of day." And that was exactly how they both liked it.

"Are you sure?"

Sophie thought of her suspicions that Mary Lucas had pulled strings to land her the job in the sheriff's department. "What are you saying, Luke?"

"Ever since I've been home, she's been dropping hints. About what a fine boy Joe is. How you've turned into an admirable woman, a good deputy and an all-around upstanding citizen. How maybe you and I should think about settling down."

"She said *that?* In so many words?"

"Just about."

Sophie lay back down and locked her fingers together under the sheets. They trembled, even so. "What does it mean?"

"I'd guess that she's assuming Joe's my son."

"Like everyone else. When the truth comes out, I won't be so *admirable*."

"No. Don't say that." He hooked an arm around her neck and pulled her to him in a clumsy but heartfelt embrace. He kissed her forehead. "The truth is that you are more admirable than any person I know. I'll set straight anyone who says otherwise. As for the details of who and when—those are no one's business but ours."

Except that he didn't know the details, she thought.

He was taking her on faith.

She must do the same. But she was scared of what would happen if she told Luke everything. It could be the end—the ultimate dead end, with no road back. Did she dare find out?

If he only knew—I'm not so brave. Sophie pressed herself along his length and whispered, "I love you," squeezing her eyes shut, wanting only darkness and Luke's warm male body, holding her close, giving her faith, keeping her safe. At least for one miraculous night.

LUKE LEFT AT DAWN. Even though Sophie hadn't asked him to sneak away before the neighbors saw, he wanted to protect her from unnecessary talk any way he could. She'd wakened when he had and they'd made love again, taking their slow, sweet time about it. She'd looked so beautiful in the morning light, with tousled hair, lazy eyelids and her lips so soft and sexy, it had been incredibly tough to make himself leave.

But he had. Because he owed her.

She'd told him she kept the keys to the shed in her sewing box. He liberated them a second time, intending only to wheel his Harley out into the rosy morning light. But the pull was too strong. He had to look again to be a hundred percent certain that he'd seen what he thought he'd seen the past night. Returning to the shed to lock up, he bypassed the lawn mower, going straight to the corner to lift a corner of the tarpaulin draped over a painted hutch.

Yep. The rifle was still there.

A Steen Scout, .308 caliber. Leaning upright against the cupboard doors. Only the butt end showed beneath the edge of the tarpaulin, if you happened to glance that way.

Last night, he'd put on a pair of Sophie's gardening gloves and checked to see if it was loaded. Evidence or not, no way would he leave a loaded weapon around a thirteen-year-old, whether or not it was kept under lock and key.

The rifle hadn't been loaded, so he'd put it back while he tried to figure out if there could be any other reason for its appearance here, and, most importantly, how to tell Sophie that the evidence she sought could be found in her very own backyard.

So far, he hadn't done a very good job.

But she'd have to be told—and soon—even if that broke her fractured heart.

Luke swiped his hands across his face in despair. He didn't… He couldn't…not again.

Maybe he was waiting for a miracle.

CHAPTER THIRTEEN

"I CAN'T BELIEVE I'm here," Sophie said under her breath. *And that I brought my son.* This was maybe the dumbest move she'd ever made in her life, and that included the time she'd stubbornly taken a dare from Skooch Haas at Jackpine Lake. She'd almost drowned, trying to swim under the mossy old wooden raft anchored in the middle of the lake. It had been Luke who'd saved her, a hand extended through the dense green water, pulling her through to the other side.

It was probably the last warm day of September, and even so there was a singing wind blowing in off the mountains. When it gusted, the red-and-white-striped tent flapped and smoke from the barbecue switched direction, making the chefs flap their aprons and wave their tongs. There was pork barbecue—an entire roasted pig—plus the usual hamburgers and hot dogs, along with a long table filled with salads and potatoes and pyramids of corn on the cob. Sophie had nibbled. The crowd around the food was a good place to get lost, especially since she'd been abandoned by both Luke and Joe.

The Lucas Ranch was more than a showplace—it was a real working ranch, impressive, but not as pretentious as she'd remembered from her teenage years. Objectively, it was a welcoming place. That didn't matter to her. She'd just as soon stay on the other side of the fence.

Except for Luke.

He'd wanted this so badly. He seemed to see it as an official announcement—as official as they could get for now—and had gone about persuading her in his own special way. It was against her every instinct for self-preservation, but, under the circumstances, how could she refuse?

I coulda. I shoulda.

Her plan was to stick with the crowd, mingling only with the distant Lucas relatives who wouldn't know her from Auntie Mame or Cousin It. She'd stay at the barbecue long enough to be polite, but that was it. Luke had insisted on introducing her to his grandmother and his father, in from the city. Luckily Heath was busy glad-handing the VIP Lucases from the East Coast branch of the family and had taken no notice of the lowly likes of Sophie Ryan. All she had to do was fly beneath his radar for another fifteen or twenty minutes and she'd be home free.

Luke appeared from a swarm of guests in pseudo-Western wear. "This isn't so bad, is it?"

She nodded. "If you can take it, I can take it."

He tucked one of her flyaway curls behind her ear. "Told you so. You're braver than you think you are."

Sophie made a face, even though Luke's position was worse than hers, in a way. Everyone seemed to know about Mary Lucas's wayward grandson, the one who'd run away one step ahead of the law, only to become a stuntman in Hollywood. They treated him like a movie star. He'd downplayed his exploits as much as possible, but there was no avoiding the notice entirely. Sophie had been happy to keep as far away from him as possible, not wanting to be drawn into a conversation that would necessitate explanations of her attendance at a Lucas family reunion.

One of the more garrulous aunts was looking their way with bright-eyed interest. Sophie turned her back to Luke, slinking toward the dappled shadows thrown by a cottonwood tree as she said out of the side of her mouth, "Can we go somewhere private—like, right now?"

He looked at her with sympathy. His eyes were more blue than gray today, saturated by sky. They made her want to melt into his arms most inappropriately, even though he'd only touched her elbow. "Sure. Why not? Private sounds good to me."

They hurried toward the house across the brick patio, avoiding the doors that led into the kitchen where there were bound to be a half-dozen happy homemakers buttering hamburger rolls and replenishing salad bowls. "Command Central is the place to go," Luke said, taking her in the side door that overlooked the barns and corrals.

It was cool and dark in the office, which was actually two large rooms, one opening off the other, separated by heavy sliding doors. Luke brought her into the second room, a book-lined study with paneled walls, leather armchairs and a few good pieces of Western art. She went to the window first, parting the slats on the plantation shutters. The reunion guests tended toward middle-aged and older, but there was a small group of young people hanging out by the corrals. She picked out Joey, perched on the top rail, hunched over as he talked to a girl with dimples and a ponytail. It looked like he was going to be a ladies' man. Wouldn't you know?

Like father, like...*son?*

"He's fine," Luke said. "No one's paying him any undue attention. You don't have to worry, Soph."

"I can't help it. I've spent so many years worrying about keeping him away from here, it goes against my grain to have brought him along. He looks so—"

"Content?"

She shuddered, recognizing that Luke spoke the truth. It was an idea she was loath to explore—that Joe would love it here. Would *want* to be a part of the Lucas and Salinger family. "I was thinking...he looks so much like a Lucas. People must be able to tell." She stopped, wanting to bite her tongue. Luckily, Luke didn't notice the slip. Or perhaps he took it to be an admission that *he* was the Lucas Joe took after.

"What the hell, Sophie. That works to our advantage, doesn't it? If he looks like me, you don't have to fret about anyone asking questions." Which was the argument he'd used to get her to bring Joe along in the first place.

"Right," she muttered, moving away from the shutters, out of Luke's reach. He didn't know; he couldn't understand.

She found herself staring at a grouping of family pictures. There was one of Luke and Heath with their parents—a formal shot taken when the boys were still teenagers. It gave her spirits a boost. The young Luke looked similar to Joe—tall, lanky, dark-haired, frozen on film as if he'd been caught in midflight. Heath was also tall, but more compact in build. His face was square, open and cheerful, like his father, Stephen's. They were both blond. Whereas Elyse Salinger had what Sophie considered the true Lucas look—like her second son.

Odd, considering the hints Luke had dropped about not being a "real" member of the family.

She quickly scanned the rest of the photos: panoramic ranch shots, old-time cowboys in hats and chaps, cattle roundups, hunting, fishing, horseback riding, Mary Lucas posed on the front steps of the house as a new wife.

Luke was watching her. He smiled a little when she glanced up. "You see? Nothing to be frightened of. None of us bite."

She winked. "Only on the right occasions."

He slid an arm around her waist. "And in the right locations," he murmured, planting a string of soft, biting kisses inside the loose round neckline of her persimmon-colored sweater.

She murmured and stretched her neck, her lids lowering as she lost focus on the photographs.

Wait. She stiffened. Her eyes opened wide.

There—in one of the hunting photos. A group of men with deer carcasses, a gray-haired Mary Lucas proudly kneeling among them with a rifle by her side.

Sophie had studied photographs of that make of rifle. It was a Steen Scout, from a rare edition of 500, produced in 1970. It was the very one she'd been looking for—the high-powered .308 that would possibly be missing its scope, if their gun expert had been correct in his evaluations of the custom-made accessory.

"You're so tense," Luke said. "Relax, so I can bite you."

She pushed him away with a coaxing laugh. "Save it for later, Luke, okay? I wouldn't want anyone walking in on us like this."

His eyes narrowed. "Sure. Sorry."

She crossed her arms, idly walking toward the chairs as if she meant to sit. She was actually surveying the room more closely. A jolt went through her when she saw the gun case, but she tried to keep her eyes away from it, feeling as obvious as an elephant in a tutu under Luke's sharp gaze. "I'm kind of thirsty. Could you be a prince and dare the kitchen for me?"

"Whatever you want," he said. "Anytime, anywhere."

She kept her face blank. "A cola sure would hit the spot. My mouth is dry from all that smoke."

Luke nodded. He stepped through to the outer room, started to roll the sliding doors shut, then paused midway. He angled his chin toward the gun rack. "Go ahead and take a look, Deputy."

Sophie's cheeks flamed. The doors rumbled shut.

She stood stock-still for a moment, gathering her thoughts. Just because Mary Lucas owned a Scout didn't mean hers was the gun that killed the mustangs. It didn't mean that only Mary used it. It didn't even mean that they still had it.

But, well…the coincidence was too big to swallow.

Sophie approached the gun case, a fancy job made of burled walnut, with glass doors and a watered-silk lining. It held six rifles, all of them polished collectors' pieces, but no Steen Scout. And no convenient empty space where the offending weapon had once hung, either.

Of course not. That would have been far too easy.

LUKE FIXED THE SOFT DRINKS with Kiki's special lemon-curl cubes while he chitchatted with the kitchen workers for a decent interval, giving Sophie time to satisfy her curiosity. He returned to Command Central at the same moment Heath came in from the patio, squinting and wiping his face with a handkerchief.

"Barbecue smoke," he said. "Got in my eyes."

At the sight of his brother, Luke's irritation flared. Pretty much as it had ever since he'd become certain that Heath had deliberately done what he could to ensure Luke stayed away from the ranch. Even if Heath hadn't outright lied, he'd definitely pussyfooted around the truth, leading Luke's assumptions about Sophie in drastically wrong directions. That made Luke wonder what else his brother was capable.

The deception alone was unforgivable, and Heath must know it. He'd been avoiding Luke as much as possible.

Heath folded the handkerchief and placed it in his pocket. One corner of his mouth twitched when he saw that Luke carried two beverages. "What's the big idea? You know Sophie Ryan doesn't belong here." A hint of whininess slipped into his tone. "I don't see why you had to invite her. People are noticing that she's out of place."

"She's no more out of place than me," Luke said evenly.

Heath's jaw bulged. "That's true," he agreed, just as evenly, daring to stare straight at his brother.

A challenge? Were they finally going to have it out?

Luke hesitated, his fingers tightening on the wet glasses. Drops of condensation trickled over his knuckles. "Are you sure you want to get into this?"

"Get into what?"

"Sophie's place. My place. The lies you told to keep us apart."

Heath backed off with upraised hands, playing the guileless card. "Lies? I don't know what you're talking about."

"What about her son, Joe? You must have known

exactly when he was born. You knew that there was at least a chance I'm his father. You should have told me.''

Heath laughed, as if the situation was just a joke among men. ''C'mon, Luke. She's cute, sure, but she's too unpolished and rough. Don't let her twist you up. Why would you want to claim the boy when he could be the offspring of any one of the Mustangs, or, hell, a good number of other local guys?''

The knife-sharp edge of anger turned Luke's voice to cold steel. ''You're wrong about that.''

''Sure, she's a deputy now, but that doesn't change what she was. After you left, it became obvious.'' Heath shrugged. ''Everyone saw what kind of woman she really is.''

Luke said, ''I wish I knew…''

Heath's chest puffed out.

''…whether you're truly that dumb or just that calculating.''

The gloating smile faded fast.

''If it's merely dumb,'' Luke went on, ''you're a pitiable fool and I can let you live. But if what you've done has been calculated all along…''

It gave him a small measure of satisfaction to see that Heath's sweat had begun to stain the underarms of his designer-label polo shirt.

''TOO MUCH NONSENSE FOR ME,'' Mary Lucas said as she came into the study from the living room, her cane sinking into the plush carpeting. She didn't seem surprised to find Sophie there, but then Sophie had noticed that the older woman missed very little. Even at a barbecue for seventy-five, she kept an eagle eye out. Sophie had no doubt that *Mary* had made careful note of her and Joe's every move.

"All that jibbering and jabbering and high-pitched squealing," she continued, settling herself into one of the armchairs with a light sigh.

Sophie stayed by the window, watching Joe lope across the lawn. He disappeared under the tent. The desserts had been brought out, including an assortment of cakes, pies and four giant tubs of ice cream.

Mary rested her head against the back of the chair. There was a long silence while Sophie covertly studied Luke's grandmother, a Lucas only by marriage, but as formidable and prideful as any of them. She could see where Luke had inherited his spirit—even at her age, Mary Lucas was a dynamo. Under other circumstances, she was a woman Sophie would have admired rather than feared.

"Now, you, girl—you don't talk much."

"No," Sophie said.

"You're strong. You take care of yourself. I like that."

Sophie fidgeted, not sure where the woman was heading with this conversation. "I had no other choice," she muttered.

Mary Lucas opened her eyes and trained the twin blue flames on Sophie's face. "Of course you did. You could have asked for child support."

A spurt of ire seared away the uncertainty. Sophie threw back her head, regarding the woman coolly. "Asking for child support doesn't make a woman weak. It takes a very strong mother to stand up in court and demand all that her child deserves, especially in the face of an unfriendly political system and critical tongue-lashings from self-righteous busybodies."

Mary's thin white brows arched higher on her lined forehead. "Then why didn't you?"

Sophie faltered. "I— Well, it wasn't—" She gave her head a small shake. "My situation was different." She could have used the extra money, but no way would she have subjected herself and her baby to the scrutiny suing for it would have entailed.

"You could go after Luke now, get yourself a fine judgment. Quite the lump sum, if it's money you're after."

Sophie narrowed her eyes, sure that Mary Lucas was toying with her, wanting to see how she'd handle the implication. "Why would I go after Luke?" she asked, all innocence.

"Do you take me for a fool, young lady?"

"Certainly not. Although I might ask you the same."

Mary cackled. She gestured to the other chair. "Come and sit by me so I can see your face."

Sophie complied. Luke had said she was brave, hadn't he? She met Mary's gaze, determined not to let the matriarch strike fear into her heart. "Are you looking for an honest woman?"

"Have I found one?"

Sophie swallowed. "I'm as honest as I can be."

"You're being evasive, Deputy Ryan."

"Uh-huh. Call me Sophie."

Mary nodded. "This boy of yours."

Tension swelled, sucking the air from the room until Sophie felt as if she couldn't get any oxygen.

"Tell me about him," Mary said, and her face softened with an emotion that looked a lot like…regret.

Wild wings beat at Sophie's throat from the inside. It was her frantic heart. She nipped her bottom lip, halfway tempted to spill out all the mothery-love stories and goofy-kid details that she'd kept mostly to herself for so, so long.

But she couldn't. Because she'd been right. Mary Lucas wanted a great-grandson. Whether it was for sentiment or to continue the venerable line, she couldn't be sure. Probably both. She did know the look in the old woman's eyes was not calculating. They brimmed with genuine interest.

For the real Joe Ryan, good or bad, moody or an eternal joy, Sophie wondered. Or for the proper young heir Mary Lucas needed him to be? The role that Heath was eager to fill, but that Luke had found so constricting he'd stayed away for fourteen years?

The wooden sliding doors parted with another rolling-thunder rumble. Heath Salinger burst into the room, followed by Luke, his hands clenched around two sweating beverages as if they were six-guns.

"Grandmother!" Heath said, startled and nervous. "What are you doing here?" He looked at Sophie in alarm, his nostrils curling in disgust. "With *her.*"

Mary was unperturbed. "It's time we got to know each other, don't you think?"

Heath patted his dark blond hair, smoothing ruffled feathers as he got himself back under control. "Whatever you like, ma'am. However, now is not the time. We have so many other guests." He aimed a second glance at Sophie, the sneer more subtle this time, as if to say *important guests.*

"I can't think of any more important than Sophie and Joe Ryan," Mary said with a surprising conviction.

The bold statement astonished Sophie. She opened and closed her mouth like a snapping turtle.

"Have a drink." Luke sat on the arm of her chair and passed the glass of cola. Cubes rattled as Sophie lifted it to her mouth. Several drops spilled onto her dress pants and she blotted them with her sleeve, feeling disconnected from herself. Her body was still there, listening to Mary Lucas stake a claim, but her head was off in the stratosphere, floating around untethered.

Luke put his arm around her shoulders, bringing her back, keeping her grounded. "You've always been perceptive, Grandmother. So I might as well say it out loud. Sophie and Joe aren't guests. They're family."

"Ah." Mary nodded sagely.

"In fact, were going to be married as soon as I can convince Sophie to say yes."

"No," Heath said. "You can't."

Luke's shoulders shifted as he turned to look at his brother. "Nothing you can say will stop me this time."

"Does this mean that young Joe is…" Mary stopped questioningly.

"Yes," Luke said. "He's my son."

"No, Luke," Sophie blurted. "Please…"

He tipped up her chin and spoke softly straight to her. "He's my son, Sophie. Believe it."

Luke's voice was a solid promise, one she yearned to accept, but helplessly her glance darted to Heath, who was growing very red in the face.

He swore bitterly. "You'll be a laughingstock, Luke. The Ryans are nothing but trailer trash. We don't marry her kind."

"Then I guess I'm not interested in being *your kind*, brother, because Sophie's better than I deserve."

"What about her bastard son? You're going to take responsibility for another man's brat?"

Luke advanced on Heath, his fists clenched. "Maybe you didn't hear me. I'll say it once more. *Joe is my son.*"

Like a cornered bobcat, Heath wasn't giving up until

he'd slashed Luke with deep cuts. There was a terrible jeering hatred in his face. "You think so? Have you asked her, huh? Has she told you how many men she spread her legs for after she ratted you out to the sheriff? *Including me.*"

A moment of harsh silence fell across the room.

Sophie couldn't believe he'd said it. She looked at her hands, carefully setting aside the soft drink as if this was a tea party and she was worried about spilling. Inside, she was reeling, ready to drop into a dead faint.

Suddenly the silence broke into action and fury. Luke let out a sound of rage and swung, connecting with Heath's jaw with a violent *crack.* Sophie leapt up, a cry of alarm on her lips, living her worst nightmare.

Mary stamped her cane on the carpet. "Luke—Heath. Stop this fighting! Immediately!"

Heath had staggered backward. One hand went to his mouth and jaw in pained disbelief. Blood had spattered his shirt. "You're just like her, aren't you? Common as dirt."

"Stop it, right now," Mary demanded. "Lucases don't fight each other. It's barbaric."

Luke was breathing hard, his fists poised to let loose again. Sophie put a restraining hand on his arm, but he shook her off, barely noticing. He looked from Heath to his grandmother. "Blood will tell, is that right?"

Mary's lips pleated. "Young man, I've warned you about that."

"Don't speak. Don't question," he said. "Hush it up, protect the family name. Well, maybe the family name isn't as noble as you like to pretend."

"Only since you came back," Heath complained. He took out the handkerchief and spat blood into it. "Don't bring us down to your level."

"You can do that on your own, just fine, can't you?" Luke said. It wasn't a question; it was an accusation.

"I'm only trying to open your eyes."

"My eyes were opened a long time ago. It's just too bad I didn't choose to see the whole picture."

Heath's gaze went to Sophie. He scoffed.

She'd backed away, toward the door. *No, no, no.* She didn't want to be a part of this family.

Luke swung around. "Sophie? It's okay. I know it's a lie."

Hot shame flooded her. She covered her face with her hands, despising Heath's smirk, but absolutely destroyed by the stunned pain that slowly came over Luke's face when she didn't deny his brother's claim.

"I'm sorry," she whispered. "I didn't know how to tell you."

He shook his head. "No, you wouldn't... Not Heath..."

Heath dabbed at his puffed lip. "Me and everyone else. Just as I told you."

Luke didn't bother to turn and look at his brother, only said, "Don't speak to me." His voice was quietly lethal.

Sophie felt disconnected again, as she often had when she was a child, abandoned in a strange place, wishing herself far away. She was vaguely aware of Mary's measuring gaze, but Luke's opinion was all that mattered. And he was withdrawing, shutting down, his face growing hard and cold, his eyes as flat and bleak as the winter plains. She knew she was losing him. He said, "Sophie," one more time, but it sounded like goodbye.

She tasted salty tears in her throat. "It was a mistake." The words were raw and bitter. Useless. There was nothing she could say to change or explain what she'd done.

She held out a hand. "Please, can't we try to—to—" Luke didn't respond and finally she gave up. Nothing left to reach for, either. Her shoulders slumped and she looked at him one more time before whispering one word: "Goodbye."

She hesitated—a split second, although the moment seemed everlasting—but Luke's expression didn't change. He didn't twitch so much as a finger to stop her. So she walked out of the room with all the dignity she could muster, not stopping, looking only straight ahead as she marched through the outer office and out the French doors that opened onto the patio.

Joe was just coming up the brick steps, carrying two pieces of apple pie topped with melting scoops of ice cream. Behind him, the barbecue continued as before—festive and gay. "Hey, Mom. I brought you and Luke some pie...."

His voice faded when he saw Sophie's face.

Dear Joe. She tried to move her mouth into a smile, but it didn't work. Or if it did, she couldn't feel it; her facial muscles were as numb as the rest of her. "We have to go," she said, her voice hollow in her ears. "Right away."

Joe faltered. "Uh, okay. Can I say 'bye to Luke?"

"No. Don't go in there. We're leaving." Even in a fractured state, Sophie was coherent enough to be grateful that Joe hadn't walked in on that terrible scene. She grabbed his arm, not caring that the wedge of pie he was carrying slid off the paper plate and splatted onto the bricks. Joe managed to place the other plate onto the low brick wall as she hauled him away.

KIKI DIDN'T KNOW if Sophie had seen her, plastered flat against one of the partially open sliding doors. Not that it mattered. After this, Sophie was toast. She was crumbs. Never, ever again would Kiki have to go on one of her visits, prying and poking at Sophie to satisfy her morbid curiosity and Heath's worries.

It was over now. They'd narrowly avoided a disaster. Or so Kiki hoped.

Though it hadn't been said in so many words, Mary's interest in Sophie and Joe had made it obvious: she'd been on the verge of accepting him as Luke's son, the Lucas heir. How fortunate that Heath had been there to put an end to that, and how gratifying that he'd vanquished Sophie entirely instead of claiming the boy as his own.

Kiki hugged herself. He was sticking with her! He loved her and he wanted to have a baby with her. Only her. Of course, whispered a small voice inside her, it helped that Mary didn't want an heir with an iffy pedigree....

That doesn't matter. Heath wouldn't have let you adopt anyway. And how right he'd been, all along.

Now that the truth about Joe Ryan was out, Heath's position was assured. As well as their baby's—who would be a *true* Lucas-Salinger.

Kiki tilted her head against the door, waiting for the elation to come—but it didn't. Funny. She should at least be relieved, and she was, just not...completely.

You dope. That's only because you're not pregnant. When you are, life will be perfect. You'll see.

Luke was talking. His words were accusing, but he sounded alienated from them, too, as if he didn't care. Kiki's heart squeezed with sympathy. Luke was an okay guy—he just wasn't as legitimate an heir as Heath. He couldn't expect to show up and take over the ranch without a fight.

"...a family tradition," he was saying. "It's getting difficult to keep track of the bloodlines, isn't it, Grandmother?"

"Don't be that way," Mary said quietly. "You were always a Lucas. There's no question of that."

"But not a Salinger."

"Hush, son."

"No. Heath had his say, so now lets get it all out, once and for all. You knew why I broke into the law office, didn't you?"

"It was a rash boyhood prank, to be sure."

"No, Grandmother. I went to get the records—the ones your attorney kept for you, about the payoff to my *real* father. I found him, you know. Took me several years, but I found him. For all the good it did me. He was exactly the man you'd expect—the type of guy who'd sleep with a married woman, get her pregnant, and then let himself be paid off to keep the situation quiet."

"Luke!" Mary said. "Stop it right now. I won't listen to this."

He went on. "What I've always wondered is...did you arrange for secret blood tests? Did my mother agree? How were you absolutely sure that my father wasn't my father?"

"Stephen Salinger comes from a fine family," Mary said tiredly, surrendering to the inevitable, "but I'm afraid they have a fatal flaw. A genetic abnormality in the seminal fluid that affects the male's ability to father children. It's why you have so few relatives from that side of the family. The Salinger strain is weak, dying off. It was a rather costly miracle that Stephen managed to father one child through an experimental insemination procedure. A second one would have been extremely unlikely.''

Even though Kiki could feel the solid carved door pressed hard against her, she was paralyzed. Heath had told her about Luke's tainted blood, how he wasn't really a proper brother. But he hadn't said a word about his own father's problem.

"Ah," Luke said. There was a long silence. Kiki waited, unable to move, afraid to think.

"Let me see if I understand. In case Heath has inherited this condition, you figured it was politic to keep me around, no matter who my father was. After all, I'm half Lucas, obviously from virile stock—I can sire a suitable heir, even if your fair-haired grandson can't. As long as no one knows about my questionable parentage, the line is intact.''

"It's not such an awful thing," Mary said.

"*You* wouldn't think so." Luke was pacing, by the sound of it. He stopped. "Why didn't you claim Joe Ryan as soon as he was born, then? Huh? Was he just your emergency heir, in case Heath couldn't get the job done? You could have told Kiki of his condition, at least, instead of blaming her for her husband's inadequacy. I'm ashamed of you, Grandmother.''

"We don't know that Heath is incapable," Mary said stubbornly. "He hasn't been tested.''

"I don't have to be," Heath said, and Kiki flinched. She'd heard *that* before. Why hadn't she seen that it was part of his disdain of weakness and imperfection? He'd never been able to admit to flaws.

"There's nothing wrong with me," Heath was insisting, getting more and more agitated.

Luke merely scoffed at him before addressing their

grandmother. "I bet Joe started looking better and better to you with every year."

Mary sighed. "It wasn't like that, Luke. I didn't know for certain that Joe was your son. And of course I knew nothing of Heath's possible involvement."

"History repeats itself, doesn't it? First my mother—"

Mary cut Luke off. "I don't want you besmirching your mother's reputation or confronting your father about any of this. He forgave Elyse before her illness. We've managed to put the unfortunate incident behind us. It's not to be spoken of in public."

"I never blamed my mother," Luke said. "You're the one who handled the bribery and secrecy."

Kiki pried her fingers off the door. Then her arms. She forced herself to take a step.

Genetic abnormalities, she was thinking. *It was the* Salinger *men who were tainted. Was that why Heath wouldn't take Dr. Cotter's tests? Because he already knew what they would show? All along he'd been saying he was the father of Sophie's son, and that was just a lie. One big gigantic lie.*

She was wild with frustration. The shrieking was building up inside her head again.

Suddenly she could move. She ran from the office, through the living room and foyer, up the wide, sweeping staircase to the grand room she shared with her husband. Tears streaming, mouth opened wide, she threw herself on the bed and buried her face in a pillow. Just in the nick of time—it muffled scream after scream after racking scream, until the pillowcase was ruined and she was limp and quiet, completely spent.

After many minutes, she rolled over to stare dully at the luxuriously appointed bedroom suite. A beautiful room in a beautiful house—the most beautiful house she'd ever seen.

Kiki jammed the pillow over her face, one last dry sob escaping her contorted mouth. How could she stay? If her position in the family wasn't secure, this would never be her home.

CHAPTER FOURTEEN

THE WHOLE WORLD HAD turned cold overnight. There was frost on the ground when Sophie got up to wander the house sometime before dawn. The yard was bleak and white and gray, like an Edward Gorey drawing from the books Joey had once loved—macabre stuff with tortured children, morose, gaunt adults, sepulchral houses and spindly trees twisted into knots and gnarls. Outside, the bare branches of the plum tree rattled like skeleton bones. Clickety-clackety-clack.

That's me, Sophie thought. Give her a shake and her shriveled heart would sound the same, rattling inside her hollowed-out shell of a body.

She turned on lights, she made coffee. She put on warm slippers and a robe. But nothing could ease her pain, nothing could chase away the blues.

I survived the first time. I can do it again.

Would Joe, she wondered. He hadn't been hardened the way she was, knowing by age six never to expect much from adults, particularly her father. She'd given her son all the love and approval she was able, but there'd been something special about his days with Luke. Joe was at the age where he needed a man around. A role model. She didn't want him emulating his grandfather, so Luke had been a godsend.

Sophie curled up on the window seat, sipping coffee and watching as a wash of soft light slowly brightened the sky and melted the frost. Soon, you wouldn't even know it had been there, except that now the bright sun wouldn't give sustenance—instead it would turn the remaining petals and leaves brittle and black.

Would Luke say goodbye, this time? Would he find the words to break it to Joe that this was the end for them? How badly would Joe be scarred by the experience?

She was unhappy with herself for opening her son to such hurt. Especially when she'd *known* the dream of a fairy-tale family was too good to be true. There were no happy endings. Just ordinary, unending life—downtrodden or precious, blessed or workaday. She would manage it. One day, she would even turn her face up to the sun and glory in it.

But for now, there was only the cold, hard frost.

"I TOLD YA," Archie said, picking over the bones of the chicken Sophie had roasted for an early dinner. "No good comes of gettin' involved with them folks. Lucas, Salinger—don't make no difference. They're all the same. High and mighty. They think the world revolves around them and the rest of us are here to jump to their bidding..."

Mentally, Sophie tuned down the Buzzsaw volume. She'd had lots of practice. Usually she could disassociate quite well from his tirades, but today, hearing the same old rant—and wondering if he wasn't a little bit right—was enough to make her scream.

How her father knew the Lucas Ranch outing had been a bust was a mystery. Maybe Joe had mentioned something. He'd been careful around her all day. Solicitous, even. In the early afternoon, when she'd been trying to take a nap on the couch—unsuccessfully, since

Luke's anguished face appeared every time she closed her eyes—Joe had come in and sat at her feet and started a tickle war. She'd laughed despite herself, and they'd wound up wrestling around the way they used to, not so long ago. Sneakily, she'd disguised her hugs as wrestling moves, and he'd been affectionate enough to let her. After she'd pleaded uncle, they'd sprawled out on the couch again and talked. He'd answered her questions and even volunteered information about his current reading material—a classic sci-fi book called *The Ender*—how his French teacher was a dope, Fletch's stupid pet dander allergy and Chelsey Greene, the girl Joe most certainly did *not* like even though she'd been calling the house six times a day.

Her son was growing up, and her father was growing old.

Sophie sighed, tucked in her uniform shirt and stooped to kiss Archie's forehead. She tapped his shoulder. "Thanks for watching out for me, Dad."

Momentarily flustered, he said, "Well, sure, you're my girl, ain'tcha? I gotta see that you keep on your toes, partickally around them Lucases."

Sophie rolled her eyes. "Whatever."

Luke had been good to her, for as long as he could. Mary Lucas, too. Heath had been vicious, but she'd given him the ammunition.

She holstered her pistol, a semiautomatic Smith & Wesson she'd bought with her tax refund, her first year on the job. The crummy department-issued revolver Ed Warren had chosen—the cheapskate—was locked away in a metal box in her closet. Watching herself in the hallway mirror, she smoothed her braided hair and put on her hat. *Put on your game face, too, Deputy. You have work to do. No distractions allowed.*

She grabbed her jacket off the hook and called out to her son. "I'm leaving for work now, Joe. Remember to do the dishes. And stay home—I don't want you out on a school night."

He appeared in the open doorway. "Can't I even go to Fletcher's to play basketball? I'll be back before dark."

Sophie studied him, finding no reason to say no except for a prickly sense of mother's intuition that she wanted him home and safe. "Not tonight. Stay and keep your grandpa company, okay?"

Big sigh. "Okay."

She kissed him. On the cheek. Gave him a squeeze. He was taller than her now, and going to be even taller in another few months. Her heart skipped a beat, just looking at him, because he was so like Luke, not Heath. Even though the Salinger brothers were tall and looked somewhat alike, they were vastly different in action and character. When she'd seen the family photograph in the office, it was apparent that Heath was a smooth Salinger, while Luke took after the active, electric Lucas side of the family. But they were still similar enough that she couldn't be certain who was Joe's father. Maybe she never would.

Don't put yourself through that torture again. You've got to stop dwelling on it.

Sophie repeated her goodbyes and walked out the door, berating herself for her weaknesses. Would she never stop hoping? She thought she had, in the coldest part of the morning. Now, she didn't know.

The temperature was dropping again. She moved briskly to the police cruiser, planning to spend as little time as possible checking in at headquarters since Ed Warren had already called her in midmorning for a testy meeting with the Bureau of Land Management folks. They thought the sheriff wasn't pursuing the case strongly enough, and Sophie was inclined to agree. A wild horse rescue group was setting up a reward for information on the killings, which was good, even though Sophie had her own ideas on how to solve the case. Too bad the sheriff was being his typical self, negative and dismissive about her suggestions. She wanted solitude and space tonight, not Ed's heavy breathing down her neck.

Kiki Salinger appeared out of the long shadows. She approached the car timidly. "Sophie?" she said, one level above a whisper. "Can we talk?"

Sophie squinted an eye at her watch. "Sure. I have some time before my shift starts."

Kiki was wearing a cable-stitched cardigan, so big it looked like she'd wrapped it twice around her body. Her arms were crisscrossed over her chest, hands tucked into the sleeves. Her face was strained; she looked wretched.

"Kiki, what's wrong?"

The slender brunette shivered. "Could we get in the car? I'm so cold."

"Of course." They climbed in and Sophie revved the engine, flipping on the heater and aiming the vents at Kiki, who was as pale as chalk with no visible makeup except for dark smudges under her eyes and faint stains around her lips where she'd chewed off her red lipstick. Sophie squeezed her friend's knee. "What's wrong, Kiki? You seem—" *Like the walking dead.* "You seem upset. Can I help?"

"I don't think so." Even Kiki's voice was faint. There was a long pause before she added, "But maybe I can help you."

"How?"

"To warn you. About the Salinger boys." Her laugh was humorless, filled only with pain and maybe a touch of angry retribution. "Heath's been playing me for a fool. I guess I am one. I've been trying to please him ever since we got married and it's all just—just—*crap*."

Sophie blinked. That wasn't like Kiki. She twisted around in her seat to get a better look at her. "What are you talking about?"

"The Salingers. The Lucases. They lie. They mislead you. They're good at it—keeping secrets, letting you know only what they want you to know, telling you what you want to hear. Heath's been doing it to me for years and years and I never even—" Her voice cracked. Her fingers clenched inside the sweater sleeves. "I have to be honest. Now. I *did* suspect. But I didn't care. I went along with whatever he asked me to do, because I really believed that he loved me and wanted us to have a b-baby."

"What did he ask you to do?" Sophie said, very carefully.

"Spy on you and Joe, mostly."

"Spy on us? For what purpose?"

"Well, because—" Kiki shook her head. "I *thought* it was because we had to keep an eye on you, to make sure either you didn't go to Mary Lucas and make demands or that she didn't take an interest in Joe. Heath also wanted to know if you were in touch with Luke, persuading him to come home."

"You *thought*? Was there another reason?" So far, Kiki wasn't revealing anything that Sophie hadn't already suspected.

"Heath told me he's Joe's father—a long time ago. I don't know if he believes it himself, because that would be pretty damn delusional, but I *did* believe him, so I decided I had to keep an eye on you two. In case Heath decided—'' A dry, gulping sob stole the rest of the explanation, but Sophie could guess. Kiki was afraid that Heath would claim Joe out of his own self-interests, just as Sophie had been.

"Oh. I see." Sophie winced. "I'm sorry I never confessed to you about that, Kiki. There didn't seem to be a point. It happened once, years before he met you...." She paused, struck by a realization. "Wait a minute. You say Heath told you he was the father, but that would be delusional. Why?"

For a moment, Kiki was baffled. Then her face cleared. "I guess you missed that part of it."

Sophie was lost. "What part?"

"Heath is—" Tears welled in Kiki's eyes. "He's sterile. Most likely."

The news slammed into Sophie like a locomotive. She was too flattened to grasp it, too stunned to believe. "Sterile?"

"We've been trying for a baby ever since we got married. I've had all the tests. Heath wouldn't, because he said he already had proof."

"Joe," Sophie whispered.

Suddenly Kiki's anger rose to a shrieking fury. "That was a lie! All a lie! He let me think there was something wrong with me, and it was him. He's the one who's defective." She let out a howl and buried her face in her hands, rocking back and forth in the car seat, muttering angry words at herself.

Sophie wrapped her arms around Kiki, soothing her with motherly words. But inside, she was cautiously rejoicing. She didn't *quite* dare to believe it completely, but maybe, maybe...

She didn't want to push Kiki when her friend was already in such a distraught state. Yet she had to know. "I still don't understand. Why are you sure *now* that Heath lied to you?"

Kiki snuffled, her head laid on Sophie's shoulder. "After you left, Grandmother Lucas admitted it to Luke. She said that was why she knew Stephen Salinger wasn't Luke's biological father—its a kind of genetic abnormality that does something weird to their semen. Most of the Salingers have it, and it makes producing babies very difficult. Heath's mother got pregnant with him only after some sort of complicated procedure." She uttered a sound that was half ironic laugh, half hiccup. "Yep. Salinger babies are very, very difficult. I should know."

Sophie patted her. "I'm so sorry for you, honey. I know how much you wanted a baby."

"It wasn't really because of the inheritance," Kiki whispered. "I just wanted a home and a family and security."

I know, Sophie thought. *Oh, God, do I know.*

Kiki moaned. "Heath always gloated about Luke not being a real Salinger. But I guess the tables are turned now."

"What do you mean?"

Kiki's head came up. "I keep forgetting you didn't hear that part. Luke's mother had an affair—Luke's not really Stephen Salinger's son. All these years, he's been mad at Grandmother Lucas for paying off his biological father to keep him quiet."

Sophie's leaden hands dropped into her lap. What? She couldn't process another revelation. It was too much to take in.

She inhaled. Heath was a Salinger. Luke wasn't.

Because he was a Salinger, Heath was sterile.

And Luke was not.

It seemed as though a huge weight lifted from Sophie's heavy heart. *Luke was Joey's father.* She had to believe it now. She had to.

But wait. If she knew it, and Kiki and Heath knew it, Luke certainly knew it too. Why hadn't he come to tell her? Did he actually believe Heath's lies about the other men?

No. She didn't think so. It was Heath Luke couldn't forgive her for. Even knowing that Joey was his son, he hadn't come to them because he couldn't stomach her betrayal.

Sophie tilted back her head, biting her lip. This was the prototype good news, bad news situation.

Sucking in a wet breath, Kiki sat up and wiped her face. "Can you forgive me for being so rotten and sneaky about you and Joe? I lied to you about so many things, just because I was scared of what would happen to me. I've been so selfish, and I'm sorry."

"I understand," Sophie said. She really did.

"Even though I haven't been a true friend to you, I feel like you're the only real friend I have. That's why I wanted to warn you about Luke."

Sophie's head snapped around. "Warn me?"

Kiki grimaced, looking guilty and uncomfortable. "When we were at the Thunderhead, I overheard Demon Bradshaw and some of the Mustangs talking about Luke."

"What did they say?"

"Stuff about you distracting Luke from their plan. Or the other way around—I forget."

Sophie gripped the steering wheel to stop herself from grabbing at Kiki and shaking the story out of her.

"Try to remember everything, exactly. It's very important."

"It was noisy in the bar, so I couldn't hear every word. Mostly they were leering after women. But then Demon mentioned guns and that got my attention. He said Luke shouldn't use such a fancy rifle, next time. I don't know what they meant, but its probably criminal."

For one instant, Sophie closed her eyes, denying it. "He called Luke by name?"

"I *think* so. No, I'm wrong. First he called him Maverick…" Kiki paused, frowning.

Sophie watched her closely.

"And then, when I could hear again, he called him by his last name. You know, the way guys do."

Sophie prodded. "Demon's exact words were…"

Kiki concentrated. "He said, 'Next time, Salinger better leave the fancy rifle at home.' Then they started talking about guns and bullets and scopes, until one of them mentioned ballistics, and, uh—" She stopped suddenly, her eyes going wide. She pressed her cuffed fist to her mouth.

Sophie barely noticed. She'd been struck by a realization—one that obviously hadn't occurred to Kiki.

Luke wasn't the only "Salinger."

Combined with the snippet of conversation she and Luke had overheard from the Mustangs—particularly the mention of the lake—it wasn't too wild a guess to assume that Heath was conspiring with Demon and his pals.

She glanced at Kiki. The poor woman was already devastated enough. How was she ever going to handle it if criminal charges were brought against her husband?

Don't jump the gun, Deputy. You haven't broken the case yet.

"Kiki, you're going to have to cooperate with me on this," Sophie said, as gently as she could. The other woman was distracted, staring blankly across the yard at the freshly painted shed. "I don't want you repeating this story to anyone, but particularly not your husband." Kiki didn't respond. Sophie's stomach dropped. "Unless you already have."

Kiki's voice wavered. "I did. I told him about Luke getting involved with the Mustangs again, and he—he—" She clamped her mouth shut, silently shaking her head.

"That should be okay," Sophie said after a moment's thought. Heath was probably thrilled that she'd fingered Luke as the co-conspirator. "But it's vital that you don't tell him that you've told me, understand?"

Kiki blinked. "Why?"

"Because this is related to an ongoing investigation. It has to be kept quiet until I find out exactly what crime they're planning." Or have already committed, Sophie added silently, thinking of the dreadful scene on the mountainside.

"Okay. Sure. I'll keep it quiet."

"Thanks for coming to me, Kiki."

Kiki turned her glistening eyes toward Sophie. "I owed you. I know you loved him, so it probably doesn't seem like I've done you a favor, but you're better off knowing the truth about Luke."

I am, Sophie thought. But it was a melancholy knowledge, because now that she was sure of Luke, the truth about her drunken tryst with Heath had destroyed his faith in *her.*

Why did they call irony delicious? she wondered distractedly. It wasn't delicious. It was sour, acid—a bitter pill to swallow.

But still not as corrosive as maintaining the secret would have been.

Sophie shook herself. She took her hat off the dash and slipped it on. "Can I give you a ride, Kiki?"

Her friend was staring out the windshield again, still preoccupied. "No," she said at length. "I have my car." She opened the passenger door and slipped out.

Sophie ducked her head to see Kiki's face. "You're sure you're okay to drive? You don't seem like yourself."

Kiki was taking in deep drafts of the cold night air. "I will be. Yes, I will. I'm going to be okay, real soon."

"You can stay over at my house, you know, any time you want."

"Thank you," Kiki said, and she smiled sadly, her needy gaze taking in the humble white cottage with its cheerful splashes of trim—plum, emerald, and pure bold electric blue.

A COUPLE OF HOURS LATER, Luke arrived at the house on his motorcycle. He'd ridden far out into the countryside, trying to get his head straight. There was still a slim possibility that Heath could be Joe's father, and Luke had to know whether or not that mattered to him. Whether or not he could get past the wretched pain of Sophie's infidelity and truly, completely forgive her.

One hundred miles from Treetop, speeding along a lonesome road that cut through a dry plain dotted with nothing but greasewood and sagebrush, he'd understood that he was running away again. Running away from the woman he loved, the son he'd grown to cherish. Running to a whole lot of lonely nothingness.

He loved them both. That was the essential truth. The rest of it was extraneous. It could be dealt with.

He'd turned around so fast he'd almost tipped the bike over on the cracked pavement, and wouldn't that have been a fine end to his rootless meandering?

That put a good scare into him, and he'd driven more safely on the way home, wearing the helmet he'd neglected to don at the start. He was a father now. He had to set an example. He had to keep himself safe so he could keep Sophie and Joe safe. He'd give up his life only for them.

When he arrived at Sophie's, he saw right off that the car was gone, but he parked anyway and headed toward the house. He was on the porch when he noticed a movement by the shed out of his peripheral vision.

The rifle, he thought at once. With all else that had happened, he'd forgotten about it.

He vaulted over the porch railing. Someone darted around the corner of the shed. He moved swiftly, grabbing hold of the lurker and pulling him—her—to her feet. "Kiki! What on earth are you doing here?"

When she couldn't wrench herself out of his grip, she went limp, begging him not to hurt her. He was baffled enough to let her go. She backed off two steps, her face crumpling as she burst into tears.

"Aw, hell." He draped an arm around her shaking shoulders and walked her toward the porch. When they stepped into the lighted driveway, she hid her face against his chest. He soothed her, patting her back like a child till she was gulping at air, trying to talk.

"I did—didn't know what I was— I shouldn't have believed— It was wrong, I know it was wrong, b-but I—"

"Kiki, calm down. Take a breath and speak slowly. Why are you here?"

Her puffy eyelids blinked. "You saw. I was trying to break into the shed."

"Why?"

"T-to get the gun."

"The rifle? Did *you* put it there?"

She gasped. "You know about it?"

"I spotted it the other day. Why did you leave it there?"

Kiki wouldn't answer.

"Because Heath told you to," Luke guessed.

She took a shaky breath, then finally nodded.

"Why did he do that?"

"I don't know. He told me it was to cause trouble for Sophie and her dad. And you. So one day when no one was home, I got the key from Sophie's sewing basket and put the rifle in the shed. Heath's going to report it stolen, because he said you'd leave town again if the situation got complicated." She lifted her face, leached of color by the contrast of black night and bright light. "When I was talking to Sophie earlier, I realized Heath was probably lying to me about that, too, so I came back to get the gun. I've done so many stupid things, but at least this one I could correct. Except the shed's still locked and I can't get the key."

"Never mind that. Sophie's on duty?"

"Uh-huh."

"What did you two talk about?"

Kiki's eyes evaded his, but she admitted in a low tone, "I warned her about you."

"Warned her?"

"About you getting involved with Demon and the Mustangs!" she said, defiant. Suddenly she stamped on

his foot, grinding her heel into his instep in an effort to
get away, but the attempt was halfhearted. He held onto
her, demanding that she repeat the conversation with
Sophie.

After she did, he knew where Sophie was. And that
she might be in trouble. He marched Kiki up to the
house and banged on the door. When Buzzsaw answered, he shoved Kiki inside and told the man to look
after her and by no means to let her go. Then he asked
for a weapon.

"I don't have one," Buzzsaw said, sort of sheepishly.
"Sophie got a bee in her bonnet about it being too dangerous now that I don't see so well."

"Glad to hear it," Luke said, and considering his
previous suspicions he sincerely meant it, even though
that also meant he was going after Sophie unarmed.

Except for the Harley, a speeding bullet composed of
hot steel and burning rubber.

HIS LITTLE WIFE WASN'T STUPID, but she was gullible
and pliable. Giving her the rifle had been a risky move,
particularly once she realized why he'd done it—to im-
plicate that foolish old man who couldn't keep his
mouth shut. No one would believe a drunk like that, no
matter what he said. When it all came tumbling down,
Kiki would back her loving husband up all the way.
She knew which side her bread was buttered on.

He paced through the house, wishing he knew where
Luke and Sophie were tonight. The two of them had
started out as annoyances that he'd easily brushed aside
by planting seeds of doubt that grew and grew and grew
with every misleading statement he'd fed them. Kiki
had come in handy there, too, cozying up to Sophie so

nicely because she believed that he'd actually fathered the brat.

Hell, maybe he had. That rubbish about the defective Salinger genes was way off base. Way off base. Luke was the brother with the abnormal bloodlines.

Even if he was the father, it didn't matter. It wasn't *supposed* to, anyway. He'd been so sure that Mary would never want to take a bastard into the family, particularly when the mother was so low class.

Sophie. The tramp was the true thorn in his side. Why couldn't she just stay in her place? She had no business trying to worm her way onto the Lucas Ranch with that brat of hers in tow.

But it wouldn't be long now. Tomorrow he'd report the Steen Scout stolen, giving Ed Warren ample reason to fire his lady deputy for withholding evidence. Without her agitating for a complete investigation, a few scrawny dead mustangs would soon be forgotten. And if he had any luck, the cheap little slut would drag his half brother down with her.

Heath strode into the study, rubbing the lump on his jaw as he remembered the satisfying scene of emotional destruction on the day of the barbecue. Ha! So much for Sophie and Luke—both of them too "noble" to realize how he'd manipulated them at every turn.

IN THE COLD MOONLIGHT, Hidden Lake glistened like a sapphire. Other than for the occasional silken ripple, the surface was placid. No wind, Sophie thought from her position on the red granite cliffside. Even the smallest sounds would carry in the thin mountain air. She'd have to be extremely cautious.

Her patrol car was parked a half mile away, hidden in the underbrush. She'd hiked in through the forest, because there was only the one narrow road and no way to hide either her or her vehicle from possible activity along the route.

She didn't have much of a plan. She wasn't even particularly expecting there to be anything to observe. Surely the mustang killers would be lying low, so soon after their last strike. But you never knew. A few hours of surveillance wouldn't hurt.

The Feds had been checking the area as well, by helicopter, and they'd reported that the remaining wild horses had moved higher up into the hills, deeper onto BLM land. It was a loss that hurt. She wondered if they'd ever come back.

Thirty minutes passed, then an hour. The air was bitingly cold. Her toes were numb, the muscles in her thighs clenched into knots. She stood slowly, keeping low behind a patch of choke-cherry as she stretched her legs, then did a few deep knee bends to limber up. After another ten minutes of deep silence, she clambered to a lower position on the cliff, sure that nothing was going to happen.

At first, she mistook the rumble for thunder. Then headlights cut through the darkness. She'd expected motorcycles, but the lights were a matched pair. A couple of seconds later a pickup truck came into view.

She ducked behind a boulder, maybe fifteen feet up the steep hillside above the grassy clearing. She'd called in her position before leaving the car and had the radio on her belt—if it would work in these hills—but decided to play it cautious and hold her position for now. No need for backup yet. Wait and see.

Two men got out of the truck's cab. When the interior light came on, she recognized Demon's fox-sharp features and tattooed forearms. The bearded driver was

Drizz. A third jumped out of the bed of the truck. She only saw him in silhouette, but the bulky shape was enough to ID Snake Carson.

Sophie's pulse was racing, but her every thought was cool and calculated. Three to one. Not the best odds. She dropped a hand to her sidearm, unsnapping the flap of the holster. Unless you counted Mr. Smith and Mr. Wesson.

Demon spat on the ground. "This is it. The perfect place. No one comes here. Hell, they don't even know about it."

Drizz scratched his sparse blond beard. He wasn't convinced. "If there's a road, someone knows."

"You saw how grown over it is."

"It's still a road on public land. I think we should stick to the original plan. Keep the stuff on Salinger's land until we're ready to transport, the way he agreed. Else ways, all the trouble you took clearing out the mustangs was for nothing."

Snake came around the truck, flexing his biceps. "Yeah, but he's weaseling out on us now that the Feds and Deputy Sophie are nosing around."

"Those damn horses." Demon swore. "Anyway, this is easier, right here by the lake. We load the crates on and off the float plane. No hassle."

Drizz's posture became defiant. The air was thick with tension and testosterone. "It's too risky. A fisherman or a tree hugger could come across the crates and get curious. We have to keep them on private land."

Sophie was crouched on her heels, her back pressed to the rock. Occasionally she risked a quick glance at the trio. They'd strutted around while they talked, and now stood so close she could have jumped down among them.

Their voices grew louder as they began to argue.

No evidence yet, Sophie thought, other than hearsay. She'd have to do better than that before making arrests. Her wisest move would be to keep hidden, listen to their plans and set up a proper stakeout to catch them with the goods. The department had long suspected Demon of dealing illegal firearms from his shabby bike shop— it would be a major coup for her to instigate sweeping arrests, even though Sheriff Warren would be sure to steal the glory.

The men were moving away, still going back and forth about the lake's suitability. "You even sure a float plane can land here?" Drizz demanded as they crashed through the border of evergreens to get a better look.

Here's my chance. Even before the thought was fully formed, Sophie was reacting on her trained instincts. Moving efficiently, she dropped down a smooth slope of red rock, landing on a ledge with a small crunch of pebbles.

"Did you hear anything?" Drizz said, his voice carrying from the trees. She crouched, exposed but motionless.

"It was nothing," Demon said. "Probably a squirrel, you girl." He laughed and continued bashing through the trees.

Covered by the noise, Sophie jumped to the ground with a soft thud. All she wanted was a peek into the bed of the pickup truck. It would take her ten seconds.

Covered by shadows, she moved slinkily to the vehicle. There were two crates inside. She hoisted herself up on her elbows to reach them, but they were nailed shut. Damn.

"Look at this," said a soft, sibilant voice behind her. A chill ran along Sophie's spine. She was in an awkward position, hung up on the side panel of the pickup truck.

The voices by the lake continued, covering the sound of rustling grass as he drew nearer. "Don't move, Deputy. I have a gun." Something hard and pointed prodded the small of her back.

She relaxed her muscles and let herself slip to the ground. Out of the corner of an eye, she saw that it was Drizz who'd circled back to come up behind her.

"I said *don't move.*"

She weakened her voice. "N-no, sir." Men always underestimated her, and she'd learned to use their gender prejudices to her advantage. The risky element was whether or not Drizz had a gun. From past experiences with Demon and Snake, she could calculate their actions and reactions. Drizz was an unknown factor.

"Hey, guys," he yelled. "I caught us a squirrel."

Demon and Snake hooted and hollered as they ran back to the truck, crashing through the trees. It was a good distraction. Sophie took the chance.

She whirled on Drizz, pulling her sidearm so fast he barely had time to realize what she'd done. He said, "Shit," his eyes narrowing as he aimed his weapon at her gut.

It was a branch.

He swung it, down low. She knocked it aside with a quick kick, lunging toward Drizz in the same motion. He was tall but skinny, unprepared for her aggression. She took his knees out with another kick and suddenly he was on the ground, yelling at the top of his lungs as she knelt over him, pinning him with a knee while she wrenched one of his arms behind his back.

Demon and Snake appeared. Sophie glanced up, checking for weapons, and Drizz managed to whip around beneath her, as wriggly as an eel. He slammed his elbow into her gut and all the air went out of her lungs. She fell back onto her rump. *"Go!"* he shouted, managing to stagger to his feet. She recovered her balance, grabbed him by the belt and the scrawny blond ponytail sticking out of his shirt collar and slammed him to the ground again.

When they saw she'd drawn a gun, Demon and Snake shot off in different directions instead of attacking her. Dumb move, but just what Sophie had hoped for. They were idiots, and they were selfish. Their first thought was to try and save themselves. She snapped one cuff around Drizz's wrist, but he was flailing the other arm and she couldn't get a hold on it. She kept on top of him, riding him like a bronco as they struggled in the grass. Right beside them, practically in Sophie's ear, the pickup truck roared to life.

Drizz's head jerked up. He shouted, cursing Demon for leaving without him. Sophie yanked him sideways, away from the wheels as the truck reversed, flattening brush and saplings with a loud crackle.

She locked the second cuff in place and gave Drizz a shove, pushing his face into the ground. She stood, panting for breath. Headlights washed over her as Demon swung the truck around. She could do nothing; she'd lost her weapon in the grass during the tussle with Drizz. Demon gunned the engine, grinding his way out of the tangled underbrush.

Snake was climbing the cliff. Or trying to. Instead of taking the easy route, he'd gone straight up and was now stuck halfway, clinging to the sheer face of the red granite. In a minute or two, he'd figure out that he had to retrace his route, but Sophie didn't have time to worry about him. She wanted Demon.

It took her only seconds to find her semiautomatic in the long grass, but every moment was precious. The pickup came free with a crackle of dry branches. It zoomed by, bucking over the rough trail as she lifted her gun and aimed for a tire.

Her finger froze on the trigger. There was another light, oncoming.

The headlamp of a motorcycle.

And it was moving fast, the driver hunched low in the saddle as the machine rocketed over bumps and gullies.

The two vehicles rushed toward each other like knights on chargers. Trailing, Sophie ran along the path at top speed. She was screaming Luke's name.

The terrible noise of racing engines filled the air. Neither vehicle was yielding. They were twenty yards apart...ten...

Time slowed for Sophie. The sound of her panting rose above the roar of the vehicles. She ran, getting nowhere. She pleaded, with nobody to hear.

A collision was imminent.

If Luke...if Luke was hit he would...

And she would die, too.

At the last moment, Demon veered the pickup to the left, tearing into the grass. He jerked the wheel, but his speed was too fast—he lost control. The truck crashed into a large boulder with a screeching crunch of metal against stone.

Sophie slammed to a stop.

Luke sped past her in a rush of wind, the motorcycle a streaming arrow of silver and black. The morning of his return came back to her with such clarity she thought she could feel the hot gush of coffee spilling down her shirtfront. The tingle of electricity. The thrill that overwhelmed her fear.

Luke, she said soundlessly, wheeling around to watch.

The motorcycle slowed, turned.

This time, he was coming back.

CHAPTER FIFTEEN

STAY IN CONTROL, Sophie told herself as she went about her job as if she hadn't just seen both her life and Luke's pass before her eyes. Demon had smashed his face against the steering wheel. His nose was already swelling; blood gushed from a gash on his forehead. He put up a token fight when she hauled him out and cuffed him to the door handle. She pocketed the truck's keys, just in case.

That was it for the handcuffs, but she had spare Flex-cuffs—a length of plastic cable tie—with Snake's name on it. She walked back toward the lake in time to see Luke greeting the old Mustang when he stumbled off the cliff side.

She ignored Snake's blustering as she secured him and ordered him to get down on the ground near Drizz, who was trying to rise to his knees. Luke gave the long-haired crook a not-too-gentle shove with the toe of his boot, sending him sprawling.

She read them their rights, all too aware of Luke watching and listening. Her heartbeat was still going like the dickens. When she'd finished, she tried her radio to call for backup, but they were out of range. She'd have to send Luke to get her car.

"Luke. Over here." She flicked her chin to a halfway point between the prisoners, who were alternating between cursing her and cursing each other. There was a certain satisfaction in seeing them trussed up like Thanksgiving turkeys.

Luke followed her, looking just as big and dangerous as his former gang members in close-fitting jeans and the worn leather vest. His hair stood on end and his scowl would have really made an impression if it weren't for his eyes.

They were burning.

Absently, Sophie rubbed the corresponding tingle in her butt before turning on him. "What was that stunt, huh? You trying to kill yourself?"

"You didn't see me in *Midnight Riders?*" he said. "I've performed the stunt before. I knew what I was doing. The risk was minimal."

"You're a maniac! What if Demon hadn't turned? I could strangle you with my bare hands for scaring me like that." She reached up for him, her teeth gritted, her fingers spread.

He caught her hands as they closed around his neck. "I had it under control. Besides, you know you don't want to kill me."

"No," she admitted. His vital life force beat beneath her fingertips. She was too relieved to have him beside her in one piece to be angry.

"You want to kiss me."

She rested her forehead against his chest. "I can't do that. I'm on the job."

"Deputies do it in uniform," he said, a small smile lifting one side of his mouth.

"You're too much." She pushed herself away from him, then changed her mind and grabbed his hand. "Let's go see what's in the truck."

They hauled Snake and Drizz to their feet and marched them over to the ditched truck. Luke found a crowbar and pried up the lid on one of the wooden crates. "Automatic weapons," Sophie said, not surprised in the least. "Machine guns—hmm, illegally altered—semiautomatics, even a few midnight specials. What do you want to bet these are all hot as blazes?"

"Which should take care of these guys for a few years."

"Yeah." Sophie dropped the lid back in place. She fingered a splinter in the rough wood.

Luke picked up on her hesitation. "What's wrong?"

"I hate to tell you this...."

He nodded. "Go on."

"These three—" she pointed to the prisoners, who were all sitting in the grass, out of earshot "—are in league with Heath. I heard them talking about it. We'll see what they say during interrogation, of course, but the way I figure it, they agreed to get rid of the wild horses in return for Heath looking the other way whenever they stashed their shipments on Lucas land."

Luke nodded, his expression dismal.

"The thing is, unless one of them caves, I have no real evidence against Heath."

The light in Luke's eyes had dimmed. It was his brother, after all, even if circumstances had turned them into rivals, of a sort. He glanced at Sophie. "Would you lock him up if you could?"

Her pulse stuttered. Was Luke asking if she had any feelings left for Heath? Or was he, like his grandmother, hoping to prevent a family scandal?

"This is my job," she said. "I'm sworn to uphold the law." She moistened her lips. "The answer is yes. I'm going to do everything I can to see that your brother is arrested. What he did was unforgivable."

Not to her. To the wild horses.

She looked at Luke. "I'm sorry. That's the way it has to be."

"The rifle you were asking about," he said. "Would that do?"

"What do you mean?"

He didn't hesitate. "It's in your shed."

DAYS PASSED. Busy days. By the end of the month, Sophie had her end of the case pretty well wrapped up and handed over to the ATF, the BLM and the Sweetwater County D.A. The rifle in her shed had been wiped clean of fingerprints, but tests showed it to be the weapon that had killed one of the mustangs. Ballistics also matched one of Demon's rifles to the second slug shed collected at the scene.

Kiki had agreed to testify that Heath had asked her to place the Steen Scout in the Ryans' shed. Demon claimed that it had been Heath who'd engineered the "removal" of the wild horses, while Heath was pleading innocence to everything, even as the evidence against him continued to accumulate. The unfortunate truth was that a high-priced lawyer would probably get him off with steep fines and a minimum of jail time. Justice was all too often truncated for those who could afford to work the system.

Sheriff Ed Warren, of course, was hogging the limelight. Sophie didn't care. She was guessing that Heath had greased Ed's palm along the way with big election donations, which was why he'd downplayed the mustang killings from the start. She also suspected that Mary Lucas knew it too…and wasn't pleased that the sheriff had misplaced his loyalties, even if it was to her own grandson. It would be interesting to see how *that* shook out.

As for her personal life, well, that was on hold. Kiki had stayed with the Ryans for a couple of days, waffling back and forth over what to do before finally agreeing to testify against Heath. She and Sophie had made overtures toward becoming true friends, with no lies between them. When Kiki mentioned moving out—there really wasn't room in the cottage for a guest—Sophie sent her to Miss Bellew's boardinghouse. Heath was trying to woo her back home with apologies and roses, but so far Kiki was standing tough, talking about finding a job and an apartment of her own.

Meanwhile, Joe had asked about Luke a couple of times. Sophie had no real answer to give him. She'd delayed telling him about the revelations regarding his parentage, hoping that it was something she and Luke could do together. *If* it was true that Heath was one-hundred-percent sterile—which they might never know—and *if*—more importantly—Luke believed, or wanted to believe, that he was the father. So far...

No Luke.

He was occupied with the ranch, she told herself. Busy settling family affairs, which had proved to be more tangled than they'd ever imagined. When he was ready, if he could forgive, he would come to her.

She hoped.

She prayed.

She dreamed.

Autumn was quickly giving way to winter. On a Friday afternoon in the first week of October, they had their first snow of the season—a swirl of powder puff flakes that melted as soon as they touched the ground. Sophie thought of Hidden Lake, the tranquil, unspoiled gem that would soon be tucked under a mantle of crystalline snow. Saturday morning, she roused Joe out of bed early and told him to get out his backpack—they were going camping one more time before winter arrived full force and the mountain roads became impassable.

It turned out to be a glorious day—crisp and clear. Hidden Lake sparkled in the sunshine, cold but shockingly bright blue. They found a small clearing on a bank above the water to set up camp, then went hiking in the mountains for a couple of hours, Joe taking great glee in the fact that he could now outpace his mother. "No fair," she complained. "You've got longer legs."

Like your dad, she wanted to say.

Maybe it was time to tell him the truth. She'd learned long ago that it didn't pay to put her life on hold, waiting for another person to tell you which direction to take.

But I only want a companion, she thought, *someone to lean on when I'm tired, to give me a boost when I think I cant make it, to share the beauty and sorrow and miracle of life.*

Well, she had her son. He even let her hold his hand as they marched, singing, into camp.

And there—there was Luke.

Sophie stopped dead in her tracks.

Joe bounded right up to him. "Hey, Luke—you should have been there! We climbed so high we saw antelope, a whole herd of them. I was wishing we'd see a grizzly too, but Mom made me wear a bell on my pack like a little baby."

"Your mom's a smart lady. You wouldn't really want to run into a grizzly, Joe."

"I s'pose not, but it might be kinda cool. I bet I could outrun one."

"Spare me from another daredevil," Sophie said,

shrugging out from under her backpack. Luke grabbed hold and lifted it away and suddenly she felt as light as the antelope that had bounded on springs through the fallow slopes. It was a good thing her tired, sore feet kept her firmly planted on the ground.

She eyed Luke. He wore sunglasses and an unbuttoned shearling jacket, with a blue bandanna covering his hair pirate-style, tied in a flippy little knot at the back of his head. "What are you doing here?" she asked, deciding to be blunt. "Looking for another game of chicken?" She leaned close to whisper, her hand on his sleeve, "I'm warning you now. If you ever teach Joey that trick, I really will strangle you."

Luke's brows rose beyond the frame of his shades. "Buzzsaw and I had a little chat. Once I finally got him to concede that maybe not *all* Lucases were bad, he told me where you went willingly enough. I thought I'd better check up on you."

"Mmm." She stayed noncommittal, keeping an eye on him while she busied herself with the camping gear.

"Joe, why don't you go and collect firewood?" Luke said, making Sophie's stomach pinch. She looked down, concentrating on unpacking the cooking supplies. Small gas stove. Cleverly fitted pots and pans. A zip-locked bag of freeze-dried veggies, followed by one of rice. Joe was going to complain when she said they were having casserole.

Minutes that seemed like hours went by, broken only by the sounds of Joe searching through the trees for deadwood. "Sophie, are you ever going to look at me?" Luke finally asked.

"Can't see you with those sunglasses on."

He slipped them off. "Is that better?"

She was drawn like steel to his magnetic eyes. For

all her declaration-of-independence resolutions, nothing had changed. Luke was her light o' love, and he would be until the day she died.

Her lips moved. "Lots better."

"Sweet Sophie." He came over and crouched beside her. "You'll always be my brown-eyed girl."

A sob caught in her throat. "I guess I will. But only if you'll be my blue-eyed boy."

He kissed her, and for the first time in days she began to believe that it was going to be okay between them. She gripped his shoulders, tasting the musk of his skin and the heated flavor of his mouth. "Mmm."

He licked his tongue along her lips. Desire opened inside her, rushing hard like an overflowing dam. Too fast, but she loved it. Their attraction hadn't lessened; they were as wild for each other as ever. As always.

Luke reached under her fleece jacket and flannel shirt, feeling for her breasts. She caught his wrists. "Luke. Joe is here."

"He's in the woods. It's okay. I have father radar."

The words stopped her for a moment, but then she tugged at him. *Had he really meant that, or was he only teasing?* "C'mon, Luke, please. This is too distracting."

"So?"

"You know we have to—" She stopped. Brushed the back of her hand across his cheek. Stubble. He hadn't shaved that morning. And his eyes were still shadowed as well. She could only guess what turmoil he'd been through lately. "You're avoiding it. Purposely diverting me."

Luke didn't answer. He wound his arms around her and held her close, his face buried in her hair.

"You've never wanted to talk about the secrets in

your past," she went on. "You'd talk about everything else, with enough zest for ten men. Harleys versus Indians. Astronomy, botany, aerodynamics. How much methane gas is emitted by cows, for Pete's sake! All that debating and arguing and persuading, but you'd rarely talk about yourself. Your inner self."

"I did with you," he said, toying with her hair. "Remember how it was? Lying together in the high pasture up at Boyer's Rock?"

"I remember lots of touching and feeling going on."

"And afterward...building castles in the sky."

"Yeah." Her voice softened. "But it turns out that wood and stone make a better shelter than vapor."

"That's okay, Soph. My dreams are solid now too."

"Good. So tell me about your biological father." It was a place to start.

He let go of her and sat nearby, his eyes getting remote until he looked at her and let them refill with emotion. "Guess what? It was Heath who started it, when we were teenagers. Somehow, rummaging around Grandmother's office—on the sly, I suppose—he'd come across a letter that contained a piece of curious information regarding me. That maybe my dad wasn't really my dad."

"And he told you?"

"He did a lot of hinting. Boasting, even. About me not being a real Salinger. I thought it was ridiculous at first. But I started to wonder. I'd always been so different from Heath and my father. You already know about the debates I had with my dad and grandma back then, about me not wanting to join the family business."

Sophie nodded. He'd fought them on their methods of logging and mining—and had even persuaded them to institute a few environmentally beneficial changes in return for his enrollment in their choice of college. A short-lived bargain, as it had turned out.

"I investigated the facts," Luke continued. "At one point, I even thought of confronting my mother, but that was when she became ill. Soon she was worse, and I couldn't worry her so I pushed the questions away. But things heated up again after she died. I had to find out the truth, but the evidence was locked away."

Sophie drew in a breath. "That was when you broke into the law office."

"It was a stunningly idiotic idea. We'd been drinking, of course. I should have known better than to take Demon and Snake, because once we were in they started trashing the place for no reason. All I wanted was the file about my biological father." Luke dragged a hand over his head, pulling off the bandanna. "The fire was an accident, but I was responsible."

She nodded. "What did you find out?"

"There was a nice, neat record of the payoffs my grandmother had made to a man named Ben Proctor. He worked for Lucas Industries at one time—in forestry management. The payments were recorded as consultation fees, but that was only a cover for the real deal. My grandmother wanted a second heir badly enough that she was willing to overlook my mother's affair and my faulty parentage, but she wasn't going to put up with even a whiff of scandal. She paid Proctor to keep quiet and leave town."

Sophie wanted to go over and sit next to Luke and hold his hand, but he was looking across the lake, his eyes distant as they studied the jarring patterns cast by the setting sun without seeing the beauty in the whole picture.

"After I left Treetop, I tried to find him. Proctor.

Took me a few years—he'd moved several times."
Luke's face twisted in disgust. "The man wasn't worth
finding." He glanced at Sophie. "You're not getting
any prize stock in me."

She did scoot over to him then, and hugged him
around the shoulders, saying, "Do you think I'm my
Dad? Damn, I hope not." She deepened her voice to a
Buzzsaw growl, stuck out a bent elbow and waved it
around. "I'd never be hanging out with one of them
high and mighty Lucases if that were so."

Luke chuckled briefly. "I guess you're right."

Joe came back with a large armful of firewood. He
threw it down before them with a loud clatter. "There.
You think that's enough? I'm exhausted!"

Luke threw him a key ring. "Too tired to go try out
my Harley?"

Joe's face brightened like a kid staring at a candle-
lit birthday cake. "Can I? Jeez! Mom?"

She made a face. "Okay. But only up and down the
trail right here by the lake. Don't go faster than fifteen
miles per hour. And wear a helmet!" she shouted after
Joe, who'd bounded away faster than a jackrabbit. She
stuck her elbow into Luke. "Are you sure that was a
good idea?"

"Not much can happen when he's only going fifteen.
I'll check on him in a minute, after I get the fire
started."

She measured out a few cupfuls of rice while he
broke down the kindling. When there were no more
voluntary confessions forthcoming, she asked, "How's
Mary taking the news of Heath's arrest?"

Luke dusted his hands on his jeans. "Well, let's just
say we haven't been a happy household. You were right
about the mineralogy reports. The land may be rich in

mineral fuels, but Heath couldn't arrange for experimental drilling while it was still listed under protected status. If the mustangs were driven from the vicinity, he figured he'd have a much better chance of getting Grandmother to reverse the designation.'' Luke snorted. ''Do you believe that? Six horses killed, and it was only about money and Heath's need to make his mark in the family business.''

''Then I take it Kiki and I are *persona non grata* at Lucas Ranch.''

''Not if I have anything to say about it. And I do.''

Sophie's eyes narrowed. That was one heck of a take-charge statement, coming from a man who'd forsworn involvement with his family.

Luke shrugged, following her train of thought. ''Someone has to run things the right way. Grandmother's ready to pass over the reins.''

''But not to Heath?''

''He's sicker in the head than we thought. It turns out that he hadn't only sent Kiki to do his spying. He's been following me since I got home, so warped in his thinking about you and me that he can't tell right from wrong. Or up from down, when it comes to gaining Grandmother's approval. And denying his own possible fallibilities.''

Sophie was freshly appalled that she'd been taken in by Heath's surface charm under *any* circumstances. She wondered if she'd ever understand why Heath had wanted to twist up her life so badly. ''The sheriff is backtracking from his association with Heath as fast as he can. He's even saying now that it was Heath who informed on you and the Mustangs all those years ago.''

''Why am I surprised?'' Luke said. ''Of course it was Heath. Never you.''

She shrugged.

"I'm sorry. He's my brother. I should have seen—"

"He fooled a lot of people, including your grand-mother."

"Yeah, well, she's paying his attorney's fees, but he's going to be in her doghouse for a good long while. When he gets out of jail, she'll probably ship him off to supervise a mine in as remote a corner as she can find. The Mary Lucas version of purgatory. She does not allow public scandal, and this is a wicked one."

Sophie said, "Whew." She couldn't think of anything else.

Luke scratched a match on the steel tip of his boot and touched the flame to the dry bark and kindling. A tiny curl of flame licked at the tinder.

He cleared his throat. "So, you know, Heath probably won't be around the ranch much. If at all. In case you decide to…" His gaze slid across her face before returning to the growing fire. He fed it another piece of wood.

Sophie's hands started to shake, rattling the metal cup and spoon in her hand. She gripped them tighter. Why was it she could take down a tattooed bad guy in black leather but one look from Luke made her shiver and shake?

She closed her eyes, following the purr of the bike as Joe drove sedately along the trail where his father had risked his life only days ago. For her and Joey, she thought. Luke had done it for them.

"Is it my decision to make?" she asked.

"I know I haven't been around. Guess I thought we both needed some time to adjust. But I still want us to be together. I've never stopped loving you, Sophie."

She looked at him through the sparkle of tears.

"There's something I have to ask. Why didn't you tell me right away about the rifle being in my shed?"

"Because I thought it was your father's, and I knew that would cause you so much pain."

She'd guessed it was something like that, because Luke was a remarkable man. "You didn't want me to suffer, yet you were willing to turn it in as evidence against your own brother."

"Heath was wrong. He had to be stopped."

She ducked her head, getting to the most difficult part. "You seem willing to forgive me for Heath, even without knowing my side of it."

"I trust you. Whatever happened, I trust you."

More than anything, she wanted to rush into his arms, but she had to get the explanation out of the way first. "It wasn't like he said. I did get pretty wild there, for a while, going out partying with some bad people. My reputation took a nose dive, and, heck, you know it was never the best to start with. I was drinking the night that Heath showed up. He offered to give me a ride home." She speeded the explanation, the words tearing out of her. "He acted so concerned. And he was so familiar. When I closed my eyes, it was like being with you. I let myself pretend I was with you. But later, when I realized what I'd done...and then I found out I was pregnant..." She doubled over. "I hated myself. It was the worst mistake of my life. But then eventually I had Joey. For his sake, I had to find a way to make myself a better person."

"That's why you don't drink," Luke said.

"Never again." She hugged her stomach. "Can you imagine how I felt? Knowing I'd been drinking alcohol with a baby inside me? I lived in terror for months, imagining I'd harmed our child."

"Our child?"

"I couldn't bear to think of the baby as Heath's."

"And now we know—within a reasonable percentage—that it wasn't. Kiki told you about that, didn't she?"

"Yes," Sophie whispered.

"Joey's my son."

She lifted her face to Luke's. Between them, the flames leapt hungrily, wafting smoke into the deepening indigo sky. She knew he wasn't asking for her to calculate the odds. He was making a declaration. And she answered, "Yes," her voice gaining strength. There was no more beautiful word in the English language.

"I don't feel as though I have the right to ask this, but I have to. Will you love me forever?"

"Yes. Oh, yes."

"And will you marry me?"

"*Yes.*"

Luke stood. "Then let's go tell our son."

A bright, pure happiness beamed out of her like the sun. Suddenly she was in Luke's arms, hugging him, holding him, kissing him. The light had been inside her all the time—it needed only Luke to turn it on.

After a few minutes, they walked to meet Joe, her arm around his waist, his hand on her hip, touching the very spot where the mustang tattoo branded her as forever his.

"Is this a happy-ever-after ending?" Sophie asked.

Luke's eyes focused on the boy riding his motorcycle. "I can't say for sure. I hope so. But I do know that it's a happy-ever-after start."

The Shannon Sisters

A Trilogy by C.J. Carmichael
The stories of three sisters from Alberta whose lives and loves are as rocky—and grand—as the mountains they grew up in.

A Second-Chance Proposal
A murder, a bride-to-be left at the altar, a reunion. Is Cathleen Shannon willing to take a second chance on the man involved in these?

A Convenient Proposal
Kelly Shannon feels guilty about what she's done, and Mick Mizzoni feels that he's his brother's keeper—a volatile situation, but maybe one with a convenient way out!

A Lasting Proposal
Maureen Shannon doesn't want risks in her life anymore. Not after everything she's lived through. But Jake Hartman might be proposing a sure thing....

On sale starting February 2002

Available wherever Harlequin books are sold.

HARLEQUIN®
Makes any time special®

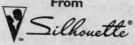

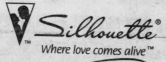

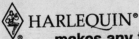

Meet the Randall brothers...four sexy bachelor brothers who are about to find four beautiful brides!

Wyoming Winter

by bestselling author
Judy Christenberry

In preparation for the long, cold Wyoming winter, the eldest Randall brother seeks to find wives for his four single rancher brothers...and the resulting matchmaking is full of surprises! Containing the first two full-length novels in Judy's famous *4 Brides for 4 Brothers* miniseries, this collection will bring you into the lives, and loves, of the delightfully engaging Randall family.

Look for WYOMING WINTER in March 2002.

And in May 2002 look for SUMMER SKIES, containing the last two Randall stories.

HARLEQUIN®
Makes any time special ®